HALO MOON

A JARED DELANEY WESTERN

HALO MOON

JIM JONES

THORNDIKE PRESS
A part of Gale, a Cengage Company

Copyright © 2022 by Jim Jones.
Thorndike Press, a part of Gale, a Cengage Company.

Thorndike Press Large Print Softcover Western.
The text of this Large Print edition is unabridged.
Other aspects of the book may vary from the original edition.
Set in 16 pt. Plantin.

LIBRARY OF CONGRESS CIP DATA ON FILE.
CATALOGUING IN PUBLICATION FOR THIS BOOK
IS AVAILABLE FROM THE LIBRARY OF CONGRESS.

ISBN-13: 978-1-4328-9269-2 (softcover alk. paper)

Published in 2023 by arrangement with Cherry Weiner Literary Agency

Printed in the United States of America
1 2 3 4 5   27 26 25 24 23

HALO MOON

CHAPTER 1

The scream of the mountain lion reverberated around the walls of the dark canyon, conjuring images of banshees and ghosts. Jared Delaney sat straight up in the saddle, his eyes wide with dread as he searched the trail for signs of the animal. His ears strained to pick up the slightest noise that didn't seem to be part of the usual sounds of the night. He scrutinized the terrain with all of his senses. There, up ahead, he saw the creature crouched on a boulder beside the pathway. It was huge, probably twice as big as any cat he'd ever seen. Its eyes burned with a malevolent amber fire. It quivered with fury and anticipation. Judging from the position of the halo moon in the sky, it was some time after midnight. Jared had a passing thought that it was odd he could see so clearly, given that it was the heart of the night. The echo of the piercing cry of the lion faded. In its place, he heard a low and guttural rumble . . . a growl.

It was the sound a mountain lion makes when attack is imminent.

He reached for his Winchester in the scabbard on the left side of his saddle. It was gone. What the hell? Panicked, he made a grab for his pistol. It was gone, too. With crystalline clarity, he saw the predator gather itself to leap. How could this be happening? Was this how it would end?

Jared came out of the dream like a drowning man swimming, desperate to reach the surface of a deep lake. As he gasped for breath and tried to collect his bearings, he felt a palpable fear and cast a frantic look around his campsite for the source of the danger. As his eyes adjusted to the darkness, he saw and heard nothing to be frightened of, nothing but the familiar and reassuring sounds of the night. Crickets. An owl hooting off in the distance. Looking up in the sky, he saw the same moon from his dream, encircled by a hazy band of light. What did the old stories say? A halo moon was an omen of things to come. Bad weather, maybe; bad luck, perhaps; trouble, probable. *Change is coming,* he thought, *and it's not good.*

Although there was an autumn chill in the air, he was drenched with sweat. As he shook off the stupor of sleep and his thoughts became more lucid, he tried to make sense of what he was experiencing. *Damn it, I just had a nightmare like the ones I used to have.* In his younger days, before he faced down his demons and married the love of his life, he had nightmares most every night. There had been mountain lions in those dreams, but it had been years since he'd awakened like this, consumed with terror.

The big cat in this dream had seemed real. He experienced an old but familiar feeling of disorientation as he tried to sort out what was real from what existed in the dark corners of his mind where those painful memories from his childhood resided. He felt naked and vulnerable as he reached first for his rifle, then his pistol. He was reassured to find his pistol in its holster not a foot away from his bedroll. The Winchester was just beyond it resting against a log.

Jared had left Raton around the middle of the day before, headed home after a tricky cattle drive up to the mining camps west of Trinidad, Colorado. His usual herds were around a hundred head but this had been a large order and he'd been trailing three hundred steers. The weather had gone to hell as they drove them through Raton Pass and he'd lost a few head in a blizzard. He had a short crew with a couple of new and very green hands. There had been a few dicey moments during the drive when he believed he would have been better off without them. They got the job done, though, and the two tenderfoots survived and learned a few things along the way. Maybe they weren't cowboys yet but they'd do until one came along.

After delivering the herd, he and his cowboy crew headed back to Raton where the young waddies proceeded to blow their hard-earned wages on the usual attractions . . . rotgut whiskey and flash girls. Jared was years past that custom and had no inclination to take it up again. He had a wife and children to support and surely didn't need to go wasting his profits on fleeting and illusive pleasures. Instead, he had stopped in at the Wild Mustang Saloon, the establishment owned and operated by his *amigo,* Big Jim Rogers.

Big Jim was a mountain of a man with a high voice and a gentle disposition along with a talent for painting wild horses. That was not to imply that he was of no use in an altercation. In the past, Big Jim had stood beside Jared to face down some dangerous men. Anyone who interpreted his artistic nature and mild disposition as being soft did so at their own risk. It was rare that an individual made that mistake more than once.

Jared had enjoyed the steak and conversation but resisted Big Jim's invitation to stay longer. He was keen to get home to his wife, Eleanor, and his two children, Ned and Lizbeth. Ned was a four-year-old whirlwind of a boy and Lizbeth, at age two, was just beginning to walk around and get into everything. They both worshipped their papa, and Jared, in turn, doted on them. The two of them were a handful for Eleanor, though, and he knew she would appreciate his returning to give her a few moments peace.

Beyond that, Jared loved his wife more than he could have imagined possible and missed her with a steady ache when he was away. She was not only beautiful; she was an intelligent and strong woman who never hesitated to share her opinions with him. That included calling him out when his thinking about some plan was a bit muddled. Though it wasn't always comfortable, he knew her honesty was good for him. She more than made up for those contentious moments by showering him with affection and humor the rest of the time. Somehow in the midst of their hardscrabble existence, they managed to enjoy life and have more fun than the law should allow. He could not have picked a more perfect partner in life.

Jared calculated that daylight was several hours away. While he was eager to get home, he had no desire to strike out in the darkness and risk wandering off the trail into a steep drop-off. He didn't know if he could go back to sleep but he crawled back into his warm bedroll to give it a shot. As he stared up at the halo moon, he had an unsettled feeling that something was wrong but he couldn't put his finger on what it might be. It took a while for him to fall into a restless sleep.

Chapter 2

The sunlight wove its way through the pine needles and caressed Jared's eyes, waking him up. He felt a moment of confusion as sleep left him and it took him a moment to get his bearings. Then the events of a few hours before flashed to the front of his mind and he remembered the disturbing dream. It had caught him with his guard down because it seemed to come out of nowhere. He still felt unsettled, as much by the fact that he'd had a nightmare after so many years of peaceful sleep as by the content of the dream.

When Jared was a child, he had witnessed his parents' murder by a gang of brutal desperados in the Texas panhandle. It was bloody and horrifying and he would never forget it. The incident had scarred him deeply and among other things, he had vivid and terrifying nightmares almost every night for most of his young life. It was only after he came to Cimarrón and met the two people who would change his life forever and for the better that he mastered the ghosts of his past. Those two people were his wife, Eleanor Delaney, and his best friend and mentor, former sheriff Nathan Averill. He was now headed home to see his bride and he hoped to meet up with Nathan fairly soon after he got back to catch up on all that had transpired while he'd been gone on this cattle drive.

Cimarrón isn't gettin' any closer with me just layin' about. Reckon I'll have a swig of water and some cold biscuits, then hit the trail.

An hour later, he had traversed several miles farther south and was moving along at a pretty solid trot. With any luck, he'd make it back to his ranch by midafternoon. His children usually took a nap in the middle of the day, which gave their mother a much-needed break. Although he missed the little ones so much that it left an ache in his heart, he was half hoping that they would still be asleep when he arrived so he might spend a few minutes of what he liked to think of as "quality time" with his wife. As he rode on, he contemplated this notion in some detail and was caught up in the thought of this pleasant prospect.

Out of the blue, his reverie was interrupted by an eerie sound that took him a moment to recognize. Somehow it was both high-pitched and low and guttural at the same time. It seemed to originate off in the distance in the direction of the higher peaks. The hair on the back of his neck stood up and a chill ran down his spine, reactions that harkened back to when men lived in caves. In a few seconds, he realized he was hearing the hunting cry of a mountain lion. That made little sense to Jared because predators mostly hunt at night. Sometimes they will continue into the early morning daylight hours but it seemed too late for one to be out and about. The ghostly high-pitched noise continued for a few more seconds followed by an unnatural hush, as if the smaller game in the vicinity had been terrified into silence. Jared could imagine animals quivering with dread in their burrows.

As Jared rode on, he kept a hand close to the Winchester in his scabbard. The scream of the lion had come from quite a distance away but he didn't want to take any chances. For the next twenty minutes or so, his senses were on high alert as he scanned his surroundings. During that time, he heard no more screams and the typical noises of the mountain forest resumed, telling him that the danger had receded. Gradually, he relaxed.

Now that he wasn't so focused on keeping watch, he reflected on the odd coincidence of his hearing the scream of a mountain lion at this strange time so close on the heels of his dream involving the nightmarish lion. He was pretty sure that a coincidence was exactly what it was and yet it left him feeling ill at ease. As he reflected on the bits and pieces that he remembered of the nightmare, he recalled the image of the halo moon, which was the first thing he saw when he awoke. He didn't think of himself as superstitious or a believer in old wives' tales but he'd seen too many examples of bad weather or some other unpleasant occurrence that followed the appearance of a halo moon. He could only hope that this one was not the harbinger of dire things to come.

"You worry too much, Chuy." Felipe Alvarado glared at his cousin, contempt written all over his face. "You are like an old woman."

Jesus Abreu took a deep breath to calm his nerves. The arrogance of this man never ceased to amaze him. "One of us needs to worry about this thing, *paisano*. You killed

16

the most famous lawman in the territory and his prisoner. You cannot believe that the officials of Colfax County will just ignore that."

Alvarado shrugged. "You said it yourself. I killed the prisoner. Pony Diehl was the only man left alive from the gang who could testify that we planned the cattle rustling. He is gone. *No problema.*"

"The problem," Abreu said in a voice taut with anxiety, "is that you failed to kill Sheriff Stallings. He suspects both of us, he and that redheaded deputy of his. You know they were asking questions all around town. They know I lied to them."

A cruel smile flickered across Alvarado's face. "They know *you* lied, Chuy. They do not know anything about me."

Abreu exhaled. "You think they cannot find more witnesses who can place you near the scene of this crime, cousin? You think they are not going to track down the man who killed Nathan Averill?"

"I think that if they try, they will meet the same end as their famous Sheriff Averill." Jesus Abreu marveled at Alvarado's arrogance. "Besides, there is a rumor that Stallings is leaving town. Ramon said he heard he was going to Texas."

"Maybe so," Abreu said, "but there are

others in Cimarrón who would avenge the death of the old lawman. And if they come for me, you know they will be on to you sooner or later."

"Not unless you tell them," Alvarado said, the same cruel smile appearing on his lips and remaining there. "You would not do that, would you, Chuy?"

Looking into the eyes of his cousin and seeing that predatory gleam there, Abreu could not help but remember how the man had come by his nickname. *Paisano,* the roadrunner. The bird that kills smaller creatures with no more feeling than if they were inanimate objects. He had seen that complete lack of emotion in his cousin's eyes far too often as he inflicted pain, torture, and death on other living beings with no more thought or remorse than if he were swatting a fly. He knew Felipe Alvarado would not hesitate to kill him if he suspected even for an instant that he would betray him . . . and he would not lose one moment's sleep over it.

"Of course not, Felipe," he said with as much sincerity as he could manage. "That does not mean they could not find connections between us and figure things out. We need to be very watchful. I suspect that Manuel will not let this drop." He frowned as he considered the mayor of Springer, Manuel Salazar. "I am certain that he suspects me as well. He will not appreciate the notion that I have been using him as a pawn."

"That is your problem, Chuy," Alvarado said with a wave of his hand. "Just do not let your problem become my problem."

"I may not be able to stop that from happening, Felipe," Abreu said. "I know Manuel is full of himself but when he decides to do something, he is stubborn and persistent." Jesus Abreu threw up his arms. "This idea you have to start up the robbing and killing so soon is not going to help things calm down. I wish you would reconsider."

"If Salazar gets in my way, I will field dress him like an elk." Alvarado spoke these chilling words in a calm voice as if he was discussing the weather. "I will leave his guts strewn all over the streets of Springer. We will see how persistent he is then."

"You cannot just kill anyone who gets in your way, cousin," Abreu said. "I think we need to let this furor die down before you start up your tricks again."

"Who says I cannot kill anyone who gets in my way?" Alvarado turned his back on his cousin and pulled out the large hunting knife he kept in a case on his belt. He

19

touched the point with the tip of his finger, drawing a drop of blood. "That has worked well for me so far." He licked his finger, turned around, and looked straight into Abreu's eyes. "So do not get in my way. *Comprendé?*"

Jesus Abreu gave a meek nod and did his best not to throw up his lunch.

CHAPTER 3

Jared struck a good clip as he made his way toward his ranch, which most folks still called the Kilpatrick place because of its previous owners and his dear friends, Ned and Lizbeth Kilpatrick. First Ned and later Lizbeth had been casualties of what people referred to as the Colfax County War, a conflict fueled by the greed of corrupt politicians known as the Santa Fe Ring. Jared, Nathan Averill, Tomás Marés, and, more recently, Tommy Stallings had battled the Ring's hired guns more than once and emerged victorious if not unscathed each time. However, as Nathan was fond of pointing out, they had never cut off the "head of the snake." The avaricious politicians who were making fortunes by stealing land from poor landowners continued to thrive. At this point in his life, Jared was resigned to the fact that corrupt politics in the New Mexico Territory would continue to flourish as long as there was land to steal and money to be made.

In 1878, Jared Delaney came to Cimarrón as a twenty-one-year-old hand looking for cowboy work. What he found instead was a full-blown range war between the small landowners and the powerful forces of the hired guns of the Santa Fe Ring. All that stood between the two factions was Sheriff Nathan Averill. It took Jared some time to sort through his personal demons and choose sides but he wound up standing with the sheriff as they overcame the cruel O'Bannon family.

Along the way, he met and fell in love with Eleanor Coulter, the woman who would become his wife. She stuck by him through the tough times as he struggled to put his difficult past behind him. Eventually, he was able to move forward in life with this brave and intelligent woman at his side. They now had a thriving cattle business as well as two fine children, named for Ned and Lizbeth Kilpatrick.

Eight years later, Jared still resembled that youthful cowboy in many ways. You had to look closer to see the lines around his eyes, brought on by the weather and the typical uncertainties experienced by those who make their living off the land. There were a few random gray hairs sprouting around his temples; you might not see them right off but they were there nonetheless. He was still whip thin, stronger than he looked, and an impressive figure of a man at a hair over six feet tall.

Those who had known him since he first came to Cimarrón would tell you that they saw a difference in his eyes. The young cowboy had possessed a haunted look, brought on by unspeakable horrors witnessed as a child. The mature rancher might have a few wrinkles but he also had an air of confidence, satisfaction, and purpose that had been missing in the young man. He also had the respect and admiration of his peers for his bravery and unwavering commitment to truth and honor. As the cowboys say, Jared Delaney was "one to ride the river with" . . . a man you could count on when a situation turned dangerous and deadly. He refused to be cowed by the corrupt and evil men who ran roughshod over the small landowners of the New Mexico Territory.

Jared pushed his horse at a quick pace, hoping to reach the ranch by midafternoon. With an ache in his heart, he couldn't wait to lay eyes on his family but something else drove him as well. Ever since he'd awakened drenched in sweat from his menacing dream, he'd been plagued by a feeling of impending peril. There was no immediate threat he could identify and it occurred to him that he was perhaps being foolish, yet his sense of foreboding was very strong. He felt an urgent need to get home and a fervent hope that his family was not in jeopardy. *Damn that halo moon, I wish I'd never seen it.*

The sun was still well above the mountains to the west when he came out of the canyon that led to the entrance to the Kilpatrick Ranch. A soft breeze caressed the autumn-golden leaves of the aspens up the hill from the ranch house, creating a rustle that sounded like whispers. Other than the quaking aspens, there was no sound of birds or any other animals. Right off, he perceived that no one was there and spurred his horse up to the front of the house.

A sense of panic spread through his gut as he dismounted and raced to the front door. As his boots hit the portal, he saw what appeared to be a note stuck in a crack in the door. The feeling of panic receded just a tad. Eleanor often left him messages in this manner when she was expecting him home and needed to be away from the ranch for some reason. He hoped that this was something as innocuous as her having loaded the children into the buckboard and made a run into town for supplies.

He snatched the note from its slot and unfolded it, fumbling a bit in his apprehension. What he read did nothing to allay his fears. *Come to town as soon as you get this.* Nothing more.

CHAPTER 4

"Do you think that Jared will make it here in time for the funeral?" Tomás Marés spoke in a soft voice to Eleanor Delaney as he helped her down from the buckboard. Young Ned hopped down and raced into the Marés Café, flushed with the prospect that Tomás's mother, Anita Marés, would offer him a honey-drenched *sopapilla* as a snack.

Eleanor accepted Tomás's assistance with her left hand as she snatched up little Lizbeth with her right before the toddler could take a flying leap off the buckboard. Once both of her feet were on the ground, she let go of his hand and smoothed her dress.

"I don't know, Tomás." She replied in a similar quiet tone to his. There was something about burying the dead that seemed to make folks want to speak in hushed tones. "I've been expecting him home any time for the past several days but you know how cattle drives go. A hundred things can slow you down." She smiled at his rueful grin of acknowledgment. He had been up the trail with Jared Delaney more than once. "I left him a note telling him to hurry to town if he gets there after we've left."

Tomás gave her a questioning look. "Did you tell him what happened?"

Eleanor pursed her lips and blew out a breath. "At first, I couldn't make up my mind. I know how hard he's going to take the news. I finally decided it would be better to tell him face to face."

Tomás shrugged. "It will be hard either way. Nathan stood by Jared back when the rest of us had all given up on him. There was no man in the world that your husband respects more."

"You're right, of course," Eleanor said. "There is no good way to break the news to him. I'm hoping he makes it here in time for the service. When will it start?"

"The service will begin at the cemetery in about an hour," he said. "Father Baca will say some words and then we will lay our dear friend to rest in the ground. After that, we will come back to the café and gather for an *estela* . . . what you call a wake." He sighed. "Somehow, I always believed Nathan would live forever. He seemed . . . what is the word? Invincible."

27

"I used to think that myself. Of course, we both met him when we were youngsters. I was convinced he walked on water." Eleanor shook her head. "After he almost died from the ambush by Tom Chapman and that wicked man, Daughtry, I got over the notion that he was immortal."

"No, he was not immortal," Tomás replied, "but he was indeed a great man. As hard and tough as anyone I ever knew and yet so honest and kind." He looked away so Eleanor would not see the moisture gathering in his eyes . . . but, of course, she did. "He will be missed."

Eleanor made no effort to hide the tears that brimmed over from her eyes. "That doesn't even begin to cover how so many of us feel about the loss of this lion of a man." She choked back a sob. "You know he became like a second father to me after my parents died."

Tomás stood there, awkward and unsure of how to comfort his friend. At that moment, his fiancée, Maria, came out of the café and saw them standing there. She rushed over to Eleanor and embraced her in an enveloping and soothing hug. Tomás watched and wondered if Eleanor Delaney would break down. Instead, she seemed to draw strength from Maria's embrace. After

28

a long moment, the two separated.

"Thank you for the hug, Maria," she said. "You always seem to know what I need."

Maria smiled at her and then turned to her fiancé with a playful look. "Unlike this man I intend to marry, who seems to have no idea what to do when a woman starts to cry."

Tomás started to protest but when both women began laughing at him, he just smiled and shook his head. "There is no question you are right about that and I can see that the two of you intend to gang up on me. I know when I am beaten. I will go inside and help Mama prepare the food."

The day was overcast and gloomy, which fit the mood. Folks had begun congregating at the cemetery on the north end of the village. It seemed as if the whole town had turned out, which meant that the crowd spilled over outside the small area where the grave markers were, enclosed by a low stone wall. Although there was a substantial crowd, they were quiet and subdued. Conversations were conducted in whispers. If you closed your eyes, you might imagine you were in the mountains standing next to a grove of trees listening to the musical sighing of the aspens. You only had to open your eyes again to realize that you were in a much darker place, not celebrating life but rather mourning death and loss.

Eleanor Delaney slowly walked arm in arm with Tomás and Maria. The three of them emanated an amalgamation of sorrow and dignity. Eleanor had left the children with Anita Marés, who refused to attend the ceremony. She said she'd had enough of funerals to last a lifetime. Since her husband had been shot not so long ago, no one was inclined to argue with her.

No words were spoken but the crowd parted to let Eleanor, Tomás, and Maria pass through toward the grave site. Off to the left, Eleanor saw Mollie Stallings standing with Tom Figgs and his wife. She wondered where Mollie's husband, Sheriff Tommy Stallings, was. The young Irish lass offered a shy smile and wave. Eleanor smiled in return and nodded to her, mouthing the words "I'll see you afterwards." The young woman nodded her head in acknowledgment.

The three walked to a place saved for them up next to the grave where they found Father Antonio Baca talking in a quiet voice with Tomás's younger brother, Estévan, and Nathan Averill's widow. In her tarnished past as a soiled dove, she had been known as Christy Quick. When Nathan offered her a way out of that life and faced down the disapproving townspeople to insist that she be given the job as assistant to the schoolteacher, she became known as Christy Johnson. It was there that she found redemption and dignity. Eleanor Delaney had been the schoolteacher and they became close friends. Once she and Nathan wed, everyone just called her Miss Christy. She was dressed in black and had a veil pulled down to hide her face.

"How are you holding up?" Eleanor took Miss Christy's hands and squeezed them.

Miss Christy took a deep breath and said, "About like you would be if you were in my shoes." She squared her shoulders. "I won't let them see me break down, though. I don't want their pity or their scorn."

Eleanor squeezed Christy's hands once more and then let go. "No you don't," she said in a firm voice. "You know you have all my sympathy and love, though."

Christy nodded. "I do. And you, more than most, know how I feel. To everyone else, he was a legend and a great man. To me, he was my gentle and kind husband. He would bring me coffee in the morning and tease me about every little thing he could think of. I don't have the words to say how much I'll miss him."

Once again, tears collected in Eleanor's eyes and spilled over. "I do know and it breaks my heart. I'll come by later and when no one is around, we'll cry our eyes out."

"I'll take you up on that," Miss Christy said.

She was about to say something else when the two ladies noticed a man walking with a resolute step in their direction. Walking wasn't the most fitting description, however. He seemed to be strutting. Since he was rather short, it made Eleanor think of a banty rooster. Her curiosity was aroused when he walked up to her, took off his Stetson, and bowed.

"Mrs. Delaney, I am Manuel Salazar, Mayor of Springer. In a moment, I would like a word with you in private." Noting her immediate discomfort with his request, he frowned. "I know this is a bad time but this cannot wait." He turned to Miss Christy and bowed once again. "I cannot tell you how sorry I am for your loss, Señora. Your husband was the greatest man I ever knew. Without his help, I would not be alive today, much less a respected public official. I owe him no less than my life."

Christy nodded at the gentleman and said, "Señor Salazar, my husband spoke of you to me on several occasions. He held you in high regard as well. Thank you for your condolences."

"I would give anything for it not to have come to this, Señora." A dark look passed over his face. "I assure you, however, that his death will not go unavenged. The men responsible for this travesty will pay, I promise you." Before Christy could reply, Salazar turned to Eleanor. "That is what I wish to speak with you about, Señora. Would you give me a moment of your time?"

Eleanor felt very uncomfortable with the direction this conversation appeared to be headed. "This does not seem to be an appropriate time, Mayor Salazar." She looked in Christy's direction.

Miss Christy cocked her head to the side as if she were curious. Then she nodded and said, "You know, Eleanor, maybe it would be all right to take a minute and hear what Mayor Salazar wishes to discuss."

"Are you sure?" Eleanor cast a cautious look at her friend. "There's not much time before Father Baca speaks."

"I think it would be all right," Christy said. "I'll be interested to hear what the good mayor has to say to you."

Eleanor shrugged and turned back to Mayor Salazar. "I suppose we can take a brief moment. I can't let this interfere with the ceremony, though. I'm sure you understand that."

"Gracias, Señora," Salazar replied. "I promise I will be brief."

They walked a short distance from the crowd. Eleanor stopped and turned to face Salazar. "What is it that's on your mind, Mayor?"

"I need to know when you expect your husband to return," Salazar said. "I understand that he has been engaged with driving a herd up to Colorado. I have a proposition to discuss with him as soon as possible after he returns."

Eleanor frowned. "A proposition? What sort of proposition?"

"I would prefer to speak with him face to face about it, Señora," Salazar said, his discomfort showing.

"And I would prefer that you tell me what it is you intend to discuss with my husband before I give you any information about when I expect him back." Eleanor found herself reacting with irritation and distrust to this man. "I don't know you and I'm not sure I approve of your discussing this with me at a time like this."

Salazar looked down for a brief moment as if hoping to find patience on the ground beneath him. When he raised his head, he looked straight into her eyes. "All right, I suppose that is fair." He took a deep breath and said, "I want your husband to help me find the men that did this horrible deed. I want him to hunt down the assassins who took the life of Nathan Averill." He paused and his eyes narrowed. "And then I want him to kill them."

Eleanor took a step back, stunned not only by the man's words but by the powerful emotion behind them. She had a vague notion that Nathan had helped Salazar out in some way when he was a younger man but she didn't know any of the details. It took her a moment to gather her wits and respond.

"Mayor Salazar, there is nobody in this old world who loved Nathan Averill more than me . . ." She paused and glanced over at Miss Christy, then continued. ". . . unless it was that woman standing over there with the black veil. But my husband is not a killer. Don't you think that tracking down and prosecuting the men who murdered him would best be left to the sheriff of Colfax County?"

Salazar shot her a puzzled glance. Then a look of understanding crossed his face. "Ah, you must not have heard the news."

"What news would that be, Mayor?" Eleanor felt her cheeks flush as her irritation rose.

"Sheriff Stallings has gone to Texas. He left with his cousin this morning."

"What?" Eleanor's voice caught as she tried to take in this shocking news. "Why did he do that? What about his wife?" Eleanor realized that she was babbling and gathered her wits. "Would you please fill me in on what happened, Mayor? And don't make me ask questions and drag this out. Get to the point."

Salazar seemed a bit taken aback by her directness but then he shrugged. "As you wish, Señora. The sheriff informed me on the day Nathan passed that he was resigning and going to Texas on personal business. It seems his cousin's family is having trouble with outlaws and they require his presence. He wished me the best but said he could not remain and hunt down these vicious killers who took the life of Nathan Averill." It was clear from his tone that Salazar didn't think much of Tommy Stallings's decision.

"So Tommy just up and left?" Eleanor shook her head in confusion. "That's not like him at all, in particular when it comes to tracking down Nathan's killers. I know

36

he would want them brought to justice."

"I would have thought the same, Señora, but he told me that 'family comes first.' " Salazar looked over and noticed that Father Baca was moving into position by the grave. "I think we may need to cut this conversation short, Señora. The ceremony is about to begin."

"One more minute, sir," Eleanor said in a firm voice. "Why would you think my husband would be interested in tracking down Nathan's killer?"

"Oh, I assumed that it was obvious," Salazar said. "I want to offer him the job of sheriff."

Eleanor felt as if she had been punched in the stomach. After all the times Jared stood up against dangerous and evil men to protect the people of Colfax County, she had convinced him to step away and focus on his family and cattle business. Now this?

She said, "You'll have to talk with him about this, Mayor. He'll make his own decision about your offer." *And if I have anything to say about it, he'll tell you to go straight to hell!*

CHAPTER 5

Jared rode over the crest of the hill and gazed down on the village of Cimarrón. He'd made good time but his horse was about done in. He intended to make a brief stop at the livery and have Julio Estrada's groom feed and water the animal while he made his way with as much haste as possible to the sheriff's office to check in with Tommy Stallings. Jared hoped Tommy would be able to shed some light on whatever this awful event was that his wife had alluded to in her note. He was so worried he felt like he had a passel of Texas fire ants crawling around in his pants. It was all he could do to sit still in the saddle. Sensing his rider's unease, Jared's horse tossed its head and snorted. He gave his mount a reassuring pat on the neck, which calmed him down. Too bad the same could not be said for Jared. His mind raced as he imagined all the different calamities that might have transpired.

As he made his way down the hill into town, he glanced to his left and saw a large crowd of people congregated in the cemetery. *I wonder who died. They must have been well loved, judging from the size of the crowd. I wonder if this is the dire news Eleanor was referring to.* He spurred his horse into a lope and made straight for the entrance to the cemetery.

As he approached, it became obvious to him that his perception had been correct. He was coming upon a funeral in progress. In the distance, he saw a woman dressed in black standing close to the grave. She was flanked by another woman and a couple who were holding hands. When he was close enough to make out their features, he saw, to his dismay, that the woman standing with the couple was his wife, Eleanor. The couple was Tomás Marés and his fiancée, Maria. At first, he couldn't make out the features of the woman in black because of the veil covering her face. As he drew a bit closer, he recognized the long blond hair falling below the veil and realized that the woman was Miss Christy. His rational mind understood the implications right away. Another part of his brain, the part where emotions lived, refused to accept them. *It can't be*

Nathan. A wave of nausea swept over him. He had to take deep breaths to prevent himself from throwing up the biscuits he had choked down earlier in the day.

Jared was torn between his feeling of urgency to find out what was happening and his inclination to be respectful of the somber event that was taking place. He did not wish to make a scene but he was desperate to find out what was happening. He brought his horse up short at the entrance gate to the cemetery and loose-tied him there. The crowd was so thick that he didn't see how he could make his way through it to join Eleanor at the graveside. He strained to hear the words Father Baca was saying. His words rang out loud and clear.

"Nathan Averill protected us from men who would do us harm, who treated us as if we were not human beings. Men who would take our lands, steal our cattle, kill us if we stood in their way. He never wavered and he never backed down. He was as brave and strong a man as I have ever seen." Father Baca paused to let his words soak in. From where he stood, Jared could hear a murmur of assent ripple through the crowd. "And yet the sheriff was a kind man as well. He treated everyone with respect. He knew all of you. He knew the names of your children;

40

he knew what dishes you would bring to the church social; he knew about your hopes and your dreams." There was a catch in his voice and again, Father Baca paused for a moment. "Sheriff Nathan Averill was a friend to all the people of Cimarrón."

Several individuals in the crowd responded by saying, "Amen." As Jared listened to Father Baca's words and tried to come to terms with the undeniable truth that Nathan Averill was dead, he couldn't help but wonder how many of those people who were now offering up their amens at this ceremony had ever bothered to thank Nathan for all he had done for them over the years. Not many, he suspected.

As if he'd overheard Jared's thoughts, Father Baca said in a firmer voice, "I am afraid that we were not as good friends to Nathan Averill as he was to us. We took his protection for granted and even worse, we took his friendship for granted."

There was more murmuring in the crowd. Jared couldn't tell if it was agreement or perhaps indignation that the good priest had pointed out a failure of character on their part. Sometimes speaking the unvarnished truth was not a popular course of action. He knew this from personal and painful experience.

Father Baca waited for the muttering to die down. Once it did, he resumed. "I know that you do not like to hear this. It means that you let a friend down, one who never let you down." There was more muttering. Again, Father Baca waited for it to subside. "If it helps you to swallow this bitter truth, I will tell you that I was every bit as guilty as any of you in taking this good man's friendship and protection for granted. I might have thanked him on one or two occasions over all the time I knew him." Father Baca's voice broke once more and he stopped to collect himself. When he resumed, he said, "I should have thanked him every single day."

Jared felt as if his heart was breaking. There was a physical pain in his chest so intense that he wondered if the term "heartbreaking" was a real phenomenon. His friendship with the old sheriff had become as comfortable as an old pair of boots, and he, like all the others, had come to take him for granted, assuming that he would always be there. This man had stood up for him when all of the other people he knew had turned their backs on him. He had believed in him when Jared didn't believe in himself and offered him the opportunity to find his way back to the pathway of honor and integrity. And in his darkest hour, Nathan Averill had saved his life when a vicious murderer was prepared to kill him. *I could never repay Nathan for all he did for me and all he gave to me but I don't know if I tried hard enough to let him know what he meant to me.*

Caught up in his reflections and recriminations, he missed some of the words Father Baca was saying. When he again focused his attention on the priest's sermon, he heard him saying a prayer in Spanish, followed by a translation in English. *Nathan would have liked that.* When he finished praying, Father Baca made the sign of the cross and looked at the crowd of mourners.

"Friends and family will be gathering at the Marés Café for nourishment for the body and the soul. Anyone who wishes to come by the church later this afternoon to speak with me . . ." he paused and looked around, ". . . you can take confession or you can just visit. You will know in your heart if you have any sin that you need to confess."

It seemed to Jared that Father Baca was laying the guilt on pretty thick for the citizens of Cimarrón. Not that he didn't think many of them deserved it. Far too many of them had taken Nathan's protec-

43

tion of them as a matter of course and never once thanked him or extended any kindness in return. For many, that wasn't the case, though. Like Father Baca and Jared himself, they had just taken Nathan Averill for granted, failing to appreciate his amazing courage and vigilance because it was so omnipresent. In some ways, he was like the mountains surrounding Cimarrón. Because they were always there, it was easy to get accustomed to their splendor and no longer see or appreciate it.

The crowd began to disperse, moving away in pairs and small groups. Jared made his way up to the grave site. Eleanor and Miss Christy were engaged in conversation with Father Baca so they didn't see him as he approached. The good Father looked up and upon seeing Jared, broke into a sad smile.

"You made it after all." Father Baca bowed his head. "I am so sorry you had to hear the sad news in this manner."

Eleanor had turned when Father Baca began speaking and saw her husband walking toward her. Although she was not given to public displays of affection, she ran to him and embraced him with such force that he almost stumbled. Without a word, he returned her embrace for a long moment.

Then he loosened his hold and stepped back, holding her at arm's length. All the pain he felt was etched on his face.

"What happened?" His voice caught in his throat and it was all Jared could do to hold back the sobs that were struggling to escape from deep inside his chest. Although he had more questions, he couldn't put them into words and remain in control, so he stayed silent, waiting for his wife to answer him.

"It's a long story, Jared," Eleanor said in a gentle voice. "Why don't we go over to the café where we can have some privacy and I'll tell you everything I know?"

Tomás and Maria came over to stand next to them. Tomás had his hat in his hands and Maria's head was bowed in silent prayer. They overheard Eleanor's last words and Tomás said, "*Sí, amigo,* let us go have some of my mother's cooking. We will tell you everything that has happened." Eleanor took Jared's arm and without a word, they turned and walked back toward the Marés Café.

Billy Gill was aggravated. He needed to get a horse saddled and head on out to where his father was gathering cattle but the paint gelding he wanted to ride wouldn't co-operate. He appeared to be intent on re-maining in the corral with his compadres, and every time Billy got close to him with his rope, the silly dink would trot away just out of reach. Billy was sixteen years old and patience was not one of his virtues. He was already frustrated because his father had made him stay behind to finish chores and help his mother load the wagon for her trip into town while he went on out with two other hands to get started working cows. Billy despised any work that didn't involve his being in the saddle. All he wanted in life was to be a cowboy.

The Gills ran a few hundred head of cattle on their place just a little north of Springer. They didn't have a lot of acreage but they did well with what they had. They delivered steers to the mining camps in the northern New Mexico Territory and southern Colorado on a regular basis and business was good. Their main competition came from Jared Delaney from just over north of Cimarrón but since the mining business was booming, there was more than enough demand for all the cattle both ranchers could supply.

That danged paint was over in the middle of a bunch of other horses, which made it tough for Billy to get a rope on him. He considered choosing another mount . . . after all, the Gills had ten mighty fine horses to choose from . . . but he refused to allow the paint to get the better of him. Anyway, he was a doggone good cow horse once you got him caught and saddled. His daddy told him, the best horse wasn't always the easiest one to catch. The paint was quick and nimble so if some old steer made a break for the brush, Billy could get on him in a heartbeat. When he succeeded in heading one off and brought it back, he could see the look of pride in his father's eyes and that meant the world to him. He tried talking in a gentle voice to the paint as he approached him once again with his rope.

Billy was getting close to the gelding and was pretty sure he could get a rope on him. He started to swing his loop when all of a sudden, the horse looked out to the south and saw something that spooked him. His eyes flashed and he took off again, which elicited a curse from Billy. He looked around, afraid he'd been caught in the act, a reflex left over from having his mother wash his mouth out with soap more than once in the past for such language. He smiled with relief as he remembered she wasn't there, then he looked to see what had spooked the horse.

In the distance, he saw a rider approaching at a swift trot. He couldn't tell much about him other than the fact that he seemed to be well mounted. Even though the man was a good quarter of a mile away, Billy could see that he was riding a large black that pranced through the underbrush. Sunlight glinted off the silver trim on the saddle. He wondered what business the man might have that would bring him out this way. As he got closer, Billy was able to make out more details. The man was wearing a fancy vest and a large black cowboy hat. He looked like a bit of a dandy but he sat his horse well and moved with a purpose. The man made straight for where Billy was in the corral but he made no call of greeting, which seemed a little odd to Billy. It was common courtesy to send out a "halloo the house."

When the rider was about twenty yards away, Billy called out, "Howdy, mister, can I help you?"

The man didn't answer but Billy could see that he was smiling as he approached. Billy found the man a bit rude for not responding, which irritated him, but he'd been taught to respect his elders so he held his tongue. The rider came right up to the corral and stepped down from his horse. He wrapped his reins around the fence of the corral and turned to face Billy. Only then did he speak.

"Good morning, cowboy," he said in a voice that seemed friendly enough. "I have come for your horses."

Billy Gill frowned. The words that he used were confusing. He figured the man must mean that he wanted to buy some horses but it seemed like an odd way to phrase it. He replied, "My father isn't here right now, you'd have to speak to him about any horse trading you were looking to do."

The man smiled at Billy again as he stepped closer. Although he was smiling, Billy suddenly felt an air of menace about the man, almost as if the temperature had dropped. Billy remembered there had been a rash of cattle rustling and horse thieving over north of Cimarrón in the past month, and while there had been none in their area that he knew of, the idea made him uneasy. It made him more nervous that he was not wearing the pistol his father had given on his sixteenth birthday a few months ago.

The man walked over to the gate of the corral and let himself in without asking for permission. Once inside the corral, he turned to Billy and said in a matter-of-fact manner, "Oh, I am not looking to trade for your horses. I have come to take them." As he spoke those words, he moved closer to

49

where Billy stood.

The man spoke in such an impassive tone that it took a moment for the meaning of his words to register. During this brief instant, the man continued to approach until he was just a step away from Billy.

Billy snorted. "I don't know who you think you are, mister, but you can't just come in here and take my daddy's horses."

Those were the last words he ever spoke. The man drew a large hunting knife and before Billy could react, he stabbed him in the lower abdomen. The young man's eyes opened wide with shock and pain as the older man yanked up on the knife. Billy Gill screamed and fell on the ground. As he writhed in agony at the man's feet, his lifeblood pouring out in the dirt, the intruder reached down and took the rope from him. Billy looked up at the man with pleading in his eyes, looking for mercy and compassion. He found none.

"You will not be needing this, I think." As Billy died, Felipe Alvarado tossed the rope over the neck of the paint gelding with a casual motion and began gathering the horses.

CHAPTER 6

Jared hadn't realized how hungry he was until Anita Marés brought him his first helping of steak and beans. He had been in such a hurry to get home that he hadn't eaten all day. Anita saw that he was famished . . . perhaps she heard his stomach growling . . . and without asking, brought him a second steak and another large helping of beans. A picture of patience, Eleanor sat beside him while he cleaned his plate. He was just devouring the last bite when Anita brought over a large slab of apple pie and a mug of coffee.

"You finish this off, Señor Jared," she said. "Then Tomás and Señora Eleanor will tell you the sad tale of what happened to Señor Nathan."

"Gracias, Anita," Jared said. "I missed your cooking while I was up in Colorado." He shot a guilty look at his wife, who was beyond a doubt the worst cook in Colfax

County. She just smiled at him and shook her head in amusement.

"Are you up for listening while you eat your pie?" Tomás had been gazing out the window but now he came over to the table.

Jared took a sip of the hot, black coffee and set the mug down. "I can do that, Tomás." He shook his head in amazement at the quantity of food he had consumed. "I reckon I didn't realize how hungry I was until I got here. Your mama still sets the best table anywhere."

Tomás chuckled. "She believes that a full stomach cures almost anything." His chuckle faded, replaced by a look of profound sadness. "I am afraid it does not cure what has happened to our dear friend."

Jared sighed. "I just wasn't ready to come home and find out that Nathan was dead. It seemed like he would live forever." He sat up. "Tell me what happened."

Tomás glanced at Eleanor and she nodded at him to proceed. "It is a long story, Jared, and it may require more explanation later." He frowned. "It involves our friend, Tommy Stallings, and some of it is confusing."

Jared managed a grin and a shrug. "Confusing is a word that often comes up when you talk about Tommy." He turned serious.

"You might as well get started with this story; it sounds like a tale that might take a while to tell."

"Es verdad." Tomás nodded. "You have been gone a long time. I am trying to remember when it was you headed north to Colorado. Had you received the news about cattle rustling raids on ranches to the north of town before you left?"

Jared pondered the question. "I do recall hearing something about a ranch getting hit just before I left." He turned to Eleanor. "Didn't we talk about that? I remember being worried about you and the children." He shook his head. "It does seem like a long time ago that I rode up the trail."

"We discussed it," Eleanor replied. "I convinced you that between me and Estévan, we would be able to handle any trouble that might come along." Estévan Marés worked as a hand for the Delaneys.

"That's right," Jared said, "now I remember. I still worried about you but I figured you were right."

Tomás continued. "After you left, things got worse . . . much worse. Several more ranches were hit and the people murdered. Donald Armstrong and his boy were shot." Anger clouded his face as he paused for a moment. "Some filthy *cabrón* snuck into

53

town and murdered Robert Woodrum. Gutted him like a hog."

"Robert Woodrum who worked for Bill Wallace?" Jared expressed his confusion. "I thought these men were cattle rustlers."

"That is what we thought as well," Tomás said. "Woodrum was closing up the mercantile in the early evening. He was by himself and this murdering dog stole the money from the day's business."

"So there were some pretty bad hombres running around Colfax County," Jared remarked. "Tommy didn't have any help either, did he?"

Tomás looked away for a brief second to hide the guilt on his face. "He asked me to help him. I refused."

Jared spoke up without hesitation. "I wasn't implying that you should have done anything, Tomás. You just lost your father to a murderer and you're about to get married. You've given more than just about anyone in these parts. It was high time someone else stepped up."

Tomás looked down before continuing. "I suppose I have given more than many of the citizens of Cimarrón but no one has given more than Nathan Averill. He stepped up once again and volunteered to serve as Tommy's deputy."

"What?" Jared wondered if perhaps he had misheard Tomas. "What do you mean he served as Tommy's deputy?"

"I mean that he offered to help Tommy investigate the rustling and murdering. Tommy swore him in and he became Deputy Averill." Tomás smiled. "He insisted on working for free. He said that way, if he decided to quit, he would not miss the money."

"Well, that beats just about anything I've ever heard," Jared said. "What did Tommy think about that?"

Tomás chuckled. "He could not stop calling him Sheriff Averill. Nathan reminded him often that Tommy was the sheriff and he was the deputy. Tommy never got used to it." Tomás resumed the story. "He had a second deputy, his cousin Rusty Stallings from Texas." Seeing the look of confusion on Jared's face, he said, "This is the part I will tell you more about later. He is the reason that Tommy left."

"Tommy left?" Now Jared was baffled. "And who is Rusty Stallings?"

"Yes, Tommy left with his cousin," Tomás replied, "that is what I will need to explain later. Right now, you need to know what happened to Nathan."

Once again, Jared shook his head. "All

right, go ahead."

"When Tommy went out to Donald Armstrong's place after it was attacked, he found the body of one of the rustlers. Either Donald or his son had shot him. He identified him as part of a thing called the White Caps Gang from down in San Miguel County."

Jared nodded. "If my memory serves me, Todd Little is the sheriff down there, isn't he?"

"That is right," Tomás said. "Tommy went down and talked with him. This is complicated so I will skip over many of the details. He traced a connection between the man who is the suspected leader of the White Caps Gang to the banker in Springer, Jesus Abreu. They are cousins. It appears that Abreu and the other hombre, Felipe Alvarado from Las Vegas, had a gang of thieves and murderers working for them up north of Cimarrón." Tomás frowned. "He knew all of this but he did not have sufficient proof of their guilt to make any arrests."

Jared nodded. "I would guess the notion of gathering proof would have come from Nathan. Tommy was not big on following procedures."

Tomás shrugged. "Believe me, *amigo,* no one knows that better than I do." Tommy had been Tomás's deputy for a time when

56

Tomás was sheriff. "I will skip ahead to the end of the story. Tommy, Nathan, Rusty, and Tom Figgs rode out and had a gun battle with the outlaw gang in Compos Canyon, which was where they were keeping the stock they had stolen. They killed all of the men except for one. They were bringing him back for questioning when they were ambushed." Tomás looked away and ran his hand through his hair. "The outlaw was killed in the ambush. Nathan was badly wounded and died two days later."

Jared took a deep breath as he considered what his friend had told him. "So does Tommy have any idea of who the shooter was?"

"He has an idea, of course," Tomás replied. "There is a strong chance that it was Felipe Alvarado. Tommy met him in Las Vegas with Todd Little and came away with the belief that he is a cold-blooded killer. It is possible that the banker, Jesus Abreu, might have done it but no one believes that. He appears to be the partner who is manipulative and devious. Alvarado was the bloody one." Tomás blew out his breath. "Once again, the problem is that there is no hard evidence that would prove either of the men did the shooting."

"How could Tommy just up and leave with

all of this hanging fire? Who's goin' to track these rotten bastards down and bring them to justice?"

Eleanor put her hand on Jared's arm to try to calm him down. "It's news I just heard about myself, Jared. Tommy made a promise to his cousin to go back with him to Texas. His aunt and uncle have been having trouble with renegades and they were in desperate straits. They need his help. I know it was a tough decision for him but he felt like his family had to come first."

Jared exploded. "What about his family here? What about Mollie? What about the debt he owes Nathan Averill for steppin' in to try to haul his sorry behind out of the fire? And who's gonna avenge Nathan's death?"

Eleanor looked at Jared with curiosity in her eyes. "I don't imagine that Nathan would want his death 'avenged,' " she said. "I think he would want these crimes solved and the murderers brought to justice."

"You know what I meant," Jared said, his voice hot with rage. "We don't have a sheriff or any deputies. Who's gonna track down these killers?"

Eleanor was somewhat taken aback by the rancor she heard in her husband's voice. She was angry as well but the prevailing emotion she was feeling at the moment was sadness at the loss of her old friend.

"Jared, we just got Nathan laid in his grave. I need some time to grieve before I begin to think about who's going to find the killers."

"Maybe that's how you feel," Jared replied with an edge of bitterness, "but as for me, I want to see the murderin' devils put down for what they did. I'll think about grievin' after that's done."

"You're entitled to your feelings about this, Jared," she said, with a bit of an edge to her own voice. "I don't appreciate the tone you're taking with me, though. You're not the only one who has lost a friend."

Jared sat there for a moment with his jaw clenched as he struggled with his turbulent emotions. Then he took a deep breath and exhaled in a slow and deliberate manner. "I'm sorry, Eleanor, you're right. If anything, Nathan meant even more to you than he did to me." He grabbed the edge of the table with both of his hands and squeezed until his knuckles were white. "It's just that I'm so damned tired of one depraved man after another killing people I care about and not being able to do anything about it." Jared's eyes held an expression similar to that of a wild animal that has been cornered.

A look of uncertainty passed over Eleanor's face as she struggled with whether or not to share with her husband the fact that the mayor of Springer wanted to enlist his aid in the hunt for the killers. As much as she wanted justice served on Nathan's behalf, she dreaded the idea of her husband being the person responsible for seeking it. He'd come close to losing his life in the past. She couldn't bear the thought of losing her husband and the father of her children. Although she wanted to focus on her own feelings of loss and sadness, she was sure that Mayor Salazar would approach Jared very soon with his request and she felt like he needed some time to consider his response.

"I need to tell you what happened at the cemetery a little while before you arrived," she said. In response to his questioning look, she continued. "Mayor Salazar from Springer told me that he planned to ask you to assume the duties of sheriff so that you could go after the murderers who killed Nathan."

Jared was perplexed. "The sheriff works for Colfax County, not the town of Springer. He can't just offer me the job." He frowned. "Not that I would take it anyway."

Tomás spoke up. "Mayor Salazar has the

60

tendency to believe he is in charge of everything that happens in these parts. You are right that he has no authority to offer you the job of acting sheriff. He does know the people who do, though, and he has quite a bit of influence with them. If you agreed, I am confident he could make it happen."

"I got no interest in bein' sheriff," Jared said. "The only thing I'm interested in is findin' the devils who are responsible for Nathan's death and squarin' the score."

There was an intensity in her husband's voice that frightened Eleanor Delaney. He seemed to be talking more about vengeance than justice.

"I'm relieved that you're not interested in taking on the job of sheriff. Heaven knows you don't have time to track down those outlaws, much less handle all the other duties of the job." She tried to lighten the mood a bit. "You've been gone quite a while, Jared Delaney. I've got a long list of chores for you and your children expect you to spend hours playing with them."

"Some of those things will have to wait, Eleanor," Jared said, a harsh tone sharpening his words. "I said I wasn't interested in the job of sheriff. That doesn't mean I don't plan to avenge Nathan's death."

Eleanor was taken aback at the acrimony

she heard in her husband's voice. "Jared, you're talking about taking the law into your own hands. You can't do that."

"Why not?" His ruthless tone frightened her. "It seems to me that these rotten, arrogant scoundrels do it all the time and they get away with it. How much longer do we go along like meek lambs accepting that? When do we stand up and say 'no more'?"

"This is not like you, Jared," Tomás interjected, a worried look on his face. "You have always been the one who said we could not act the way these *cabrónes* do lest we become just like them."

Jared stared hard at his friend. "Maybe I was wrong, Tomás. Maybe becomin' more like them is just what I need to do. They got no respect for the law. Maybe it's time they learn to fear the vengeance of good, decent people."

"What you're talking about is neither good nor decent, Jared," Eleanor said with conviction. "Once you get over the shock of Nathan's death, I'm sure you'll see that."

Jared turned his gaze on his wife. "I wouldn't count on that, Eleanor. I'm about done with dependin' on the law to protect us. You can see how well it's worked out for folks like Nathan, Juan Suazo, Ned and Lizbeth Kilpatrick. Your father too, Tomás."

His laugh had a bitter ring to it. "Besides, we ain't even got any law right now. There is no sheriff in Colfax County."

They had been so deep in their discussion that neither Jared, Eleanor, nor Tomás had heard the door of the Marés Café open. Manuel Salazar had walked in on the end of the conversation and it was clear that he'd heard Jared's last remark.

"You could solve that particular problem if you were of a mind to, Señor Delaney." Salazar took off his hat and bowed. "Pardon me for interrupting; I came to pay my respects. I could not help but overhear your remark, though, Señor Delaney, and I want you to know that if you are so inclined, I promise I can make it happen that you will be appointed acting sheriff. That would give you the authority to pursue these *pendejos* who murdered our dear friend."

Jared stood up and extended his hand to Salazar. "We haven't been introduced, sir, but I know who you are. My wife had just informed me of your offer to make me sheriff."

"I am pleased to make your acquaintance, Señor Delaney. I, too, know you by reputation." Salazar took Jared's hand and shook it vigorously. "I hope you will give my proposal serious consideration."

63

"First off, there's no need to call me Señor Delaney. Call me Jared." He let go of Salazar's hand. "Second, I appreciate your offer but I got no interest in bein' sheriff of Colfax County. I'm afraid you're gonna have to look elsewhere to fill that job."

Salazar put his hat back on. "Are you telling me that you have no interest in seeing justice done for Nathan Averill?"

Jared glanced at Eleanor. "I didn't say that, Mayor. I just said I wasn't interested in bein' sheriff."

Salazar gave Jared a long appraising look. He nodded and said, "I see. Perhaps we have more to discuss in the future then, even if you are not interested in the job of sheriff."

This time, Jared avoided looking at his wife. "I'd say that was a distinct possibility, Mayor. This ain't done yet."

"You are right about that, Señor . . . please excuse me, I mean to say, Jared." Salazar bowed once again to Eleanor and Tomás. "I have taken up enough of your time. Please accept my condolences for your loss. I share your deep feelings for Nathan Averill. I will miss him a great deal."

Salazar turned and walked out of the café. Jared sat back down at the table, looking everywhere but at his wife. It was clear to

Tomás Marés that the two of them needed to have a private conversation so he stood up and excused himself. He headed toward the kitchen. When he was a safe distance away, Eleanor spoke in a strong voice to Jared.

"Did you not hear a word that Tomás and I said? Do you intend to pursue this vendetta outside the law?"

Jared sat in silence, his eyes like slits. Childish laughter rang out from the kitchen. Jared and Eleanor glanced in that direction. The rage on Jared's face was in stark contrast to the innocence of that sound. For the first time in their marriage, Eleanor felt concern about the children being around their father. She had no idea how he might react.

"I intend to do whatever it takes to make those murderers pay for their deeds," he said.

"What about your children? What about me?"

Jared continued to avoid his wife's look. His jaw was set and Eleanor recognized the stubborn and willful look in his eyes that she hadn't seen in years. She felt a wave of fear pass through her body. She prayed that the children would stay in the kitchen. She didn't want them to see their father in this state.

After a moment, Jared met her gaze. "What about Nathan?" Without another word, he got up and stalked out of the Marés Café.

A moment later, Ned ran into the room and asked, "Where's my daddy?"

Eleanor struggled to hold back her tears. "He had to go, honey. He'll be back." *I hope he'll come back to us.*

CHAPTER 7

"What have you done, *paisano*?" Jesus Abreu could not believe the recklessness of his cousin. "I told you how important it was to let things die down. Instead, you murder a boy and steal his horses. What were you thinking?"

The two men were meeting at the shell of a cabin where they had spent many hours together in their youth. When Abreu heard about the murder and horse thievery, he had sent a coded message to Alvarado through his nephew, Ramon, that they needed to meet. Alvarado reached out and dug the fingers of his right hand into the muscle of Abreu's left shoulder. The banker winced and tried to shake his grip off. Alvarado would not let go and Abreu cried out in pain. Only then did Alvarado release him.

"You do not speak to me in this manner, Chuy," he said in a low and cold tone. "If any other man spoke to me this way, I would have already killed him. You I will warn first. I have done so. Do not ever do it again."

Abreu knew he had overstepped his bounds and hastened to make up for it. "I am sorry for my tone, *amigo;* I was out of line." He stepped back out of reach of his cousin. "I am so concerned, though, that you have brought more attention to us when we needed to lay low for a while."

Alvarado laughed, his insolence apparent. "I have no need to 'lay low' as you say. Who is going to stop me? There is no sheriff in Colfax County. Now is the perfect time to act."

Abreu sighed with frustration. "There is no sheriff but our old friend, Manuel Salazar, is not going to let this rest. You must not underestimate him, *amigo.* He has some powerful friends. He can be quite determined."

"He is a strutting rooster," Alvarado said, his voice dripping with contempt. "He crows and makes noise like he is cock of the walk. When the time comes, I will kill him without a second's hesitation."

Abreu shook his head. With great caution, he spoke. "Please do not take this wrong, cousin. I am afraid that all this killing you are talking about will bring the attention of too many people. What do we have to lose by staying out of sight for a while?"

"I do not stay out of sight, cousin," Alvarado said. He looked down his nose at Abreu. "I do not run and I do not hide. I will do as I please, when I please and where I please. Those who do not like it will pay the price."

Jesus Abreu could not think of any way to respond that would not result in his being injured or killed by his rapacious cousin.

"As you wish," he said, doing his best to keep the resignation out of his voice. In his head, he began plotting ways to extract himself from this disaster without losing his life.

Eleanor breathed a sigh of relief when she saw her husband feeding and watering his horse as she arrived back at the ranch with the children. It was comforting to see him engaging in normal, everyday activities. When he stalked out of the Marés Café, she had no idea where he was headed, and considering the frame of mind he had been in, she had worried that he might not go home. As she directed the buckboard through the gate, he looked up and smiled at her and the children. She noticed that the smile seemed rather tight and there was a haunted look in his eyes.

As she came to a stop and the children saw their father, it was all she could do to contain them from jumping down from the buckboard and racing to his side. She managed to grab Lizbeth but Ned did launch himself from the seat and tumbled as he hit the ground. As usual, this didn't faze him. He raced over to the corral, whooping like a wild savage.

Jared's face broke into a wide grin as his son leapt up at his father. He caught him in midair and hugged him tight. In the meantime, Lizbeth was squirming in her mother's arms, saying one of the first words she had spoken . . . da da.

"Yes, my darling," Eleanor said, "your daddy is home. Do you want to go see him?"

In response, Lizbeth squirmed with even more vigor and Eleanor set her down, in part because she was afraid she would drop her otherwise. The little girl took off in the funny wobbling gait that toddlers have, hollering "da da" at the top of her lungs as she went. Jared saw her coming and bent down to scoop her up. With two wiggling youngsters in his arms, he decided it would be smart to move away from his horse. The gelding was a solid mount and good around the children but he didn't want to risk spooking the animal. He walked toward the gate of the corral to where Eleanor was standing.

"Can you tell that they're happy to see their father?"

Eleanor smiled at her husband. She was concerned about the way he had left the Marés Café without a word but she didn't want to start an argument right then, particularly since the children were so excited to see him. In her experience, Jared would come around sooner rather than later and let her know what was on his mind.

"And their father is mighty delighted to see them," Jared said. He smiled but Eleanor was still aware of that strained look on his face.

"Do you want me to finish grooming Jake?" Eleanor had been around horses most of her life and was quite comfortable with all aspects of their care.

"I was pretty much done," he said. "If you'll give him a few flakes of hay and then shut the gate, I'll take these ragamuffins inside."

"I would be happy to do that," Eleanor replied. "I'll unhitch Daisy from the buckboard and take care of her while I'm at it. You entertain the little savages. When I'm done, I'll get dinner ready." When Eleanor saw the hesitation in Jared's eyes, most likely a reflection of his unease about her lack of culinary skill, she laughed. "Don't worry," she reassured him, "Anita packed a basket of food for us. She knew it would be getting on past dinnertime when we got home."

"That was nice of her," he said, trying to keep the relief he felt off of his face. "We'll head on in now."

As she watched Jared walk to the ranch house with the children in his arms, she wondered about the best way to approach him. Of course, she had expected for him to be devastated by the news of Nathan's death. She was surprised, however, by the bitterness with which he had talked about seeking vengeance. It was a side of him that she hadn't seen for many years and it brought back painful memories. She thought it might be best to talk of other topics and let him take whatever time he needed to get around to discussing how he wanted to deal with the murder of the old lawman.

When she came in carrying the picnic basket Anita Marés had packed for them, she saw that Jared had lit the lamps in the house. He was setting the table, letting Lizbeth carry utensils that wouldn't break if she dropped them. Ned had the more demanding job of carrying plates. She smiled as she saw the look of concentration on her son's face as he carried each plate with great care to its place. His tongue was sticking out the side of his mouth as he focused on his task.

She laid out the spread that Anita Marés had packed for them. The biscochitos in the basket were a surprise for when the children finished their main course. They were also an expression of the woman's love for them as well. Jared had a sweet tooth, too, and she knew he would be pleased to find out there was a treat at the end. Before they began eating, they joined hands and said a prayer of thanks. Once that was done, she passed out the tamales, removing the corn shucks and cutting up Lizbeth's serving for her.

Eleanor had not wanted to discuss anything controversial during the meal and Ned helped in that regard. He quizzed his father about the cattle drive from which he had just returned, asking how the young cowboys had done with their first trip up the trail. Although he was not quite five years old, Ned Delaney already knew that he wanted to be a cowboy just like his father. Jared often took Ned with him when he went out to check the cattle, placing him on the saddle in front of him. Ned had extracted a promise from his father that once he reached his fifth birthday, he would get his own horse.

As she had anticipated, the children and their father were delighted to discover that Anita Marés's biscochitos were in the bottom of the picnic basket waiting to be devoured. Lizbeth squealed with delight and Ned had a grin plastered all over his face. She parceled out two to each of them and poured a cup of coffee for herself and Jared. They munched for a few happy minutes and then Eleanor noticed that Lizbeth had laid her head down on the table and fallen asleep in the middle of her second biscochito.

She smiled at Jared and said, "I'll put Lizbeth to bed if you'll take care of your son." Ned was never pleased at the prospect of retiring for the night, although he never failed to fall asleep within minutes after his head hit the pillow.

Jared smiled back and said, "I'll get this little buckaroo tucked away in his bedroll, don't you worry."

Ned immediately began complaining that he wasn't tired but Jared was having none of it. In a firm voice, he explained to his son that a cowboy needs his rest if he wants to do his job well the next day. That was all the persuasion the boy needed. He got up and accompanied his father into the small bedroom that he shared with his sister. Eleanor found herself feeling a tad bit jealous of her husband that he was able to get their son to comply with so little difficulty. She often found herself butting heads with the strong-willed youngster. It was good to have Jared home.

Once the children were in bed, they set about cleaning up the dishes and putting things away. When they were through, Eleanor asked Jared if he would like to join her on the front porch sitting in their rockers. The moon had just appeared in the sky and the night air was cool but not cold. She noticed a halo around the moon, something she had seen from time to time in the past. There was something about it that made her feel uncomfortable, and a slight shiver passed through her body.

"I'll get coffee for us and join you," Eleanor said. "Maybe I can tell you more about Tommy Stallings's state of affairs. A lot of things have happened during the time you were away."

Jared frowned when Eleanor alluded to his abrupt departure and she wished she had not said anything about it. She didn't want to fight with her husband. She considered trying to qualify her statement in some way and realized that she would only dig herself a deeper hole. Instead, she went to the stove and poured two cups of hot coffee. When she took them out on the front porch, she found Jared standing by the rail rather than sitting in his rocker. He was staring up at the moon.

"Don't you want to come over here and sit?" Eleanor spoke in the most inviting and affable voice she could manage. "A lot has gone on since you left for Colorado. I'll fill you in."

With his back to her, Jared said, "I'm sure a lot has happened. The only thing that matters to me right now, though, is to hunt down the murderers of Nathan and bring swift justice to them."

Eleanor Delaney loved and respected her husband but she was strong-minded and never one to be timid. She wasn't seeking a confrontation with Jared but if it came to that, she would not back down and be submissive.

"Jared, it concerns me a great deal that you are taking this single-minded approach to handling Nathan's death. I'm in complete agreement with you that his killers need to be brought to justice but you sound like you're ready to mete out vigilante justice. That doesn't sound like the man I married."

Jared whirled around. "And what justice will Nathan get if not the vigilante kind?" The words came out harsh and accusing. Eleanor was taken aback but she was not about to allow her husband to intimidate her.

"I don't appreciate you taking out your anger and grief on me, Jared," she said, a hint of steel in her voice. "I understand that you're upset but I will not stand for being the target of your anger."

He turned back to the rail and gripped it with both hands so hard that his knuckles turned white. He took a deep breath and seemed to be trying to get himself under control. He turned around again and said, "You're right, I got no call to take this out on you. It ain't your fault and I know you want to see justice done. It's just that the situation is so jumbled up, what with Tommy bein' gone and all." He frowned and shook his head. "You said you were gonna tell me about that. I reckon I might be a little less confused if you went ahead and did that."

"Why don't you come on over and sit," Eleanor said. "I know this is distressing for you but I would feel a whole lot better if we could talk it out rather than fighting about it."

Jared hesitated for a moment, and it seemed as if he wanted to continue on the contentious path he had started down. Then he nodded and walked over to sit down in his rocking chair. He closed his eyes and leaned back in the rocker, his feet braced, then he began to rock in a slow and gentle manner.

"I don't want to fight with you, Eleanor darlin'," he said, reverting to his old term of endearment for her. "I'm just so confused by all that's happened in such a short time." He closed his eyes and said, "Reckon you ought to try to explain to me what in thunder has got into Tommy Stallings that he's headed off to Texas."

Eleanor sat in her rocker and handed Jared his cup of coffee. "I can do that," she said. "I'm not certain that I understand the whole thing myself, having just heard about it from Tomás this afternoon. I need to talk with Mollie to find out more details."

"I'll let you handle that part," Jared said. "Mollie wears me out. I'd bet she ain't happy that Tommy took off."

"They were having a rough go of it anyway," Eleanor said, "what with Tommy being over in Springer."

"What was Tommy doing in Springer?" Jared was confused.

"I guess that's right, you don't know," Eleanor said. "I forgot this all happened after you left for Trinidad. You were gone for quite a while."

"So what was Tommy doing in Springer?" A note of impatience crept into his voice.

Eleanor filled Jared in on the specifics of the Colfax County governing body's decision that the sheriff's office be transferred to the county seat in Springer with no further delay. This had taken place just as Tommy had begun to investigate the rash of rustling and murders that had swept through the county north of Cimarrón. She told him about Tommy's confrontations with Mayor Salazar regarding the suspicion that he had accepted a bribe to back off on the investigation. As she was telling him about the role of Nathan and Tommy's cousin, Rusty Stallings, as his deputies, Jared broke in.

"So this mysterious cousin Rusty just appeared out of the blue?"

"From what Tomás told me," Eleanor replied, "Rusty came to Cimarrón to enlist Tommy's help. Renegades had been victimizing ranchers over their way. Apparently, they felt like they needed Tommy's assistance in standing up to them."

"Don't they have lawmen in Texas?" Eleanor could hear the frustration in Jared's voice. "Why did they need to come to the New Mexico Territory?"

"I think there was more to it than that," Eleanor said. "Tommy lived with his aunt and uncle after his parents were killed. From what I heard, he didn't leave there on good terms. This was a chance for him to go back and make things right."

Eleanor figured that Jared would understand this since he, too, had alienated some folks in his younger years when he first came to Cimarrón. It had taken him some time to make amends. His response shocked her.

"The hell with that! What about makin' things right for Nathan?" Jared sat up straight and rigid in his rocking chair. "He left when he should've been here doin' his job just to go back and help out folks he hasn't seen in years. That ain't right."

It took Eleanor a moment to collect herself. After a pause, she said, "It seems to me that you, of all people, would understand and respect Tommy's need to make things right with people he had treated with a lack of respect in the past."

Jared glared at her. "Are you gonna drag

up things out of the past and throw them in my face? This ain't the same at all."

"How do you know that?" Eleanor was angry now and not willing to back down just to keep the peace. "You're so busy plotting your revenge, I don't believe you listened to half of what I said. And I wouldn't bring up your past if you weren't treating me with a lack of respect right this moment."

Jared stood up stiff-legged and looked at Eleanor. "I'm done talkin' about this. I'm goin' to bed." Without another word, he stalked into the house.

Eleanor sat there for a while longer. Bit by bit, her shock and anger were replaced by a fear that something was wrong with her husband. She knew him to be a kind and loving man but she had also seen his dark side many years ago. It disturbed her a great deal that she was catching a glimpse of that dark side returning.

Chapter 8

From his hiding place, Jared watched as the outlaw raised his pistol and began to exert pressure on the trigger. He tried to move and felt like his feet were stuck in a quagmire of mud. He cast a fleeting look to his right where the gun was aimed, expecting to see his father. Instead, he saw Nathan Averill. He felt like he should do something to save Nathan but he was just a little boy. What could he do? He heard the sharp crack of the shots and saw Nathan fall. As the old lawman crumpled to the ground, he glanced in Jared's direction with a look that was equal parts entreaty and condemnation. Did his eyes play tricks on him or did Nathan mouth the words, "help me" as he fell? Jared was consumed with guilt.

Jared awakened to the clink, clank, and sizzle of his family going about their daily routine. Eleanor was serving eggs and bacon to Ned and Lizbeth while mediating their conflict about who got to sit in which chair. As a rule, Lizbeth wanted to sit in whichever chair her brother chose to plop down in. Sometimes Ned would shake his head in resignation and let his baby sister have her way, but this morning he was having none of it. Sometimes a fella just has to make a stand, even if he's sitting when he does it.

A feeling of foreboding pervaded Jared's consciousness. He suspected that he'd had another nightmare but he had no clear memory of it. He tried to recall details but after a moment, he gave up. Why did dreams always seem so vivid until you tried to recall them? He had a full day's ride ahead of him to Springer where he intended to meet with Manuel Salazar and discuss plans for their vigilante mission. He faced the conversation he was about to have with his wife with trepidation.

"Mornin'," he said in a subdued voice as he walked into the kitchen and grabbed the coffee pot off the stove.

Eleanor nodded in a perfunctory manner but didn't speak. Ned and Lizbeth made up for her lack of enthusiasm by greeting him with whoops and hollers. For a moment, he basked in the glow of his children's adoration, giving each of them a hug and kiss. Eleanor continued to make a point of ignoring him. Jared figured he might as well get the confrontation over with.

"I'll be gone for a couple of days," he said in a quiet voice. "I'm headin' over to Springer. I should be back day after tomorrow at the latest."

Eleanor looked at him for a long moment before she replied. "I suppose you'll be meeting with Mayor Salazar. I had hoped you might reconsider that decision."

"Reckon I need to hear what he has to say," Jared said. "Least I can do is listen to him."

Eleanor glanced at the children, uncomfortable at having a confrontation in their presence. She spoke in a low voice. "But your mind is already made up, isn't it? Regardless of what Tomás and I had to say to you, you've already decided what you're going to do."

He started to deny it but stopped himself. She was right. He shrugged. "I won't stand by any longer doin' nothin'. I'm done with that."

Eleanor tried hard to keep the exasperation out of her voice but her efforts were only partly successful. "If you're dead set on doing something, you might at least take the mayor up on his offer to be acting sheriff. That way what you're about to do

84

would at least be legal."

"Dammit, Eleanor, can't you ever just agree with me about somethin' rather than questionin' every thing I do!"

The children stopped their recreational arguing and looked over at the parents. Ned said, "Daddy said a bad word."

Eleanor glared at Jared and walked over to the table. "Daddy is a little bit upset, Ned. It's all right. Why don't you be a good big brother and take your sister to get dressed." Ned perked right up at the prospect of having a chore to do that made him feel grown-up and allowed him to boss his sister around. He led Lizbeth away to the bedroom.

"I don't know what you think you're doing," she said, once the children were out of the room, "but this is not the way you usually act. It's been a long time since you've told me I need to keep my opinions to myself."

Jared knew she was right but he couldn't bring himself to admit it. Rather than continue a losing argument, he got up and walked over to where his hat and rifle were hung on the wall.

"I don't want to talk about it anymore," he said. "Like I told you, I should be back day after tomorrow."

"That's it?" Eleanor stared at him in disbelief. "No discussion, you just walk out the door."

He looked at her for a long moment. "Reckon that's the way it is." He walked out the door.

Jared felt bad about how he'd treated Eleanor but it was clear to him that she just didn't understand. He had no choice but to do this thing . . . avenge the death of the man who was the closest thing to a father he'd had since his own father was shot down before his eyes by renegades when he was a little boy. He had been helpless to do anything about it at the time but that was not the case now. He refused to do nothing while waiting for the wheels of justice to turn, creaking along in the same old manner as always in the New Mexico Territory, with the same end result. The wicked and powerful would have their way and the common folk would once again be victimized.

Not this time. I will do this different than in the past. I won't depend on lawmen to do their jobs in spite of all the obstacles placed in their way and I won't depend on the courts to dispense their twisted version of justice in which the corrupt and lawless always seem to prevail. Let's see how they like it when one of the victims takes a page out of their book. They may not have to answer to the law but, by God, they will answer to my wrath.

Jared arrived in Springer at dusk. He found his way to the livery and left his horse to be cared for while he went to the Brown Hotel to get a meal and a room. He was tired from the long day of travel so he bedded down pretty soon after finishing his meal of steak and beans. His sleep was restless but if he had any nightmares, he didn't remember them when he awoke just after sunrise. After a breakfast of ham and eggs, he set out to find Manuel Salazar.

If he'd thought he might have difficulty tracking down the mayor, he soon found out he was mistaken when he walked out the front door of the Brown Hotel. Almost straight across the street, he saw a large sign with bold letters proclaiming the office underneath the sign to be the workplace of Manuel Salazar, attorney at law and mayor of Springer. He couldn't help but chuckle. Clearly the mayor was not lacking in self-confidence.

The sun had not risen much above the horizon but he had a hunch that the mayor would be an early riser who charged out each morning to meet the day. He walked across the street and after knocking on the door, he opened it slowly. As he did, a voice within called out for him to enter.

"Mornin', Mayor Salazar," he said as he stuck his head through the opening. "It's Jared Delaney from Cimarrón. I've come to talk with you about the topic we discussed day before yesterday."

Salazar looked him up and down for a moment, taking his measure. Then he said, "Welcome Señor Delaney, come in and have a seat. Can I get you some coffee?"

"Thank you, sir, coffee would be a fine idea," Jared replied. "And I think we agreed the other day that you can call me Jared."

"You are right," Salazar said as he poured two mugs full of steaming coffee. "I will call you Jared and you may call me Manuel."

He handed Jared a mug and took a seat behind his desk, motioning for Jared to do the same on the other side of the desk. As Jared made himself comfortable, Salazar took another moment to study him.

"Am I to believe that you have reconsidered my offer to have you appointed acting sheriff?" He smiled. "I was under the impression that neither you nor your wife had any interest in that."

Jared flashed a polite smile in response, although he didn't find the topic especially amusing. "Your impression was correct,

Manuel. I'm not the least bit interested in being sheriff of Colfax County. I only have one interest in this matter."

Salazar tilted his chair back on two legs and studied Jared with care. "And what would that interest be?"

Jared leaned forward in his chair. "I intend to track down the vile bastards who killed Nathan Averill. When I find them, I intend to make them pay for their actions."

Salazar also leaned forward in his chair and looked into Jared's eyes. "When you say you will 'make them pay for their actions,' am I to assume that by that, you mean you will kill them?"

"Yep." Jared nodded. "If it comes to it, that's what I mean to do. And the chances are mighty good that it will come to it. We're talkin' about men who are killers. If I go after them, that's what they'll try to do to me. I'll just have to be better than they are." Jared took a deep breath and exhaled. "You have a problem with that?"

Salazar sat back in his chair and smiled. "No, I have no problem with that at all. You are just the man I am looking for." He chuckled. "That is, of course, if you are better than these men at killing."

"So the fact that what we're talkin' about is against the law doesn't bother you?" Jared glanced around the room at the law books. "That seems like an odd position for a public official to take, particularly one who is an attorney."

Salazar laughed out loud. "How long have you lived in the New Mexico Territory, Jared? If you have been here very long, you know that it would be odd for a public official *not* to take that position. The primary difference between me and many of my contemporaries is that I am willing to break the law in order to see justice done. Most often, it is the other way around."

Jared laughed in spite of himself. "Reckon you got me there," he said. "Far as I can tell, you wouldn't make any money from this thing we're discussin'. There doesn't appear to be much in the way of a profit in it for you that I can see."

The smile disappeared from Salazar's face. "Nathan Averill saved my life when I was young and foolish. He showed me a path to success that was built on hard work and honesty, on doing things the right way. He gave me a chance." For a moment, Salazar gazed toward the window in his office. "I know people think I am prideful. They see me as arrogant and brash. And you know what? I *am* proud. I rose from nothing and with the help of a good man, I turned my life around to become something I am proud of."

Jared was struck by the similarities in their stories. Every word that Manuel Salazar had said in describing what Nathan Averill had done for him also applied to Jared's life. He had given him a chance and a choice to be better. At a time when everyone else was ready to give up on him, Nathan Averill refused to give up. This was the debt he owed Nathan. It would seem that it was the same debt Salazar owed.

"Looks to me we're of a similar mind on this matter, Manuel," Jared said. "Reckon we ought to get to work doin' the job. Why don't you tell me what you know or suspect."

Salazar nodded but didn't begin talking right away. Instead, he sat there with a pained expression on his face. Jared waited. At last, Salazar spoke.

"There are two men who are responsible for the murder of Nathan Averill. One is Felipe Alvarado who lives in San Miguel County. I have never met the man but his reputation is noteworthy. He is acknowledged as a vicious killer and more than likely, he is the one who pulled the trigger. I will tell you more about him in a moment." Once more, Salazar paused as if he was trying to collect his thoughts, and again, Jared waited. Salazar shook his head as if exasperated with himself. "The second man is someone I believed I knew well. It would seem that I was wrong."

Jared was becoming impatient. "I ain't here to judge you, Manuel. If you misread this man's character, you made a mistake. That's somethin' we've all done on more than one occasion. Why don't you go ahead and tell me about this fella."

"I misjudged this man's character because I was blinded by ambition," Salazar said. "If I had paid closer attention to what was actually happening instead of my own hopes and dreams, I might have seen the truth sooner. And Nathan Averill might still be alive."

"And maybe if I hadn't gone off to Colorado, I might have been around to help Nathan and Tommy Stallings track down these buzzards before they could do the foul deed," Jared replied. "Whatever mistake you made, I doubt you did it on purpose."

Salazar nodded his gratitude. "You are right, my error was not committed on purpose but it was an error nonetheless. The man, Jesus Abreu, was my personal advisor. He was guiding my political ambitions." A look of disgust crossed his face. "Little did I know that I was his puppet."

"Jesus Abreu? He's the banker, ain't he?" Jared tried to move the discussion along. Although he understood Salazar's regret, he wasn't inclined to waste any time wallowing in it. There was a job to do. "What would a banker have in common with a man like Felipe Alvarado that would bring the two together?"

"They are *primos* . . . cousins," Manuel replied. "They grew up together and have remained in closer contact over the years than most of us realized. From working with Abreu for a number of years, I am guessing he was the one who came up with the strategy of raiding ranches north of Cimarrón while leaving the people around Springer alone. He assumed I would be less concerned if Springer was not involved," Salazar said, a look of chagrin on his face. "He was right. I played right into his hands."

"We can't change that now," Jared said, "but we can dang sure try to catch up with these two skunks and make 'em pay for what they did. Tell me what you can about their raidin' the ranches."

"As far as I know, they had a gang of men operating under their orders," Manuel said. "When Sheriff Stallings and Nathan raided the gang's hideout up in Compos Canyon, they killed all the men except for the leader, an hombre called Pony Diehl. They were bringing him in for questioning when he and Nathan were shot. They were hoping Diehl would give up the leaders of this band of outlaws to save himself."

"And that's why we got no proof against these no-good villains, I reckon," Jared said. "They killed the man who could turn on them." He shrugged. "That's why I ain't interested in bein' sheriff. This way, I don't need proof. I'll just take your word for it." He stared hard at Salazar. "Just how sure are you?"

"I am as certain as the day is long, Jared," Salazar said. "These *cabrónes* are behind all of the stealing and killing. They are the ones who murdered Nathan Averill."

"If they're smart, though, they'll lay low for the time bein'," Jared reflected. "That might make it harder to track 'em down."

"It would if that is what they were doing," Salazar responded. "However, I was just notified by the acting town constable that a boy was murdered and his family's horses were stolen a ways north of here the other day." His eyes narrowed. "They say the boy was gutted like a hog. That sounds like Felipe Alvarado to me."

"Did the constable go out and look at the place? He might have found somethin' we could use to tie these boys in."

"The constable has no jurisdiction outside of town. He just got word of the crime and passed the information on to me," Manuel said. "I promise you that he wants nothing to do with trying to solve this murder. With no sheriff, we are basically on our own here."

"Then I'd better get to work," Jared said. "Is Abreu still hangin' around town? I'd be interested in havin' a little talk with him to see what I can shake loose."

"No one has seen Jesus for days," Salazar said. "I do not know where he is hiding but he seems to have figured out that I am onto his game."

"Well, maybe I'll head down to Las Vegas then," Jared said. "I know the sheriff down there. He may be able to help me locate these boys."

"And I will be on the lookout for Jesus Abreu," Manual said. "If I see him before you do, we may do more than just talk."

Jared chuckled. "I think I'm gonna enjoy workin' with you, Manuel. I like the way you think."

It was torturous for Eleanor as she stumbled through the day's chores while keeping an eye on her vigorous and energetic children.

95

Jared's behavior since he arrived back from Colorado was alarmingly similar to that of the younger man she had known eight years ago. He had been a young cowboy then, handsome and dashing but always with a shadow of pain and suffering lingering in the background. When he arrived in town, she felt an immediate attraction to him but he drove her to distraction with the inconsistencies in his behavior. She finally had her fill and told him she didn't want to see him anymore.

Back then, Jared had seemed to lack a moral compass. He knew the difference between right and wrong but at times, he seemed incapable of making a decision about which path to follow. For a time, Jared had ridden with an evil man, Morgan O'Bannon. That was a dark period for Eleanor. She feared she'd lost her young cowboy forever. Nathan Averill had stepped in to provide him with the direction and encouragement he needed to get on the straight and narrow trail and he had remained there ever since . . . until now. Nathan was gone, torn from their lives by a vicious murderer. Jared appeared determined to track down and kill that man, the law be damned.

One of the things that disturbed her most about how her husband was acting now was his unwillingness to listen to her and engage in a dialogue. Over the years that they had been married, they had developed the ability to have spirited debates about topics, often arriving at different conclusions at the end of the discussions than either one would have predicted. They respected each other's opinions and that had always kept the talks from turning contentious. With Nathan's death, something seemed to have shifted in Jared. Right now, he wasn't even listening to her, let alone talking it out.

By sundown, she was feeling angry, hurt, and helpless. Always before, during her marriage, she would have discussed these feelings with her best friend . . . her husband. This time that wasn't an option. Her husband was the source of those feelings.

CHAPTER 9

"Who is this Jared Delaney and what is he talking with Salazar about?" Felipe Alvarado paced back and forth over the floor of the cabin, clearly agitated.

"I do not know what he talked with Manuel about," Jesus Abreu said, speaking with caution. More and more he was becoming concerned that his sadistic cousin was spinning out of control with his violent actions. "My assistant could only tell me that he saw him go into the mayor's office and come out some time later. He was not present at the meeting."

Alvarado whirled around. "Do not treat me as if I am a child, Chuy. I understand that your man was not at the meeting. And you did not answer my other question. Who is Jared Delaney?"

Abreu held his hands up in a placating gesture. "I meant no offense, *paisano*. I was only trying to explain that I did not know the topic of their conversation."

"Of course you did not." Alvarado exhaled. "Now, you worthless *pendejo,* would you please answer my other question?"

Recognizing both the futility and danger of challenging the slur his cousin had just directed his way, he continued. "But of course. Delaney is a rancher who was a close friend of Nathan Averill. Perhaps he was only trying to get more information from Manuel about the circumstances of the old man's death."

"And why would he want that information?" Alvarado pursed his lips as he contemplated his question. "You have told me that you think your mayor is considering trying to avenge the death of his old friend. Might he not be attempting to enlist the assistance of this Delaney hombre?"

"That is a possibility, *paisano,*" Abreu said. "I believe Delaney tracked down some cattle rustlers with the old sheriff in the past. I think it would be wise for us to keep an eye on him to see what he does next."

"How do you propose to do that, Chuy? You are hiding up here in this cabin, afraid to show your face in town."

Abreu was stung by the disdain in his cousin's voice but he was careful not to challenge him when he responded. "I have

99

chosen to keep a low profile at this time, *primo.* I want to let things die down a bit. That does not mean I do not have resources. I can have my assistant follow Delaney."

"Does your assistant have the skills to do that without being seen?"

Abreu nodded. "I chose him with care, Felipe. He is an ambitious young man who has not been a bank clerk all of his life. In fact, he has worked in the past outside the law on more than one occasion. He is counting on me to help him further his career in return for his doing, shall we say, 'odd jobs' for me. He will do what I tell him."

"All right then," Alvarado snapped. "Tell him to follow Delaney and find out what he is up to. If it appears that he is attempting to investigate the death of the old sheriff, I will have to dispose of him."

Abreu heaved a deep sigh. As he feared, his cousin seemed determined to continue down this path of slaughtering anyone who got in his way. Jesus didn't think this was an intelligent approach to handling the problem but he was afraid to challenge his cousin in any way. His biggest fear aside from being killed by Felipe Alvarado was that he would be taken down by his cousin's impulsive and violent actions. He needed to think of a way out of this trap that he found himself in. He had to find a way to insulate himself from his cousin's rash actions but he knew he couldn't challenge him directly. *I may need to leave the New Mexico Territory and find a place to start over.* As long as Alvarado was alive, though, he would never tolerate that. *I may need to arrange an accident for my primo. Otherwise, he will bring me down with him.* He said none of this to Alvarado.

Alvarado flared up at his cousin. "You have a problem with what I said?"

"No, of course not," Abreu said, beads of sweat popping out on his forehead. "I will tell my man to do that, Felipe. I will let you know what he finds out."

As Jesus Abreu rode back to Springer, he thought hard about his limited options. He would put his assistant, Davey Good, on the task of following Jared Delaney like he told his violent cousin he would. He didn't dare cross Alvarado in the open and besides, he figured Felipe was right. They needed to know what Delaney was up to. That didn't solve his bigger problem, though, which was to find a way to extract himself from this huge mess.

If Delaney was in fact tracking them down

for killing Nathan Averill, he knew his cousin would never allow himself to be taken into custody and given a trial. He would go down in a hail of gunfire and either kill or be killed. At this point, Abreu considered it would be better for his own long-term survival prospects if Felipe Alvarado was killed. His challenge was to find a way to manipulate his cousin into a situation where that would happen without Alvarado's becoming suspicious. That would be difficult. Difficult but not impossible.

South of town just past where Salado Creek ran into the Cimarrón River, Abreu veered off on a trail that took him to the east so that he could ride up to the back of the bank without being seen. Although it wasn't official that he was wanted for any crimes, he knew that Manuel Salazar had been looking for him and was eager for a confrontation. Whatever sway he'd held over Salazar as his political consultant was gone. Manuel had information about his role in the planning of the cattle rustling and murder spree that Alvarado's White Caps Gang had been on, and while Abreu didn't think anything could be proven in a court of law, he knew that Salazar was convinced he was guilty.

Reflecting on his state of affairs, Jesus

Abreu concluded that his days in the New Mexico Territory were numbered. He needed to figure out how to stay out of jail, set up his cousin to be murdered, and find a way to abscond with sufficient funds from his bank that he could set himself up in another town far away. He had contemplated going to Denver but he thought there might be some interesting prospects in Fort Worth as well. The idea of a new start buoyed his spirits a bit. Perhaps this could work out after all.

The bank that he owned and operated was located on the east side of Colfax Street in Springer. Coming from the east, he could slip into the bank through the entrance off the alley without anyone seeing him. He tied his horse at the hitching post and entered the back door, which opened on a hallway that led to his office. Once inside his office, he opened the door a crack so he could look out into the lobby of the bank and see if anyone he needed to avoid was there. To his relief, there were only a couple of customers there and none were any threat to him. He quickly slipped out into the lobby and signaled to young Davey Good to join him in his office.

"Come in," he said in response to the knock on his door.

"You wanted to see me, sir?" Good stepped inside the office but stood by the open door.

"Come on in and close the door," Jesus said in a brusque tone. "I do not want everyone in the lobby to hear our conversation."

Good shut the door and walked over to Abreu's desk. He stood there shifting from one foot to the other, his anxiety obvious.

"Go ahead and sit down," Abreu said. "I have something I need for you to do for me and it will take me a few minutes to explain it to you. No need to stand." The young man sat on the edge of the chair and waited, his eyes alert. "I need for you to follow Jared Delaney, the man you saw meeting with Mayor Salazar." He smiled in a friendly manner at the young man. "Good job, by the way, of finding out who he was. That was smart to check at the livery."

"Thank you, sir," Good said with an air of caution. "I could tell he was from out of town. I figured he had to have left his horse there 'cause it wasn't out front of the mayor's office. Lucky old Arturo Garcia knew who he was."

"Arturo knows most of the people who go in and out of town. He is both friendly and curious . . . nosy, some might say. If he did

104

not know Delaney before, he most certainly would have introduced himself when he left his horse there. Again, that was clever of you to check with him."

Good nodded in acknowledgment. "How am I supposed to follow Delaney, sir? He left here two days ago and I don't know where he went."

"Delaney owns a ranch north of Cimarrón. I suspect that he returned there after he left. If not, he may be in Cimarrón." Abreu frowned at the young man. "Delaney is well known. Use those skills you learned growing up down south. Ask questions, get information, do not make anyone suspicious."

When Davey Good applied for a job as a teller at Jesus Abreu's bank, there was something about him that made Jesus wary about the young man. He had a furtive look that made Jesus wonder if he had a shady background. At first, he was concerned that the young man might be trying to get a job at the bank so he could figure out how to steal money.

Although there was no sheriff occupying the office at this time, wanted posters still appeared on a regular basis as sheriffs around the territory notified officers of the law of outlaws who were on the loose. Jesus

Abreu had looked through the wanted posters and found a reasonable likeness of Davey Good along with his father and two brothers on one that had been sent by the sheriff down in Mesilla. Turned out the Good family had been up to "no good," robbing the local bank.

When he brought this up to Davey, the boy feared that Abreu was going to turn him in. It took a while before he understood that the banker was only using the information for leverage so that he could recruit him to do his dirty work. He wasn't happy about that fact but he didn't have any good alternatives so he went along with his boss. He tried telling Señor Abreu that he was sincere in his wish to change his life and get out of the outlaw trade but the banker didn't seem to care. Davey Good was in a bind and he couldn't see any way to get out of it.

"When do you want me to leave, Mr. Abreu?" Davey was concerned about leaving his actual duties as a bank clerk unfinished. It would appear he was more concerned about it than Abreu.

"Was I not clear?" Abreu raised his voice in an imperious tone. "I want you to leave right now. This is very important to me. I need to know where he is going and what he is doing."

"Yes, sir," Davey said. After a pause, he asked, "How do I let you know what I find out?"

Abreu considered the question. "You will have to send me telegrams. Delaney is often in Cimarrón and has been seen down in Las Vegas as well. Both of those towns have telegraph offices, use them." He frowned. "It is important that you keep your messages vague. Refer to him as 'our friend.' Tell me where he has gone but do not mention who he has seen or talked to. I can figure that part out myself."

Abreu figured that in all likelihood Delaney would be coming back to Springer to talk to various individuals but it occurred to him that Jared might make a trip down to San Miguel County to see what he could find out about Felipe Alvarado. If he did, there was a good chance that his cousin would kill Delaney, which would solve at least one problem. However, he still needed to find a way to take his leave from the New Mexico Territory without incurring the wrath of Felipe Alvarado. As far as he could see, that would require his manipulating someone into killing his *primo*. This would not be an easy task. Delaney probably had the best chance of anyone involved in the game of accomplishing the feat.

Seated behind his desk, Abreu had been lost in reflection. Now he looked up and noticed the young man still standing in front of him, his anxiety evident.

"Do you have a question for me?" Abreu waited for a response from the young man.

"Uh, well, yes, sir, I reckon I do," Good stammered.

"Well, what is it?" Abreu's patience was wearing thin.

"You . . . um, you don't want me to do anything to this fella, do you? I mean, like trying to hurt him or something? I mean, you just want me to follow him and tell you where he's been, right?"

It occurred to Abreu that this young man was a bit less enthusiastic about his job than he would have preferred. "You are not getting squeamish on me, are you, Davey?" Abreu's smile did not reach his eyes. "No, right now I do not want you to do anything except keep track of Delaney. Keep me informed of his actions and whereabouts. If I require more of you, I will let you know." Standing up, he said, "Now, please get moving. Do not even stop at your station; I will have someone else count your money for you. Go!"

With a distressed look on his face, Good

turned and walked out of Abreu's office. Jesus Abreu sat back down behind his desk and continued to plot his getaway. He was busy contemplating whether to go north to Colorado or east to Texas when he heard a big commotion in the lobby of the bank. The door to his office burst open and his secretary, Roberto, rushed in.

"Señor Abreu, the mayor is insisting on seeing you. I tried to tell him you were not in but he said he knew you were here." Roberto shot a nervous glance over his shoulder.

"I am just leaving, Roberto," Abreu said. "Please tell the mayor I will have to see him another time." Jesus wondered how Manuel had known he was in town. He figured Salazar must have spies on the lookout for him. There was more noise from the lobby and then Manuel Salazar pushed past Roberto and confronted him.

"There you are, you filthy *cabrón,*" Salazar shouted at him. "You worthless *pendejo,* you thought you could sneak in here and I wouldn't know."

Abreu stood up. He was sick and tired of being called names. He might have to tolerate it from his homicidal cousin but not from this man. "You cannot burst into my office and insult me, Manuel. I have done

109

nothing wrong. I do not have to take this abuse from you."

Salazar was shaking with rage but with an effort, he calmed himself. "Do not try to play the innocent with me, Jesus. I know what you did . . . you and your vile cousin, Felipe. You will pay for your transgressions, I give you my promise."

Abreu decided to try to bluff his way through the confrontation. "That is fine, Manuel. Let me know when your new sheriff, Señor Delaney, has the evidence he needs to take me in front of a judge. In the meantime, you need to leave my office and stop disrupting my place of business or I will file a complaint with your sheriff."

Salazar looked puzzled for a moment and then he smiled. "You think Jared Delaney is the acting sheriff? That is humorous." He laughed for a moment. "You are not that fortunate, Jesus. Jared Delaney is working as an independent citizen to track you and your *primo* down and make you pay for your foul deeds. He needs no evidence to do that because we already know what you did and we know you are guilty. He will not bring your case in front of a court; he will serve as judge, jury, and executioner."

Jesus Abreu was speechless for a moment. When he gathered his wits, he said, "If he tries to do that, Manuel, he will be committing murder. He will be an outlaw himself. He cannot just ignore the law."

Salazar shook his head and laughed again. "It is amusing to me to hear those words come out of your mouth, Jesus, considering to what degree you and Alvarado have ignored the law for all these years. How do you like it now that the tables are turned?"

"You have nothing on me, Manuel," an indignant Abreu said. "I repeat, you cannot just ignore the law. You are the mayor of this town and are sworn to uphold the law."

"I am not the one you need to fear, Jesus," Salazar said. "As much as I would like to exact my own revenge, I have indeed sworn to uphold the law. I will not lay a finger on you." He glared at the banker. "The same cannot be said for my *amigo,* Delaney, however."

"Your threats do not scare me, Manuel," Abreu responded. "They are only talk. In the meantime, you need to leave my office or I will have my employees escort you out."

Salazar aimed a cold stare at the man for another moment, then he said, "I will leave you alone for now. Just know that you have been warned. It would be in your best interests to speak to a lawman and confess your foul deeds. Perhaps you can make a deal." He smirked. "Making deals is what you are good at, *qué no?*"

CHAPTER 10

As Davey Good rode along the trail from Springer to Cimarrón, he shook his head as he pondered his situation. Once again, he was at the mercy of someone who was older and more powerful. One more time, he was being forced to engage in actions that he did not want to be a part of. He knew that if he got caught, he would be the one to suffer the consequences, not the man who forced him into it. As he contemplated his helplessness, he felt as if he might throw up.

His circumstances with the banker, Abreu, were not that much different from what he experienced growing up in his family. He was the youngest of three sons and for as long as he could remember, his father, Bill Good, had embraced the life of an outlaw. As a young boy, he watched as each of his older brothers was brought into the fold. Their father began taking them along on his forays to steal horses when they were only ten years old. Both brothers embraced the life with enthusiasm and by the time they were in their teens, they were full-fledged criminals.

Davey had no desire to follow in his father's and brothers' footsteps but as far as he could see, it was inevitable. When his father started taking his brothers with him, Davey's mother had mounted a weak protest but to no avail. She was not a strong woman and seemed to have given in to her husband's will long ago. Davey held little hope that she could prevail with his father and convince him not to include Davey in the family business, and even this tiny bit of hope was dashed when she died of pneumonia when he was nine years old.

Sure enough, soon after his tenth birthday, his father informed him that he was going along when he went out on a raid to rustle cattle. For the first time in his life, Davey stood up to his father and told him he didn't want to go. Faster than the strike of a rattlesnake, his father lashed out and slapped him across the face, knocking him off his feet. As Davey lay there trembling, his father told him that if he ever challenged him again, he would kill him.

With his future as an outlaw now solidified, Davey discovered that he had skills that were a good fit for the job. He could move with stealth and his father frequently sent him ahead to scout out ranches in order to count the stock and assess how well-armed the folks were. Davey was a good shot with a pistol and a rifle but he made a point to miss on the few occasions they became involved in the exchange of gunfire. He didn't like stealing and he had no stomach at all for killing. He reckoned his father suspected as much so he kept those views to himself.

When he was seventeen, his oldest brother, Bob, was killed as they were in the process of robbing a bank in El Paso. They were riding away with the money when he was shot out of the saddle. As a terrified Davey spurred his horse to a greater speed and hunkered down in the saddle, he noticed that his father never even looked back. Even as he hurtled along, he resolved that as soon as he saw a chance, he would find a way to leave the family business.

His opportunity came less than a month later. He, his brother, and his father were robbing another bank, this time in southern Arizona. A bank guard with an itchy trigger finger and a desire to be a hero pulled his pistol on them as they were leaving the bank with the money they had stolen. The guard managed to get off one shot before his father shot him dead but his actions emboldened the others in the bank. In a heartbeat, bullets were flying thick and fast as hornets around them as if someone had beat on a nest with a stick.

They jumped on their horses out front of the bank and his father and brother rode at breakneck speed toward the south. In a split second, Davey saw his chance. He turned his horse north and rode as if the devil was chasing him. In fact, he was sure that if his father figured out that he had run, Davey would wish the devil was on his trail because he could expect more mercy from Old Scratch than from his father. His lone hope was that the man would assume Davey had been shot attempting his getaway. Davey assumed that his father would spend even less time mourning his loss than he had that of his older brother.

Davey rode north and east through Arizona, up towards Springerville. He pushed his horse as hard as he could but after two days of riding, he let up for fear that the gelding would become lame. He headed east from Springerville across the San Agustin Plains toward Magdalena, then headed north from there. He wasn't sure where he was headed, he just knew he had to put as much distance as possible between himself and his father.

He had lived off the land during this trek, shooting small game and drinking from streams. When he got into the northern part of the New Mexico Territory, the land they called the Big Empty, game got scarce. He realized that he needed to stop in a town and find a way to make some money. He would prefer to do it in an honest manner. He was fervent in his hope that his outlaw days were behind him.

Once he made this decision, the nearest town turned out to be Springer. He had a small amount of cash on him from his family's ill-gotten gains and he used it to get a room at the Brown Hotel. He purchased a large meal of steak, potatoes, coffee, and apple pie. After spending extra to get seconds, he paid for a bath and soaked himself for a long time to get the trail dust off his weary body. He then fell into the fluffy feather bed in his room and slept for twelve hours straight.

The next morning, he went downstairs to the front desk and asked the man there if he knew of anyone who was looking to hire a good worker. The man looked at him with a critical eye and told him that he'd heard they were looking for a teller at the bank but he doubted that Davey was the man for the job. Davey did his best not to smile as he told the man that he, in fact, had some experience working in banks. He thanked him and walked over to apply for the job.

Dusk was coming on as he reflected on his misfortune. In his naiveté, he had walked into a snake pit at Jesus Abreu's bank. At the time, he had no way of knowing the man was as crooked as a rope or that he would somehow discover Davey's shady past and use it against him. He wondered if he would ever find a way out of these traps he kept falling into. He found himself sinking into despondency as he looked for a place to camp for the night.

Davey made a fire and ate the last of the jerky he had brought with him. With a heavy heart, he laid down in his bedroll and tried to sleep. He looked up at the sky and saw that there was a misty halo around the moon. He recalled something his mother told him many years ago, that a halo around the moon meant that change was coming. It occurred to him that it would sure be nice if this time it was a change for the better.

As he dozed off, an encouraging thought crossed his mind. The last time he was in Abreu's office, he had noticed the man had some numbers written on a slip of paper.

He managed to see what they were and committed them to memory. Although he wasn't sure, Davey Good suspected that he now had the combination to the safe at the bank. He didn't know when, how, or even if this would prove useful to him but he figured that at least now, he had one chip to play.

CHAPTER 11

"You agreed to do what?" Eleanor Delaney exploded with anger when she heard the news from her husband that he had agreed to become Manuel Salazar's vigilante. "How can you do this? If you have no regard for me, do you not care about your children?"

Jared set his jaw and tried to face his wife but he had difficulty looking her in the eye. As he responded to her outburst, he heard a sullen tone in his voice that he didn't like. This made him feel even angrier and more obstinate.

"I can't believe you think that way, Eleanor," he said. "I've gone out before to catch outlaws and you didn't question my love for you or the children."

"The difference is that you were going out with the sheriff and had been legally deputized, Jared." Eleanor was aggravated and it was apparent in her tone. "You must be able to see the difference. I hated that you were risking your life back then but I knew you were on the side of the law. Now you are choosing to break the law and act like a criminal. If you do this, how are you any better than the men you hunt?"

Jared threw up his hands in anger. "How can you say that to me? These men killed Nathan Averill, the closest thing you've had to a father for most of your life." He was so upset that he was quivering. "You're gonna compare me to those men and say I'm like them. That ain't right."

Eleanor did her best to calm down. She knew her best chance of getting her husband to listen was to be reasonable. "One of the things I love about you, Jared, is that you stand up for what is right. When Juan was killed, you went through the trial and kept your temper in check even when it was clear the judge was in the pockets of the Santa Fe Ring. You respect the law even when the people charged with enforcing it come up short." She laid her hand on his arm. "What you are doing now is different. You're acting as if the law doesn't matter, like you can just disregard the parts you don't like. That's not the Jared Delaney I know."

Jared pulled away from the touch of her hand. "Maybe the Jared you knew wasn't gettin' the job done, Eleanor. In case you haven't noticed, good people keep gettin' murdered and nothin' seems to ever get done about it." Jared's voice quivered with indignation. "You say I care about what's right. Well, that ain't right."

Eleanor took a deep breath. "Of course it's not right. But if your answer to what is wrong is also wrong, how can you show your children how to be good, moral people? And how can you look at yourself in the mirror?"

"Dammit, Eleanor, these men murdered Nathan," Jared thundered. He was on the verge of losing control. "They need to pay for their evil deed. The law ain't gonna make that happen so I either have to stand by like a helpless sheep or do somethin' about it. I'm done waitin' on the law to do what's right."

"Please don't yell at me, Jared," Eleanor said. "That's not like you either. Can't you see that you're not being true to yourself?"

Jared glared at his wife. "More like I'm not actin' like you want me to. You just can't stand for me to think for myself."

Eleanor stared at her husband in astonishment. "How on earth can you say that? Are you so muddled in your thinking that you can't stand for me to challenge it? When did this start?"

Jared stood there with his fists clenched, searching for an answer. Finally, he said, "I ain't discussin' this any more. I got to go down to San Miguel County and talk to the sheriff there. I'm sorry you don't understand but I got to do this my way." With those words hanging in the air, he left.

Eleanor stood there speechless as the sound of the door slamming echoed in her ears. She could feel the tears welling up and she struggled for control. She heard a noise from the loft and when she turned, she saw her son climbing down the ladder. He ran over to where she was standing, a worried look written all over his young face.

"Mama, what's wrong with Papa?"

Eleanor knelt down in front of him and looked into his innocent eyes. "I don't know, Ned." She reached out and pulled him into a fierce embrace. She felt the tears run down her face, and with a great effort, she managed not to sob. "I just don't know."

CHAPTER 12

Eleanor did her best to stick to her usual routine with Ned and Lizbeth, not only to provide comfort to them during this stressful time but also to soothe herself. She knew something was wrong with her husband and that it was having a terrible and destructive effect on their marriage and family. She fed the children and set them on their way to do the simple chores they had. The house was in mild disarray and she went around straightening things up and dusting a bit.

Engaging in these undemanding tasks helped her calm down and take a more objective look at the state of affairs. Although she was very concerned about Jared, she knew he was a good man and that he loved both her and his children. At this moment in time, she couldn't think of anything more she could do or say to persuade him to handle things in a different way. As hard as it was, she figured she would just have to trust him to come to his senses.

In the meantime, however, she wasn't sure how to handle the questions the children were asking her about why their father was so angry. Ned had asked her what he had done to make his daddy so mad at him, which broke Eleanor's heart. She reassured the boy that his father was not angry with him but she wasn't sure if he accepted her explanation. Although they were used to their father being gone for stretches of time when he drove cattle to Colorado, they seemed to be able to sense that this was different somehow. She couldn't help but be angry at Jared for his callous disregard of their children's fears.

As she thought about Jared's need to come to his senses, she realized that she, too, needed to take stock and reassess her priorities. She had been so focused on Jared's distress that she had completely forgotten about a person who was in desperate need of her support and comfort. She had not kept her word to Christy that she would come and join her in grieving for the loss of the man who had been so special in both of their lives.

Eleanor stepped out onto the portal and looked at the sky. She figured it was midday from the location of the sun. If she fed the children promptly, she could gather them up and they could make it into town by midafternoon. She knew she could count on Maria Suazo and Anita Marés to look after her two wild and woolly imps. Ned and Lizbeth loved spending time at the Marés Café and would be delighted for the opportunity to be spoiled with treats and attention. They could make an outing of it, spend the night in town, and come back to the ranch in the morning. She also considered that focusing on a problem that she could do something about would make her feel less helpless.

When she told the children of her plan, they were beside themselves with glee. It was all she could do to get them to sit still long enough to wolf down a few bites of the leftover stew she reheated on the woodstove. Eleanor was confident that Estévan could manage without her. Soon they were on their way into town, singing songs and playing word games. She felt better than she had at any time since learning the news of Nathan's death.

Leaving the buckboard at the livery for the night, Eleanor did her best to keep up with Ned and Lizbeth as they skipped toward the Marés Café singing a song. When they burst in the front door, she saw

Anita and Maria working to clean up and restore order to the establishment following the noon meal rush. When Anita saw the children, she threw up her hands and laughed out loud.

"Look who has come to help me out. Come, *mi chilitos,* let us run into the kitchen and see what work there is to be done there." She leaned over towards the children and winked at them. "Maybe we will find some biscochitos that did not get eaten. *Quien sabé.* I suppose we can throw them out for the birds to eat. You do not like biscochitos, do you?"

"Yes, we do," screamed Ned and Lizbeth in unison. "We love them."

"I did not know that," Anita said in faux amazement. "Maybe we will not give them to the birds after all. Do you know anyone who might want to eat them?"

"We'll eat them, *Tía* Anita," Ned said. Lizbeth squealed with laughter.

She took the children by the hand and said, "Let us go then." As they walked toward the kitchen, she looked back and smiled at Eleanor.

Eleanor shook her head in wonder. "How did she know to do that?"

Maria smiled. "She is full of wisdom, that one. She knows what her family needs, sometimes even before they do." Her smile faded. "What can I do for you?"

"Get me a cup of coffee and talk with me," Eleanor said as she walked over to a table. "I need to know how Christy is doing and I need your advice on something else."

Maria grabbed two cups of coffee and joined Eleanor at the table. "I took some food over to Miss Christy this morning. I do not think she has been eating. Who can blame her?" She shrugged. "I could see that she had been crying and she did not have much to say. I did not push her to talk. I remember all too well how it was for me when Juan was murdered." Maria looked down at the table. When she looked back at Eleanor, her eyes were misty. "It took some time before I was ready to speak with others about my thoughts and feelings."

"I think I understand," Eleanor said. "There is a time to talk but words alone are not enough. Sometimes, you just need to grieve." She took a deep breath. "I told her at the funeral service that I would come by and we could cry together. She seemed to think that was a good idea. Do you think now is the time to do that?"

Maria nodded. "Miss Christy knows and trusts you, maybe more than anyone. She knows you loved Señor Nathan as much as she did, in your own way. I think this could be good for her."

Eleanor nodded. "All right, then, I'll do that when we're through here."

Maria gave her a quizzical look. "You said you needed my advice on something else. What is it?"

Now it was Eleanor's turn to stare down at the table. She took a breath and responded. "Maria, I'm worried about Jared. He's acting like he did when he first came to Cimarrón all these years ago."

Jared had worked with Maria's late husband, Juan Suazo, when he first came to town. Juan was a top hand for the Kilpatricks. In the beginning, he and Jared had a friendly rivalry, and in the end, a deep friendship. After Lizbeth Kilpatrick, who died from wounds inflicted by the outlaw, Gentleman Curt Barwick, left the ranch to Jared, he made Juan his partner. Maria had known Jared through the bad times and the good.

Maria frowned. "He was very confused back then. He had much trouble choosing between the paths of good and evil, as I recall." She sipped her coffee and thought some more about what Eleanor had said. "He got straightened out, though. Between you and Sheriff Averill, he found his way."

129

A look of understanding crossed her face. "The death of the sheriff, it has taken him back to those bad times, *qué no?*"

Eleanor nodded. "I'm afraid so, Maria. He is angry and insists that he is going to track down the men who murdered Nathan and kill them. He refuses to listen to anything I have to say. He won't listen to Tomás or Estévan either." She blew out a harsh breath. "I don't know if I want to take him in my arms and comfort him, kiss him, or just straight out shoot him. I'm so frustrated, I don't know what to do."

Maria smiled. "As tempting as it is, shooting him is not a practical solution. Although you might feel better in the moment, in the long run, it does not work out so good."

Eleanor laughed. "I know, and you're right . . . it's not a good solution but I think it might make me feel good to do it. I swear, he can be the most stubborn man in the world. I might as well talk to a fence post."

Maria chuckled. "I know that feeling. Juan was like that and as it turns out, Tomás can be quite stubborn as well. It is as if our men were crossbred with mules, *qué no?*"

"I hadn't thought about that possibility," Eleanor said with a smile, "but you might be right." Her smile died away. "I still don't know what to do, though."

Maria cocked her head to one side. "Maybe there is nothing you can do. Perhaps you have already done all there is to do by loving him and telling him what you think. It is possible that your words have sunk in even though he cannot accept them yet." She leaned back in her chair. "Maybe the only thing you can do now is be patient."

"In case you hadn't noticed, Maria, patience has never been a virtue I have cultivated," Eleanor said, laughing. "Although it galls me something fierce that I can't fix this, I'd already had the same thought. I guess I just needed to hear it from someone I trust." She reached over and took Maria's hands in hers. "Thank you for being my friend."

With a smile, Maria squeezed Eleanor's hands and stood up. "Enough, this is all I know to share with you. I will go help my future mother-in-law with your wild children while you go comfort Miss Christy."

Eleanor nodded as she rose and headed for the door.

The small cottage behind the school that Christy and Nathan had shared was dark and silent as Eleanor approached. Although it appeared that no one was home, Eleanor thought it unlikely that Christy was out strolling about the village. She went to the door and knocked. It was a moment before she got a response and when it came, she found it hard to understand the muffled words.

"Please go away; I don't want to see anyone." At least that's what Eleanor thought she heard.

"Christy, it's me, Eleanor," she said. "I told you I would come see you."

Her words were met with silence and Eleanor was afraid Christy would not let her come in. Then she heard shuffling inside and the door opened. Eleanor took a deep breath, shocked by what she saw. Christy was still wearing the black dress she had worn at the funeral several days ago and she looked as if she had aged thirty years. Her face was drawn and there were dark circles under her eyes.

Christy noticed her reaction and a brief smile flitted across her lips. "I know I look a fright. I haven't paid much attention to my appearance these past few days because I haven't been accepting company. I figured I'd make an exception for you."

Eleanor and Christy had been friends for too long for her to lie. "You look like someone who just lost her husband, Christy. There's no shame in that." She glanced past

Christy and saw the food that Maria had brought over sitting untouched on the small dining table. "May I come in or would you rather I come back another time?"

Christy took a step back and said, "No, come on in. It's not like there's going to be a better time any time soon."

Closing the door behind Eleanor, Christy then walked over to the divan and sat down. Eleanor sat beside her without speaking. Soon, tears began sliding down Christy's cheeks. Her face twitched with her effort to hold back the emotions that were roiling inside her. Eleanor reached out to her and Christy collapsed into her embrace. Her outpouring of grief was so intense that she shook, wracked by sobs that came from deep within her soul. Eleanor planted both her feet for balance and held on tight to her friend for what seemed like a very long time. At last, Christy's tears were spent, at least for the time being. Eleanor loosened her hold and Christy sat up.

"Thank you," she said to Eleanor. She took a deep breath. "There's no one else in the world that I would let myself go with like that." One solitary tear trickled down her cheek. "Well, there was one other but he's no longer here."

"I know what you mean, though," Eleanor

said in a quiet voice. "Nathan was the strongest man I ever knew but he had a kindness about him that made you know you could trust him. It was like you could let yourself go because you knew he wouldn't let anything or anyone hurt you."

Christy nodded. "You know, he saved my life. I was nothing but a whore when he met me yet he treated me with respect. He saw something in me that I didn't even know was there." She frowned. "That's not altogether true. When I was a young girl growing up, I thought I was meant for great things. With the lousy hand fate dealt me, though, I guess I forgot those big dreams." Her frown faded and was replaced with a smile. "He helped me remember them."

Eleanor smiled as she thought back to the time when Christine Johnson had been Christy Quick, the crown jewel of the ladies of the evening who held court at the Colfax Tavern. It seemed like a lifetime ago.

"It seems a little odd to me that with all the despicable acts Nathan witnessed as a lawman, he could manage to imagine a better life for you or me," Eleanor said. "I'd lost both of my parents and was still a young girl with no skills or prospects. He could see a life for me that held promise and respect. It would have been easy to have gone astray without him."

"But you didn't go astray," Christy replied, "and that's a credit to you as much as him."

"The same could be said for you," Eleanor said. "Still, who knows where either of us would have wound up if he hadn't believed in us and given us an opportunity?"

"I just don't know what I'm going to do without him, Eleanor." Christy's eyes brimmed over with tears and yet she smiled. "Who's going to bring me my coffee in the morning?"

Eleanor reached out and took Christy's hands in hers. "Why you're going to do what he would want you to do. You'll grieve for his loss and you'll never forget him but you'll carry on."

Christy nodded. "I know you're right but it seems hard right now . . . maybe too hard."

"You'll not be going through it alone," Eleanor said. "Those of us who love you will be right beside you every step of the way."

"I know," Christy said, a sad smile on her lips. "That doesn't change how hard this is but it does give me a tiny bit of hope." She took her hand away from Eleanor's grasp and wiped her eyes with her sleeve. "I know you realize it but you are so lucky to have Jared."

"That's true, you're right," Eleanor said in a flat voice. At the same time, she looked away from Christy.

Christy looked at her quizzically. "What's going on? There's something wrong, isn't there?"

With a deep sigh, Eleanor responded, "I don't want to burden you with my troubles. They're nothing compared to what you're going through."

Shaking her head, Christy said, "Nonsense. I'm your friend as much as you're mine. We're there for each other. What is it?"

Eleanor was quiet for a moment as she collected her thoughts. "You and I are not the only ones deeply affected by Nathan's loss. Jared is taking it very hard. I think it's changing him."

"Changing him?" Christy frowned. "How so?"

"Christy, he's acting much like he did when he first came to Cimarrón. He's determined to hunt down Nathan's killers and seek vengeance. When I try to reason with him, he won't listen and becomes angry." Eleanor shook her head. "It's as if the good man he's become over the years . . . a loving husband and father . . . has vanished and been replaced by the angry and confused young man he used to be."

"Maybe Tomás could talk some sense into him," Christy said. "I know Jared respects him."

"Tomás has tried. Jared wouldn't listen to him." Eleanor stood up and walked over to look out the window. "Estévan tried as well. Nothing seems to get through to him." She turned back to Christy. "He's formed some sort of dangerous partnership with that Salazar man from Springer. Together, they're determined to kill the men that murdered Nathan."

"I am so sorry, Eleanor, I had no idea," Christy said. "Here you are comforting me when you've got plenty of trouble of your own."

Eleanor shrugged. "I don't think it compares with what you're faced with but it hasn't been easy. He's been gone most of the time. There's work to be done. Estévan can't do it all by himself. As for Jared, the children wonder why he's gone so much and why he's so angry when he is home. I don't know how to answer their questions."

Christy put her head down. When she looked up, she said, "I wish I knew what to tell you, Eleanor. I'm worried about you and the children but I'm afraid this is all more than I can handle right now. It's all I can do to get out of bed in the mornings."

Eleanor took Christy's hands again. "I know, my friend, I'm not asking you to do anything. It's just that you asked and I felt like you should know."

Squeezing Eleanor's hands, Christy said, "These are some dark days we're in. I don't know how we'll get through them."

Eleanor squeezed back. "We'll get through them together, Christy. That's how we'll do it."

CHAPTER 13

Jared felt an urgency to get down to Las Vegas so he could talk with Todd Little, the sheriff of San Miguel County. He only had one horse, though, and he knew he couldn't afford to wear him out, so he rode at a judicious pace for two full days and camped out about ten miles north of the town. He was up with the dawn on the third day and made it into town late in the morning. He found the livery and left his horse, then he walked over to the sheriff's office. He knocked and then opened the door. Little was seated at the desk and broke into a smile when he saw him.

"Why it's Jared Delaney, showing up out of the blue," Little said. "What in the heck brings you down our way?" He rose from his chair and said, "Come in, fill me in on the news."

Jared walked over to the chair Little had motioned him to and had a seat. "The news ain't good, Todd. I reckon you heard that Nathan Averill got murdered."

Little's face fell. "I did hear that, Jared. I guess I wasn't thinking real clear when I made light of getting filled in on the news. That's a terrible thing."

"It is that," Jared said in agreement. "You know he got bushwhacked, right? Those murderin', thievin' cattle rustlers that Tommy Stallings was chasin' all over the canyons northwest of Cimarrón, they were workin' for someone else. Some yellow dog, or maybe a couple of yellow dogs, was plannin' every move they made. It was one of them that pulled the trigger. They were bringin' in the last one of 'em left alive as a witness when someone shot both the prisoner and Nathan. That fella was the only one who could've put the finger on the bastards who planned that whole reign of bloodshed."

"I know," Little said. "Tommy talked with me quite a bit about the case. We both had a damn good idea about who was behind it; we just didn't have enough proof to arrest anyone."

"Well, that's why I wanted to talk with you, Todd," Jared said. "I was interested in hearin' your ideas about who the brains of the outfit is. I ain't lookin' for evidence that would stand up in a court of law; I just want to know what you think."

Little looked puzzled. "Well sure, Jared, I suppose I could tell you what I think and what I know. I'm a little confused about what your interest is, though."

Jared's eyes blazed. "My interest is that I'm gonna track those sons of bitches down and make 'em pay for killin' my friend. I just need to know who they are and where to find 'em."

Little couldn't hide his shock. "Why, Jared, you can't go taking the law into your own hands that way. Like it or not, this is a job for the lawmen."

"And how's that worked out so far?" Jared made no attempt to keep the contempt out of his voice. "No offense, Todd, but you fellas been trackin' these scoundrels for a long time and you ain't got nothin' to show for it. I won't settle for that anymore."

Todd Little sat back in his chair and took a deep breath. "I don't know what to say to you, Jared. I sympathize, that's for dang sure. We lawmen have rules we've got to play by. The outlaws have no rules. It's not fair but it's the law."

"I ain't worried much about the law anymore, Todd," Jared said. "I'm mostly interested in justice these days. And justice demands that these murderers pay for their crimes. It's as simple as that."

"I don't know, Jared," Little said, uncertainty in his voice. "As you probably know already, one of the men me and Tommy suspected is Felipe Alvarado who runs the Imperial Saloon here. There's some folks who think he's just a regular businessman. They wouldn't take it well for me to be accusing him of a crime without proper evidence."

"Fact is, Todd, you ain't accusin' him of anything, you're just sharin' your thoughts with me. And I won't be tellin' anyone about our conversation so you won't have to worry about any blowback from the good citizens of Las Vegas." Jared smiled. "Tell me the truth, wouldn't you like to see justice done with this?"

Little took a deep breath. "Well sure, Jared, I reckon I would. It gets down right frustrating to try to do the right thing and do it the right way only to see some cold-blooded killer get away scot-free, either for lack of evidence or because he had some judge in his pocket."

"That's what I'm talkin' about, Todd," Jared said in his most convincing tone. "I don't think about this as bein' a vigilante, I just figure I'm changin' the rules on these *pendejos* and beatin' them at their own game."

"When you put it that way, it don't sound all that bad," Little said. "The truth be told, I'm downright certain that Felipe Alvarado is a killer and cattle thief. Just because I couldn't prove it in a court of law doesn't mean it's not true."

Jared nodded. "I think we're beginnin' to understand one another, Todd. You don't have to do much of anything, just fill me in on what you suspect."

Little sat quietly for a moment and then he began to talk. "There's folks that hint around that they know people who've ridden with Felipe Alvarado when he's rustled cattle. They say these men have seen him murder people. They also say the men they're talking about are part of the White Caps Gang and that Felipe is the leader."

"Well hell, Todd, if you got people who're sayin' things like that, it sounds to me like you got some real evidence after all," Jared said. "How come you haven't pursued it?"

Sheriff Little appeared to be stung by the remark. "What are you saying, Jared? Are you saying I don't have the guts to go after Alvarado?"

"No, not on your life, Todd," Jared hastened to say. "That ain't what I meant. I'm sure you got a reason not to do it but I didn't figure lack of guts was it."

Mollified, Little continued. "I do have a good reason, Jared. Fact is, none of those folks who've hinted around about all this are willing to make an official statement and they dang sure aren't willing to testify against Alvarado in a court of law."

Jared nodded. "So why is that, Todd? What is it about this man that has everyone so spooked?"

Little grunted. "Probably has to do with the fact that he may be the meanest son of a bitch you've ever encountered. He's scary."

"You know about the men I've gone up against, Todd." Jared frowned, his skepticism obvious. "Morgan O'Bannon, Daughtry, Jake Flynt, a few others, too. You think this Alvarado fella is worse than any of them?"

Todd Little nodded. "Except maybe for that loco Jake Flynt scoundrel, I'd say Felipe Alvarado is worse than the rest of 'em put together."

Jared pondered that notion. He knew Todd Little was not a coward or easily intimidated. The fact that he believed what he'd just said didn't necessarily make it true but it was sure worth considering. Best not to underestimate your foe.

"All right," he said, "I'll take you at your word. Sounds like anyone who tries to go up against Alvarado had better be mighty good and mighty careful."

"I'd say that would be a good way to approach it," Little said.

Leaning forward in his chair, Jared asked, "What about the other one? What about Jesus Abreu? What's his stake in all this?"

"I don't know as much about Abreu," Little said. "He lives in Colfax County, which as you know, is not my problem. Plus, I don't know the man or any folks who do. Anything I could tell you would just be hearsay."

"Hearsay is fine with me, Todd," Jared said. "Like I said, I ain't interested in pursuin' this in a court so I don't have to be able to prove a case. I just want to know who and what I'm up against."

"Fair enough," Little replied. "First off, Abreu is Alvarado's cousin. I hear they grew up together and were close like brothers. The biggest difference is that Abreu went on and got some education. I think he was a lawyer first but he went on to become a banker. You know he owns the bank in Springer, right?"

"I did know that," Jared said. "I also know

145

that until all this rustlin' business came down, he was advising Manuel Salazar, the mayor of Springer, on how to get elected to higher office here in the territory." He chuckled. "That ain't the case anymore, though. I reckon if Manuel catches up with him, there's gonna be one heck of a fistfight at the very least."

"It doesn't surprise me that he was advising Salazar," Little said. "I hear he's the kind of man who likes to work behind the scenes, pull strings and such, kind of like a puppet master."

"Well, he's a lawyer and a banker," Jared said with a chuckle. "What else would you expect?"

Todd Little grinned in response but then his grin faded. "If you want to know what I think . . . not what I can prove but what I think . . . it seems to me that these boys are in this together up to their necks. With someone like Abreu involved, it makes sense that this might be more than just old-fashioned cattle rustling. Abreu knows too much about how those lousy bastards in the Santa Fe Ring operate, the way they figure out how to steal folks' land and such. I think Alvarado is in it for the killing but I think Abreu is looking for a big payday."

Jared nodded again as he took all of this

information in. Then he stood up and put his hat on. "I sure appreciate this, Todd, I can't tell you how much. I intend to bring justice to these murderin' bastards. They been gettin' away with breakin' the law for so long that they think nobody can touch 'em." With a grim look on his face, Jared said, "They're about to find out different."

When Jared walked out of Little's office, he was convinced that he knew who was behind the murder of Nathan Averill. His challenge now was to run these men to ground and rain vengeance down on their heads.

"What do you want, Ramon? Can you not see that I am busy?" Felipe Alvarado was already in an irritable mood and being interrupted by his nephew did nothing to improve that. He was looking over the bar receipts from the previous week at his Imperial Saloon and his income was down. Perhaps he would have to start putting less water in the whiskey.

"Sorry Tío Felipe, I thought you would want to know about this as soon as possible."

"Know about what, Ramon?" Felipe wanted to get back to his business but Ramon was a smart and observant young

147

man. If he had seen something that he assumed his uncle needed to know about, it would be worth Felipe's time to listen. He made a circle with his finger to indicate that his nephew should get on with sharing his news.

"I happened to be walking down by the square, close to the sheriff's office," Ramon said. "I saw a man walk out. I think it was this Jared Delaney you told me to be on the lookout for."

Alvarado had never laid eyes on Delaney but Jesus had described him. "He was tall, dark hair?"

"*Sí, Tío.* I do not know this for sure but I think there is a chance that he is the man you told me about. He had the look of a cowboy, like you said he would. He got on his horse and headed out of town to the north. It appeared to me that he had been meeting with Sheriff Little." He put his head down. "I am sorry that I do not know any of the details of the meeting. If I had known it would be taking place, I would have tried to find a way to listen in."

"There was no way you could have known, Ramon. Do not worry about it." Ramon was the son of Felipe's youngest sister. She was not happy that her youngest boy had taken up with her cruel older brother but Felipe was not concerned with his sister's happiness. The young man showed promise. He was loyal and willing to do whatever his uncle told him to do.

"Now that I have seen this man, *Tío* Felipe, I will be better prepared to watch for him." Ramon was anxious to curry favor from his uncle. He was an intelligent young man, unencumbered by scruples. While he did not know the full extent of his uncle's criminal enterprises, it was obvious to him that the man was very successful.

"You are right, Ramon," Alvarado said with approval. "I want you to be on guard. If you see this man again, try to get as close as you can without being discovered and find out what you can."

"*Sí, Tío* Felipe," Ramon said as he backed out the door. "As you wish."

After Ramon left, Alvarado contemplated this new information. From the sound of it, this cowboy, Delaney, was serious about trying to avenge the death of the old lawman. Now he was enlisting the assistance of the sheriff of San Miguel County, which could result in some difficulty for Felipe's trade if the man looked more closely at his business activities. *I think someone else will have to die.* As this notion crossed his mind, Felipe Alvarado smiled. There was no merriment

in the smile. There was only pure malevo-
lence.

CHAPTER 14

"Dammit, Tomás, we got to have a sheriff. What's gonna happen when word gets out that there's no one enforcing the law in Cimarrón?" Bill Wallace, mayor of the village of Cimarrón, paced back and forth, his agitation apparent. Standing in the mayor's office where he'd been summoned, Tomás Marés, the former sheriff, found himself to be the focus of his displeasure.

"Just to be clear, Mayor," Tomás said in a gentle voice, "it is not only Cimarrón that has no one enforcing the law. The sheriff is employed by Colfax County and serves the entire area."

"I know that, Tomás," Wallace snapped. "I just don't give a damn about the rest of the county."

And I know that. He didn't say it, though. Instead, he said, "I believe the county officials are looking at possible candidates to appoint as acting sheriff, Mayor."

Wallace exploded. "Those idiots couldn't find their behinds with a map, Tomás. Besides, they're just waiting to see what Manuel Salazar wants them to do and you know he's only interested in what happens in Springer."

Much like you only care about Cimarrón. Again, he kept that thought to himself. "Of course Mayor Salazar will try to influence the county people. You can do so as well." Tomás hesitated to make his next statement because he knew where it would lead but he figured it was best to get it over with. "You only have to find a qualified candidate. The sooner you do that and present him to the county, the better your chance of getting a man that you want."

Wallace stopped pacing, turned around, and put his hands on his ample hips. "You know who I want, Tomás. You are the most qualified candidate I know. You've done the work already and you did a damn fine job of it. Why won't you at least consider it?"

Might it be perhaps that I lost my father because of the job? Maybe it has to do with the fact that I am about to get married and I want to live long enough to enjoy my bride. Once again, Tomás held his cards close.

"I have not changed my mind since the last time we had this conversation, Mayor, and I will not change my mind in the future. We are wasting valuable time. You need to look elsewhere."

Wallace cursed under his breath. Then he shrugged. "All right, Tomás, I get your message. You can't blame me for trying, though." He squinted in concentration. "That means you have to help me come up with someone else."

Tomás wasn't sure why it had become his responsibility to help the mayor in his search but he figured the sooner the position was filled, the sooner people would stop bothering him about taking the job again. He knew his fiancée, Maria Suazo, was worried that he would cave to the pressure.

He had given some consideration to possible contenders for the job but each one was complicated. The most qualified man was his friend, Jared Delaney. Regrettably, he was not only unwilling to take the job, he was at this time working with Mayor Salazar from Springer as a vigilante attempting to track down the men responsible for the death of Nathan Averill. Tomás was worried about his friend. He seemed to have lost his moral compass.

"Have you spoken with Tom Figgs?" Tomás knew Tom was a good man, honest and brave, but he lacked both the skill and

153

the desire for the job. That being said, he was still one of the best options available.

"Yes, I did," Wallace answered. "I don't know that he's up to the job but he was clear with me that he's not interested anyway." Wallace paused. "What about Jared Delaney? Do you think you might convince him to take the job?"

Tomás shook his head. "Jared has been very up front that he will not take the job." He chose not to share his other concern about the trouble Jared might be getting himself into.

"I know," Wallace said, his weariness plain. "He was clear with me, too. I just hoped maybe you could convince him." When Tomás remained silent, Wallace continued. "I had another idea and I wondered what you would think about it."

Now Tomás was curious. He had pondered the question of who might be able and willing to do the job and Wallace had already mentioned the men on his short list. "Who are you thinking about?"

Wallace winked at him. "Why I'm thinking about your brother, Estévan."

Tomás's eyes widened in surprise. His brother had a reputation, well earned, as an impulsive hothead but in more recent times, he had settled down. He worked as a hand for Jared and Eleanor Delaney and had tempered both his wild ways and his consumption of tequila a great deal. He also had demonstrated his value as a member of the posse that tracked down and killed the vicious outlaw, Jake Flynt. Tomás had not considered his brother as a possible candidate for the job and now he wondered why that was.

"Estévan had not occurred to me at all as a candidate," he said in a thoughtful voice. "I have no idea if he would have any interest in the job."

Wallace smiled at him. "Would you be willing to discuss it with him?"

Tomás was silent for a time as he considered the request. He had a surplus of opinions and emotions about the possibility of his brother becoming sheriff of Colfax County, even if it was on a temporary basis. His number one concern, of course, was for his brother's safety. The fact that able men like their father, Miguel Marés, and Nathan Averill had died in the line of duty spoke volumes about the perils inherent in the job. This frightened him. Although they'd had many conflicts over the years, he loved his brother and couldn't bear the idea of losing him.

Beyond that however, it occurred to him

that his brother might need and perhaps even benefit from such a challenge. As the younger son in their family, he had not often had the opportunity to step forward and become a capable person in a position of authority. Although by all accounts he was doing an excellent job in his work for the Delaneys, he still remained in a subordinate position. As sheriff, he would be required to assume responsibilities far beyond any he had encountered so far in his life. The prospect might provide him the chance to flourish as a leader.

As he pondered the possibility of Estévan taking the job as sheriff, it occurred to him that his brother might be the only person in a position to bring Jared Delaney to his senses before he did something that could ruin his life. There was a time when his younger brother had been full of rage toward Jared for what he perceived as his role in the death of their mutual friend, Juan Suazo. However, they had worked through that quarrel quite a while ago and during the time he had worked for Jared, Estévan had come to respect and admire him a great deal. Delaney felt the same way about Estévan and Tomás hoped that this might give him some leverage that the rest of Jared's friends did not possess. It would be worth a try.

Wallace had waited while Tomás considered his request, demonstrating patience that was out of character. "I would be willing to speak with my brother about this," Tomás said. "I have no idea if he will be interested since it had never occurred to me that it might be an option. He may not have ever considered it either." He smiled. "If you had asked me this question two years ago, I would have laughed in your face. Estévan has grown up a great deal in the past few years."

"That he has," Wallace nodded in agreement. "It's been a couple of years at least since I last saw him all liquored up on tequila, down at the Colfax Tavern looking for a fistfight."

Tomás laughed. He recalled a number of unpleasant occasions when he'd had to take his brother into custody and have him spend the night in jail courtesy of Colfax County.

"He has changed a great deal since those days, I think," Tomás said. "Being away from town has been good for him. Having the steadying influence of Jared and Eleanor has done much for him as well."

"They may have been a steadying influence on him but I, for one, don't know how he tolerated Eleanor's cooking. Maybe that's how he learned to be more patient." Wallace chuckled at his attempt at humor. Eleanor Delaney had many sterling qualities but her epicurean skills were not among them.

"You know he will not move to Springer," Tomás said. "If he is even willing to think about accepting the job, that will be one of his conditions."

Wallace waved his hand as if brushing away an annoying gnat. "I don't think that'll be a problem, Tomás."

"Why do you say that?" Tomás looked confused. "You know as well as I do that Mayor Salazar insisted that Tommy move the office of sheriff to the county seat in Springer. Why would he now change his mind?"

"Because now, old Manuel has his very own vigilante working for him. I believe the last thing he's going to want is the actual sheriff breathing down his neck in Springer." The mayor of Cimarrón grinned. "I think we can work that part out without much trouble."

Tomás sat and contemplated what the mayor had said. Then he stood up. "Very well, Señor Wallace, I will ride out and speak with my brother."

Bill Wallace reached out and shook Tomás's hand as they walked toward the door.
"I appreciate it, Tomás. I knew I could
count on you."

As Tomás rode out to the Kilpatrick Ranch,
he mulled over how he might broach the
subject of the sheriff's job with his brother.
Although he hadn't discussed the topic with
him, it occurred to Tomás that Estévan
might harbor some of the same concerns
that he did in regard to having just lost their
father to a murderer not long ago. His
brother was fearless, almost to the point of
recklessness, and would not let fear for his
own personal safety stop him from doing a
job that needed to be done. He might,
however, be concerned with how their
mother would feel about another member
of her family putting his life on the line. If
that were the case, Tomás resolved that he
would say nothing to try to encourage his
brother to change his mind.
He had not had a chance to speak with
Estévan about Jared's current situation as
Manuel Salazar's vigilante. He didn't know
if his brother had seen the wild look in
Jared's eyes when he talked about hunting
down the men who murdered Nathan
Averill. When Eleanor had filled him in on

159

the details of Jared's course of action a few days before, she hadn't mentioned whether or not she had discussed any of this with Estévan. Tomás knew there was a time that his brother would have considered Jared's quest for vengeance the proper way to proceed. With his newfound maturity and stability, that might no longer be the case. He figured he would find out soon enough.

Tomás was still several hundred yards away from the front gate at the ranch when he recognized his brother working with a colt in the round pen. That was yet another one of the ways Estévan had surprised his family. He was notorious for his impulsivity and lack of patience and yet he had become a fine trainer of young horses. He had the knack for working gently with them to allay their natural fears and gain their trust. Tomás suspected that this skill was in part an acquired one that he had learned from his relationship with Jared Delaney, who had patiently tolerated Estévan's anger and distrust of him until he came to trust him in the end.

"Hola, hermano," Tomás called out. *"Qué paso?"*

"Nada de nuevo." He grinned. "Nothing new. Every day is the same."

Recognizing an opportunity when he

160

heard one, Tomás replied, "That could change for you if you wish it to."

Estévan frowned, a curious look written across his face. "What are you talking about, brother?"

Tomás reined in at the round pen, dismounted, and loose-tied his gelding to the fence. "Finish up what you are doing and I will tell you more."

Estévan nodded and then walked over to the skittish colt, taking his time. He spoke soothing words to the animal and as he stroked its mane, it calmed down. He then led it over to the stables and brushed it down before offering it a carrot from his pocket. When he was done, he walked out to where his brother was standing.

"I know you are always careful about what you say and how you say it, brother," he said. "Am I going to have to drag this out of you or will you just come out and tell me?"

Tomás chuckled. Estévan, always the impetuous one, was right. He was by nature a cautious man. His brother never tired of teasing him about this trait. He shrugged. "You will not have to resort to violence with me, *hermano*. This is too important and immediate for me to speak in riddles."

"Good, I am pleased to hear that, at least,"

Estévan said. "So what in the world are you talking about?"

"I think I can get you a new job," Tomás said.

Estévan looked sideways at his brother. "I am not seeking a new job, Tomás. For once in my life, I feel very satisfied with what I am doing. And our *madré* is happy that I have settled down."

"Yes, she is," Tomás replied with regret in his voice. "She is pleased that you are not wasting your money and your life drinking tequila at the Colfax Tavern every night."

"You are right, of course," Estévan said, his impatience obvious, "but now you are doing exactly what I feared you would do. You are drawing this out. Would you please explain to me what you are talking about?"

"All right," Tomás said. "Colfax County needs a sheriff. Mayor Wallace would like to put you forward as a candidate for the job."

Estévan stared at him in stunned silence. It took a moment before he found his voice. "What are you talking about? Why would I want to do that?" He shook his head. "Why would Bill Wallace even want me to do that?"

"I can answer some of your questions, *hermano*. Bill Wallace wants a man who is brave, honest, and has some experience tracking outlaws. You are all of those things." Tomás looked down at the ground for a moment and then looked his brother in the eye. "He knows that I will not take the job again. Other candidates are few."

"So everyone else turned him down?" Estévan smiled at his brother.

"I do not think that is the case, *hermano,*" Tomás said. "It had just not occurred to anyone to consider you for the job because you appear to be very settled and happy where you are."

"That is the truth, Tomás, I am happy here, which brings me back to my other question. Why would I want to take this job? I saw how it wore on you and we both know that we lost our father because he was so willing to stand up and defend people in Cimarrón who had not the guts to stand up for themselves."

"There is no doubt you are right. It should be someone else's turn to do this dirty work." Tomás frowned and shook his head. "It is sad but you know as well as I that this will not happen."

"What about Tom Figgs?"

"Tom turned down the job when Wallace offered it to him," Tomás said. "Unlike most of the people you were referring to who have never had the nerve to take a stand, Tom

Figgs has done so on more than one occasion. He has a wife and family and a thriving business. I do not blame him for refusing."

"Nor do I, Tomás," Estévan replied. "So I hope you will not blame me for refusing either."

"I would understand that, *hermano,* and I would not blame you at all." Tomás took a deep breath. "There is more to consider, however."

"With you, there always is." Estévan rolled his eyes.

"You may be the only one who can save Jared Delaney from himself."

Estévan stared at his brother and then nodded. "I am afraid I have an idea of what you mean."

"You know what Jared is up to then?" Tomás cocked his head. "You know that he and Salazar are planning to take the law into their own hands?"

"I am not deaf, brother," Estévan responded. "I have heard some of the arguments between Jared and Señora Eleanor. I have also seen the haunted look in his eyes and I know that he has been gone more than he has been here of late."

"*Sí,* he is tracking the men he suspects of killing Nathan." Tomás made a wry face. "If he catches them, he will attempt to kill them. I know he and Salazar have no interest in bringing these desperados to trial. I am afraid that he will either be killed in his attempt or will be tainted as a murderer."

Estévan asked, "Have you considered that perhaps these murdering *cabrónes* should be tracked down and killed?"

Tomás snorted. "If these men were killed, I cannot say that I would mind in the least. It is not them that I am concerned about. They deserve no better fate. My only concern is for my friend. I believe that in the end, he would regret his actions and that he would never be the same."

Estévan nodded. Then he said, "I fear that as well, *hermano.* And I worry that he would lose his wife and family in the bargain."

"Then you will think about it?"

Estévan was rapidly losing his patience. "Even if I was willing to consider taking the job of sheriff on a temporary basis, *hermano,* I will not move to Springer. My family and friends live here. I cannot do that."

"I said the same thing to Bill Wallace," Tomás replied. "He thinks he has that problem solved."

Estévan looked at his brother with suspicion. "What sort of deal has that *cabrón* come up with?"

165

"With Jared working for him now as a hired gun, Wallace believes that Mayor Salazar will not want anyone looking over his shoulder. Bill believes he can use that to convince Salazar to not make an issue of the sheriff's office being located in Springer."

Estévan stared at his brother, conflicted emotions written all over his face. The brothers stood there like statues. Then Estévan spoke again. "All right. I will give it serious thought, brother. I cannot promise anything but that."

Tomás reached out and pulled his younger brother into a quick embrace, then without a word, untied his horse, mounted up, and rode away.

Eleanor had been up in the north section doctoring some cows. When she finished, she planned to head back to the house and pull some weeds in her vegetable garden. She helped Ned up on his little gelding and then hauled Lizbeth up to sit in front of her. As soon as she was settled in, the girl began complaining that she wanted her own horse. Eleanor had heard all this before and gave her usual response, which was that Lizbeth could have a horse of her own when she was five years old and not a day before.

They headed back towards the house in a gentle trot, in no big hurry.

As they rode into the yard, Eleanor saw Estévan standing over by the round pen. He was leaning against the fence and didn't seem to be doing anything in particular. This was unlike the young hand who, for the most part, was in constant motion, finding some chore to do almost every waking minute of the day. She rode over to where he was standing and saw that he appeared to be deep in deliberation. She dismounted and helped Lizbeth down, which seemed to shake him out of his reverie. He helped Ned down, tickling him in the process, which sent the boy into peals of giggling.

When Estévan was done messing with Ned and let him go, Eleanor looked at him inquiringly. "You look like the weight of the world is on your shoulders, Estévan. Is something bothering you?"

"*Sí,* Señora Eleanor, there is something bothering me. I expect we should get these horses taken care of and then I will tell you about it."

Eleanor nodded and took the reins of her mare to lead her to the stable. Estévan enlisted Ned's assistance in leading his pony to the stable as well and then he snatched up Lizbeth and gave her a good tickle. He put her up on his shoulders and she hollered giddy-up at him as he loped ahead of Eleanor and Ned. He put her down when they got to the stable and assisted Ned in brushing down his horse while Eleanor attended to hers. Once they were done, they walked over to the house and Eleanor shooed the children to their room to play. Then she turned to Estévan.

"Let's get some coffee and go out on the porch. You can tell me what's on your mind."

It just took a few moments to heat up the remnants from the morning pot of joe. Coffee was about the only thing Eleanor could "cook" that was tolerable. They filled their mugs, walked out, and sat in the rockers on the porch. They both gazed at the mountains to the west for a while before Eleanor broke the silence.

"Has something happened?"

Estévan continued looking at the mountains for another moment before he responded. "Tomás rode out to see me this morning. He talked to me about taking another job."

"Another job?" Eleanor's concern was apparent. "I thought you were happy here. Why would you be interested in another job?"

"I am happy here," Estévan replied, a note of resignation in his voice. "I would never have considered leaving except for the nature of the job Tomás was offering."

Eleanor was confused. "I don't understand, Estévan. What kind of job would make you want to leave a place where you're happy?"

"I know that it is a bit perplexing," he said in a subdued voice. "I have never felt more contented at any kind of work I have done. You, Jared, and the children have become my second family. I could imagine doing this for the rest of my days."

"Well then why on earth are you considering taking another job?" Eleanor's frustration was evident in her voice.

"Because it is a job someone has to do and I may be the best . . . maybe even the only . . . person who can do it the way it needs to be done at this time," Estévan said.

"I have no idea what you are talking about, Estévan," Eleanor said, her voice rising as her frustration increased. "Would you please tell me what this job is?"

"Sorry, Señora Eleanor, I sound like my brother, talking in circles and never getting to the point. *Sí,* I will tell you." A wistful smile crossed Estévan's lips. "Mayor Wallace would like for me to take the job of acting sheriff of Colfax County. He sent Tomás out to make me this offer."

Eleanor responded with stunned silence. When she found her voice she asked, "I don't mean any offense, Estévan, but why would they ask you to do that job? There are several other men with more experience who are probably more qualified."

Estévan laughed. "Not to mention that there are several men who are nowhere near as hotheaded as I am, *qué no*?"

"That's not what I meant," Eleanor said, shaking her head. "I know very well how hard you've worked to curb your temper rather than flying off the handle. And as I think about it, I know that you've had experience in the past riding with Tomás when he was hunting outlaws. I'm not saying it's a bad idea, it's just that there are others who I would have expected to be in line for the job before you."

Estévan shrugged. "There were others. None of them was willing to accept the job." He gave her a long look before he spoke again. "Your husband was one of those men."

Eleanor sighed. "I know that. He turned down the job."

"I think it would be more accurate to say that he both did and did not turn down the job," Estévan said. "Of course you realize that he is working with Manual Salazar to track down the *pendejos* who killed Nathan Averill."

Eleanor looked away, her discomfort evident. "You have been paying attention then, haven't you?"

"*Sí,*" Estévan replied. "And like you, I am very worried about Jared. I do not see this ending well, no matter how it turns out."

"He's changed overnight since he found out that Nathan was murdered," Eleanor said, a tremor in her voice. "He's acting the way he did when we first met . . . willful, stubborn, evasive. He won't listen to reason. He's bitter and angry in ways that I haven't seen in years. He won't listen to me when I try to talk with him about this."

Estévan cleared his throat. "Tomás thinks that he might listen to me. That is why he wants for me to take this job."

Eleanor cocked her head, curiosity written on her face. "Tomás thinks you might be able to talk Jared out of going down this crazy path? That's why he wants you to take the job?"

"*Sí,* that is part of the reason," Estévan replied. "He also believes that if I can bring these *cabrónes* to justice before Jared has the chance to face off with them, we might be able to avoid a tragedy."

"You would take this dangerous job to try to rescue Jared from himself?" Eleanor had tears in her eyes as she looked at the young man who had become a part of their family.

Estévan took a deep breath. "*Sí,* Señora Eleanor. I believe that I would do that."

CHAPTER 15

As Felipe Alvarado reflected on Jared Delaney's visit with Sheriff Little, he could feel his face heating up, a sure sign that his rage was mounting. The nerve of that *pendejo*, Delaney, to talk about him with Little. He knew that Delaney was working with Salazar and he figured the man would make a run at him sooner or later. A cruel smile crossed his lips. *Let him come. He will not live to see another sunrise if he is foolish enough to try it.*

Although he was not afraid of Delaney, Felipe reasoned that it would be wise to know more about what his foe had been up to. He decided that a visit to the good sheriff of San Miguel County was in order. He considered wearing his *pistolero* but decided against it. No reason to tip his hand before he was ready to do so. At the last minute, he did strap on his imposing hunting knife. Perhaps just a touch of menace might be in order.

Alvarado strolled up the street and walked into the sheriff's office without bothering to knock. Todd Little was sitting at his desk reviewing some papers. Felipe slammed the door. Startled by the noise, Little glanced up. A look came over his face . . . fear, uncertainty? It was hard to say. He made a quick recovery, though.

"You don't bother to knock?" He leaned back in his chair and viewed Felipe with an expression bordering on open hostility.

"Please excuse my lack of manners, Sheriff," Alvarado said, his voice dripping with sarcasm. "I tend to forget them when someone is prying into my private business."

Little looked away, his uneasiness apparent, then returned Alvarado's stare. "I'm not sure I know what you're talking about, Señor Alvarado. Perhaps you could be a bit clearer."

"I can be clearer, Sheriff," Felipe said, raising his voice in anger. "I understand that Jared Delaney was here in your office recently asking questions about me. I also understand that he is not an officer of the law and has no business inquiring about another private citizen. To be blunt, I have heard that he is working with Manuel Salazar from up in Springer. They say that they

174

are pursuing some kind of vigilante justice." He shook his head and shrugged. "Whatever that might be."

Little noticed the large knife on Alvarado's hip and a look of apprehension crossed his face. He glanced away again for a brief moment before sitting forward in his chair.

"Jared is an old friend of mine, Señor Alvarado. He was down here on business and stopped in to say hello. Nothing more, nothing less."

"You deny that he was asking questions about me?"

"I don't recall your name coming up, Alvarado," Little said. "I don't know where you get your information but this time, it's just flat out wrong."

Alvarado favored the sheriff with a long, cold stare. "Somehow I doubt that, Sheriff." He shrugged. "Still, if you will not be honest with me, then I suppose I will have to pursue other avenues to get to the bottom of this problem."

Little stood up, taking his time. His pistol was in a holster on his desk. He leaned forward and put his hands on the desk, his right one a scant few inches from the gun.

"I'm going to overlook the fact that you called me a liar . . . this time . . . and invite you to get yourself out of my office pronto."

175

The sheriff glared at Alvarado. "In the future, though, don't come barging in here making false accusations against me."

Alvarado glared back at Little for a moment and then he nodded. "I see how it is, Sheriff. I promise you, the next time we meet, I will not bother with accusations." He turned and headed for the door. As he opened it, he turned toward the sheriff and said, "You have been warned."

After Alvarado left, Todd Little sat back down at his desk. His hands were shaking and he was sweating so much his shirt was soaked. It wasn't only the words the man had said when he warned him, it was the predatory look in his eyes. It was clear to the young sheriff that to Alvarado, his life meant nothing. He would kill him with as little concern as he would step on a bug that blundered into his path. Little shivered.

As he walked back to his saloon, Felipe Alvarado was thinking, *I believe it is time for the sheriff to die.*

On the way back from his visit with Sheriff Todd Little, Jared rode along the trail through the foothills south of Cimarrón. He was lost in thought as he considered what he had learned from the conversation. From everything Manuel Salazar had told him about the death of Nathan Averill, he'd been pretty certain that the two men responsible for the murder were Jesus Abreu and Felipe Alvarado. Clearly, Todd Little shared that suspicion. However, he was bound by rule of law to collect sufficient evidence to convict those men in a court of law. Jared was not. He intended to be judge, jury, and executioner.

His challenge now was to determine how best to mete out his version of justice. Both men were cagey and he figured they would know by now that he was hunting them. From all he had learned about the two men, he knew Alvarado was more dangerous in a head-to-head fight. By all accounts, he was a vicious and sadistic killer who enjoyed his work. Jared wasn't sure he could take the man in a fair fight but then he had no real stake in fairness. Whichever one of the two men who had fired the shot that killed Nathan had not been interested in fairness. He had ambushed him and shot him in the back. If that was what Jared had to do in order to even the score, he didn't mind at all.

Although he wanted Alvarado more, Jared was committed to taking down both men. His concern was that if he killed Alvarado, Abreu would hear of it and vanish. If he went after Abreu first, he worried that Alvarado would catch wind of it. Jared figured that unlike Abreu, Alvarado would not be inclined to run. Instead, he would be prepared and alert to the likelihood that Jared was coming for him. In fact, he might take the offensive and come after Jared. Knowing ahead of time that it was a strong possibility, Jared might be able to turn it on the man. If Alvarado was as reckless and arrogant as he'd heard, Jared might be able set a trap for him. So much to ponder.

The sky overhead was a brilliant blue. For a moment, Jared looked around and took in the splendor of the southwestern landscape. In the past, this sight had never failed to lift his spirits and make him appreciate this beautiful land in which he was privileged to live. Those musings always led him to contemplate how lucky he was to have a loving wife and two beautiful and healthy children. Now, however, they resulted in his experiencing a twinge of guilt followed by a sense of resentment. He had a job to do, one of which his "loving wife" did not approve. He didn't know why she couldn't understand that he needed to avenge the death of Nathan. He did his best to push both the guilt and the resentment out of his mind.

As he cleared his mind of the distractions, he became aware of a feeling that he was being followed. It was hard to identify exactly what had tipped him off. A tingling feeling in his lower back? A subtle noise that seemed the slightest bit out of place? He didn't know but he didn't care. He knew with absolute certainty that there was someone on the trail not far behind him. He took a deep breath and considered what his best course of action might be.

Up ahead, he saw that the trail narrowed as it entered a canyon. There were boulders on both sides and a stretch of trail that appeared to be solid rock where his horse would leave no tracks. It was the perfect place for him to slip off the trail up into the boulders and wait to see who was following him. He dismounted and led his horse behind a large rock and waited for more than an hour. He heard and saw nothing during that time. Whoever it was that had spooked him did not appear, so he decided to continue up the trail towards Cimarrón. He made frequent stops to listen but whatever noise had alerted him before did not recur. It was tempting to chalk it up to his imagination but that would lead towards carelessness. *Maybe I'm hearing ghosts, but I don't think so.*

■ ■ ■ ■

Davey Good had learned many lessons from his outlaw father and one of them was to proceed with the utmost caution whenever you were following someone. Although he was a sizable distance behind Delaney, he detected when the man entered the stretch of rocks, hearing the hooves strike the hard surface. As a result, he heard that noise stop and figured that he was up to something.

Unlike the rocky stretch ahead where his quarry had stopped, a blanket of pine needles covered the trail where he was and he was able to rein his horse in without making a sound. Pausing in the middle of the trail, he waited. He knew the rocks would tell him if Delaney began moving again and he would be able to discern whether he was moving towards him or away from him.

In addition to caution, Davey had also learned patience from his father. He sat motionless in the saddle for what he reckoned was an hour, based on the position of the sun in relation to the mountains to the west of him. During that time, he listened to the steady sounds of the forest . . . birds chirping, squirrels chattering. He also listened for indications that the man he was tracking was moving. Finally, he heard hoofs striking rocks as a horse and rider moved away from him. He concluded that somehow he had spooked his prey. Moving forward, he would be even more wary. It was time to retreat and figure out a new plan. He rode back the way he had come.

For the first hour or so after he started back up the trail toward Cimarrón, Jared listened for the sound of hooves on rock. He didn't think there was any way that the man on his trail could get through that rock stretch without making noise. He finally decided that whoever it was, the man had given up tracking him, at least for now. That didn't stop him from pulling off the trail from time to time to watch and listen. With another part of his brain, Jared pondered who might be following him. He figured it was likely that word of his visit with Sheriff Little in Las Vegas had gotten back to Alvarado and now he was stalking Jared at the same time Jared was hunting him. So be it. Let the superior hunter prevail.

CHAPTER 16

"What?" Manuel Salazar was livid. "These *cabrónes* who govern Colfax County must have taken leave of their senses." He crumpled the telegram that Jim White had just handed him.

"I couldn't rightly say, Mayor," White said with an injured air. "I'm just bringing you the message I received. No need in your being rude to me, it ain't like it was my idea."

Salazar smoothed out the telegram and read it again. It said the same thing it had said the first time he'd read it. The county officials had made the decision to appoint Estévan Marés the acting sheriff of Colfax County. He figured that scoundrel Bill Wallace was behind this latest insult. Although he didn't know for a fact, he presumed this man was related to the former Sheriff Marés. He took a deep breath and tried to regain his composure.

"You are right, Señor White, this was not

your doing." Realizing he had been short with the man, he said, "I apologize for my bad manners."

Mollified, White replied, "That's all right, Mayor. It don't sound like you're any too pleased with their selection."

"It is not your concern, Señor White." Salazar had no interest in discussing his thinking with the nosy telegraph operator. He wanted the man out of his office so he could reassess his strategy. "If that is all you had for me, you can take your leave now."

White was disappointed not to get more details from the mayor. He stomped out without another word and stalked back to the telegraph office. Salazar was deep in thought and didn't notice. He was trying to make sense of this latest action and anticipate how it would impact his plan of utilizing Jared Delaney as a vigilante to extract his revenge on Jesus Abreu and Felipe Alvarado. He'd hoped that the position of acting sheriff would remain vacant for the time being, giving Delaney room to operate without official scrutiny. He had no idea of the nature of the relationship between Delaney and this Estévan Marés and how it might affect Delaney's mission. He hoped to discuss this topic with Jared Delaney as soon as possible.

■ ■ ■ ■

Jared had just gotten back to Cimarrón and was hoping to find Tom Figgs in order to catch up on what had transpired in town while he was gone. As he walked toward the blacksmith's shop, Bill Wallace stepped out of his office and intercepted him.

"Jared, I'm glad to see you," he said. "I wanted to fill you in on what's happened with the job you turned down."

Jared was baffled. "What are you talking about, Bill?"

"Well, the job of acting sheriff that you turned down. What did you think I was talking about?" Wallace put his arm around Jared's shoulder and practically drug him back into his office. "You and a number of other folks turned that one down."

As he realized what Wallace was talking about, he responded with curiosity. "Who wound up taking the job?"

As if it had just dawned on him, Wallace said, "In fact, this'll mean you need to find a new hand out at the ranch."

Once again, Jared was puzzled. "What are you saying, Bill? I got a fine hand in Estévan Marés . . ." All of a sudden, he understood what the mayor of Cimarrón was telling him. "You're tryin' to tell me that Estévan took the job, aren't you?"

"Yes, indeed, Jared, that's what I'm telling you." Wallace preened like a peacock. "When I thought about him as a possible candidate, I never thought he would consider it. If Tomás hadn't talked him into it, I doubt that he would have."

"I'm a little surprised myself," Jared said. Wallace apparently didn't notice the tension in Jared's expression. "When does he plan to start?"

"Soon, I believe. Last I heard, he was out at the ranch getting his belongings together and taking care of a few odds and ends for Eleanor. If you're headed home now, I'm sure you'll have a chance to catch him before he rides this way." Wallace was oblivious to the fact that Jared was stunned by the news. "He's going to stay at his mother's place. For now, we're letting Mollie Stallings stay in the house where the sheriff would normally live. It didn't seem proper to put her out right now when she's got no place else to go."

There was something about this whole thing that made Jared suspicious. He was amazed that Tomás had not only supported the idea but had, in fact, talked his brother into accepting the job. He wondered what

Eleanor thought about it. He had a feeling that his wife and his friend might be conspiring against him. He would get to the bottom of it.

"I need to get home, Bill," Jared said. "Sounds like I've got some planning to do so I can make sure I can manage all my cow work. I don't know where I'll find as good a hand as Estévan."

As he turned to walk back to his horse, Wallace called out. "Oh, wait, there was another thing."

Turning back, Jared asked, "What else?"

"A young man was asking about your whereabouts yesterday."

Recalling his vivid feeling of being followed, Jared snapped, "And you're just now thinkin' to tell me this?"

With a hurt look on his face, Wallace replied, "It didn't seem like a big deal, Jared. He was a nice enough kid. As far as I know, he might've been looking for work. Heck, he might be the answer to your ranch hand problem."

"Maybe," Jared responded. As he turned to go, *but I doubt it.*

Jared stewed the entire ride out to his ranch. After a cool fall morning, the weather had warmed up under a cloudless blue sky. The aspens were turning but the beauty and serenity of the countryside was wasted on him. The more Jared thought about it, the more he was convinced that Estévan, Tomás, and Eleanor were conspiring against him. Just from a practical standpoint, losing Estévan would necessitate his having to spend more time at the ranch to take care of his cattle business. He felt certain that this whole thing was a ploy to divert him from the mission he had taken on of tracking down Nathan's killers and dispensing justice. He felt betrayed by his wife and friends. An old yet familiar anger boiled up inside.

As he rode through the gate that led to the house, Jared spied Estévan in the round pen and Eleanor on the porch. Both saw him approaching and waved. He stared straight ahead, ignoring them both. When he got to the corral, he dismounted but did not unsaddle his horse. Eleanor reached him first and sensed that something was amiss right away.

"You've heard the news about Estévan becoming acting sheriff," she said in a quiet voice. "I can tell you're not happy."

Jared's eyes flashed. "Would you be happy if I stabbed you in the back? If you were tryin' to do somethin' that meant the world to you and I interfered, how would you feel?"

Estévan arrived in time to hear Jared's declaration. He looked at his friend and shook his head. "No one is trying to stab you in the back, *amigo.*"

Jared whirled on Estévan. "You dare to call me *amigo!* You're in this, too. You think I'm so stupid I don't understand what y'all are doing?"

Estévan stepped back as if he'd been punched in the gut. It took him a moment to recover and collect his thoughts. After a moment, he spoke.

"No one thinks you are stupid, Jared, and no one is trying to stab you in the back. My brother asked me to consider taking the job of sheriff on a temporary basis. I agreed as a favor to him."

"You think I don't know why Tomás was so all-fired hot to have you take the job? I'm doin' everything I can to bring justice to the men who are responsible for Nathan's death and all y'all can do is get in my way."

Estévan frowned. "I didn't take this job to get in your way, *compadre;* I took this job to enforce the law. As long as you are not breaking the law, you and I will have no problems."

Jared glared at the man. "I've known you

since you were a pup, Estévan. We've been friends for a long time. But if you hinder me, I'll make you wish you'd never been born."

Estévan took a step towards Jared. He and Jared had indeed known each other for many years and Estévan had come to admire and respect Jared a great deal. It was only this high regard that made him pause rather than lash out. He stepped back and looked at his friend.

"I do not know what happened to the man I knew but you are not him," he said. "The man I knew was not consumed with anger and bitterness. The man I knew did not confuse justice with vengeance. The man I knew understood the difference between right and wrong."

"How dare you question my character?" Jared was livid. "I been standin' up for the people of Cimarrón for years and look where it's got me."

Estévan studied his friend. "You ask how I dare to question your actions. You are so blinded by your rage that you forget who you are speaking to. Every time you stood up for these people, who was right there at your side? Do you not recall that I lost my father to a vicious killer not long ago?" He took a deep breath. "The man who killed him is dead. That did not bring my father back."

Jared did not respond right away as he considered what Estévan had said. Perhaps if he had acknowledged the truth his friend had spoken, things might have taken a different course. Instead, he lashed out again. "Yeah, but at least you had the satisfaction of seein' that son of a bitch die. Don't tell me that didn't mean somethin' to you."

Estévan stood there, sorrow reflected in his countenance. "I say it again. I do not recognize you."

Eleanor had been standing by without speaking. Before Jared could respond to Estévan, she spoke up. "Jared, you're letting your anger and grief cloud your judgment. You must know that what you're doing is not what Nathan would have wanted."

Jared whirled around. "How dare you act like I can't make up my own mind about how to handle this?" He clenched his fists and glared at her. "Nathan is gone. I'll decide how I deal with that. You don't get to tell me how to do it."

Eleanor struggled between reacting with anger or sadness. Opting for the latter, she responded in a quiet voice. "For years now, we've been deciding things together. I never tell you what to do; I give you my opinion.

Up to now, you've been willing to consider it. I don't know why that has to change."

Jared threw up his hands. "And I don't know why you don't understand what I'm tryin' to do. It's like you're workin' against me." He shook his head. "I can't take any more of this. I'm leavin'."

As Jared got back on his horse and turned to leave, Eleanor spoke. "Jared, I love you. You know that. But I'll not stand by and watch you do something that is wrong. We need to discuss this and you need to listen to what other folks who care about you have to say."

Jared stared at his wife. "The time for listenin' has passed, Eleanor. It's time to do somethin'." He spurred his horse and rode away.

Eleanor's eyes followed her husband until he disappeared over the rise. She turned to where Estévan stood and they stared at each other.

"I do not understand, Señora Eleanor. I have never seen him this way."

"I have," Eleanor responded. In a hushed voice, she continued. "He was this way when he first came to town all those years ago. It's like a ghost from the past has come back." A tear trickled down her cheek.

"I did not know him well in those days,"

Estévan said. He frowned. "As I said, I do not understand."

"He's got scars, Estévan." Seeing the bewildered look on his face, she continued. "They're scars that you can't see . . . on the inside. But they hurt just as much."

Estévan looked as if he had more to say and Eleanor waited. After a moment, he shrugged and turned to go. Looking back over his shoulder, he said, "I must get my gear and head into town. Is there anything you need for me to do before I go?"

A melancholy smile played on Eleanor's face. "Maybe find my husband and bring him back to me. Not the man that just left but my 'true' husband, the man I love."

"I will do my very best, Señora Eleanor," Estévan said, a note of sadness in his voice. "I hope we can find that man again."

Eleanor watched Estévan walk away. When she turned back toward the house, she saw the children standing on the porch. Shocked, she raced over to where they stood and embraced them.

"I thought you were taking a nap," she said for lack of any better words to say. "How long have you been standing here?"

She could feel Lizbeth tremble. The child had tears in her eyes and she looked terrified. When Eleanor looked at Ned, she saw

192

anger and defiance in his eyes.

"You made Papa go away," he said. "I hate you."

Eleanor felt a stab of terror. "No, Ned, that's not what happened. Your Papa and I are just angry at each other right now. He'll come back, you'll see."

"No, he won't." Again, he said, "I hate you." Then he turned and ran out to the corral.

Eleanor straightened up and started to run after him when Lizbeth burst into tears. Torn, she didn't know which child to try to comfort. Finally, she decided she could do Lizbeth more good if she took her in her arms and held her. She kept her eye on Ned to make sure he just went as far as the corrals. Standing there cradling her daughter, she wondered how in all the world they would get past this horrible state of affairs. And in her heart and mind, she cursed the evil men who had murdered Nathan Averill and stolen her husband's soul.

CHAPTER 17

Jared heard the piercing hunting cry of the mountain lion and grabbed for his pistol. His holster was empty. He whirled around and caught sight of the huge cat as it launched its body at him. He screamed.

The sound of a scream shocked Jared awake. He bolted upright, scanning his surroundings for the source of the scream. As he made the transition from dream world to reality, he realized that the noise had emanated from his own throat. He was sweating and his body shook. As the shaking abated, he remembered that he had made camp for the night off the trail to Springer. He looked at the sky and reckoned dawn was an hour or so away.

He lay back and rested his head on the rolled-up shirt he'd used as a pillow, trying to collect his thoughts. With a stab of remorse, he recalled leaving his wife and one of his best friends standing next to the round pen, hurt written all over their faces as he rode away in a rage. The remorse was fleeting, though. When it passed, it was replaced by a long-lost companion, bitterness. The two of them had connived against him, throwing up obstacles to impede him in his quest for justice. They wouldn't succeed, though. He would not be stopped. The men who killed Nathan Averill would pay for their transgression. The price would be dear.

He dozed fitfully until the sun's rays cut through the pine needles and shone in his eyes, waking him up. Taking a deep breath, he hauled himself out of his bedroll. He added some kindling and stirred the embers from the fire he'd made last night. He hoped coffee would wash away the fog in his brain.

Jared intended to make his way to Springer and see if he might catch up with the crafty banker, Abreu. He knew the man was neck deep in the plotting that resulted in the death of Nathan Averill. He hoped that if he could take him captive, he could use him to get to the actual assassin, Felipe Alvarado.

After washing down his beans and tortillas with coffee, Jared felt ready to face the day.

The recurrence of the nightmare involving the mountain lion continued to disturb him. In his younger days when he first came to Cimarrón, he was plagued by such nightmares on a regular basis. It was only after he faced down the dangerous outlaw, Morgan O'Bannon, and accepted the love of his beautiful wife that the nightmares vanished from his nights.

Jared knew their reappearance had to be connected to his reaction to the murder of Nathan Averill but he didn't know any way to make them go away other than to seek retribution on the men who committed that murder. For a moment, he considered the thought that he was pushing his wife away in the same manner that he had as a younger man. Consumed as he was with seeking revenge, he only considered it for a moment.

Setting an easy pace, Jared made his way east toward Springer. Years of experience on cattle drives had taught him the trick of keeping one part of his mind alert and focused on his surroundings while allowing himself to relax in the saddle. This skill allowed him to hear a sound that was out of place . . . a horseshoe striking a stone somewhere on the trail behind him.

Under different circumstances, Jared

might have ignored the noise. Having experienced the feeling that he was being followed when he returned from Las Vegas, however, he was on guard. He remembered what Bill Wallace had said about a young man asking questions about him in Cimarrón the day before. He had no idea who this hombre was but he intended to find out. As he went around a bend, he directed his horse into the trees off to the right. Once he was well off the trail, he dismounted and loose-tied the reins to a low-hanging branch so that his horse could graze. He then moved closer to the path and hid behind a boulder to wait. His vigilance was soon rewarded.

Davey Good was daydreaming about the future. For the time being, he would do his employer's bidding and track this Delaney character. It was clear to him that the man was headed for Springer, and once he got there, Davey would slip into the bank to let Abreu know he was there. He was thinking about the possibility of slipping around Delaney and beating him to town when he heard a noise off to his right. As he turned to look, a man stepped out from behind a rock. He had his pistol leveled at Davey.

"Hands up, mister," the man said. "Slow

and careful. Don't make me nervous or I'll shoot you right out of that saddle."

Davey moved slow but thought fast. He raised his hands up with great care and said, "Mister, I don't have anything worth stealing. I doubt that I'm worth your time and effort to rob."

"I ain't plannin' on robbin' you," the man said. "We're gonna have us a talk."

With what he hoped was a winning smile, Davey said, "You don't need to pull a gun on me to get me to talk, sir. I'd be happy to visit with you."

The man did not return his smile. "I want you to get down from that saddle and walk to the middle of the trail. Soon as you're off your horse, put those hands back up. Move slow as drippin' honey if you don't want to get a bullet in you."

Davey complied. He did as he was instructed, his mind racing. His eyes never left the man's face as he dismounted and he realized that the man looked somewhat familiar. It dawned on him that this was, in fact, Jared Delaney, the man he had been tracking. Somehow things had gotten twisted around in a horrible muddle.

"Mr. Delaney, I know who you are," he said. The man appeared surprised to hear his name. "I know you got no official standing here. You can't stop me and ask me questions or anything like that. You're not a lawman."

Jared Delaney looked the young man up and down. "No, I'm not. But I do have questions for you and I will get answers."

Davey shook his head. "There's nothing to stop me from just riding off right now."

"If you try that, boy, I'll throw a rope around you and drag you right out of the saddle," Jared said. He glared at him. "Then I'll beat the hell out of you. Reckon that'll stop you?"

Davey chuckled. "I hate to tell you, Mr. Delaney, but my daddy beat all the hell out of me a long time ago. There's nothing you can do to me that's worse than what he's already done."

Jared raised his pistol and pointed it at the young man's head. "Well, then I guess we'll skip the questions and I'll just shoot you right here and now."

Davey wasn't sure how to play this. With great care, he walked to the middle of the trail and turned at a snail's pace to face Delaney, wondering as he did if there might be a way to turn this to his advantage.

"Well, when you put it that way, I guess that would be a bit worse than what my old daddy's done to me." He stood very still as he contemplated his options. After a moment, he grinned at Jared. "I think maybe we can do some business."

Jared glared at him. "What makes you think I'd want to do business with a young punk like you? And what would you have to offer me if I was so inclined?"

Davey smiled. "Because I have information that you need. The man who hired me is a son of a bitch. He had me trailing you but I figure you're trailing him. Maybe I can be of some help to you in catching up to him."

His brow furrowed, Jared studied the young man for a moment. Then he said, "Lower your hands ever so slow and pull that pistol out of your holster. Set it on the ground and then walk over towards me. When I tell you to stop, I want you to sit down with your legs crossed. Then maybe we'll talk a bit."

"Yes, sir," Davey said. His smile got wider. "I think we have a lot to talk about."

Felipe Alvarado sat in the comfortable chair behind his desk in his office in the Imperial Saloon. He was smoking a cigar and sipping an expensive whiskey, one that was not available to the clientele of his establishment. He'd had the office added to the structure once his business ventures, both within and without the confines of the saloon, began to be more profitable.

There was an expensive rug covering the rough wood floor and he'd ordered the furniture from an upscale store in Denver. Consulting with an artist in Santa Fe, he had purchased a number of rather expensive paintings, which he kept to himself rather than display in the main room of the saloon. It was his custom to keep his pleasures . . . in all things . . . to himself.

He was deep in thought about a couple of things his devious cousin, Jesus Abreu, had said to him. First, he'd said that the officials in Colfax County would not look the other way in regard to his killing one of the most famous lawmen in the New Mexico Territory. Second, he had said that Felipe could not kill everyone who got in his way. He pondered those two statements. *Right about the first, wrong about the second.* He smiled.

This hombre Jared Delaney had his attention. He didn't know much about him but he knew that he would have to dispatch him as soon as he found the opportunity. Delaney had the backing of Manuel Salazar and it appeared he was on a mission to avenge that old sheriff. Felipe would have to find a way to kill him that not only resolved the immediate problem but also sent a message to others who might be tempted to follow in his footsteps. This would require some planning.

As he contemplated his next steps, it occurred to him that one way to begin sending a strong message to the fools that dogged him would be to dispatch the man with whom Delaney had parleyed when he came to Las Vegas. He'd never believed that Sheriff Todd Little accorded him the respect he deserved and for that reason alone, he needed to die. In addition, he had always seemed a little too suspicious of Alvarado's activities. Although he'd never come up with any hard evidence, he hadn't been inclined to let it drop. Perhaps taking Little out of the picture could accomplish two goals. He would no longer be an irritant with his snooping and Delaney would get the message that Alvarado was deadly serious.

Alvarado thought back on his childhood days when he and Abreu, his cousin Chuy, would spend weeks at the family's cabin in the mountains to the northeast of Las Vegas. They never took supplies but instead depended on their skills to acquire food by hunting and fishing. Abreu had been a superior fisherman, in part because he was smaller and better able to negotiate the trees and brush around the streams that wound through the mountains. The main reason for his success as an angler, though, was because he was far more patient than Felipe. By the time Alvarado landed a trout, he would be so frustrated and angry that more often than not, he would smash the fish against a rock.

For some reason, Felipe had more patience when it came to tracking game. He would stalk an elk for hours, soothed by the anticipation of putting a bullet through its heart when he was in position for a clear shot. Whereas Abreu was never interested in anything more than acquiring the meat, Alvarado relished the kill itself. It was as if time stood still. He could see the startled look on the face of the elk and see the bullet tear through its flesh as it shredded its heart. Sometimes when he went to field dress the animal, it was still clinging to life. This was his favorite part. He enjoyed gutting the animal as the last of its lifeblood drained into the dirt. He liked the blood.

Felipe Alvarado was not a mindless animal. He was aware that he had a sadistic streak and that he took delight in inflicting pain and suffering on other living beings. Something about their helplessness and agony satisfied him in ways that nothing else did. He knew that he was different from most people in that regard. He didn't care.

To Alvarado, stalking and killing Todd Little would be no different than tracking and shooting an elk in the wilderness. He had no more regard for Little's life than he did for the life of a wild animal. He would follow the sheriff's trail and when the time was right, he would shoot him down without a second thought. *And then I might just field dress him.* He smiled.

CHAPTER 18

Tomás and Estévan Marés and Tom Figgs rode three abreast up the trail towards the Kilpatrick Ranch. Tomás talked while the other two gave him their full attention.

"I believe our only hope of convincing Jared to not go down this dangerous path is to have Eleanor on our side. It is plain that he is not willing to listen to any of us."

Tom Figgs cleared his throat before speaking. "I got to confess, fellas, I never seen Jared act like this. I understand that he's mighty upset about Sheriff Averill gettin' killed but he's actin' like he's plumb loco."

"I forget that you did not know him when he first came to Cimarrón," Tomás said. "He was very different back then. You may not know that he rode with a powerful rancher who was stealing cattle and murdering people around Colfax County."

Estévan swatted at a horsefly that was buzzing around his horse's ear. "I was sixteen then, I do not remember him all that well either. That just does not describe the man that I have come to know and call *amigo*."

"He has changed a great deal since that time," Tomás said. "The two people responsible for that change are Eleanor and Nathan Averill." He took a deep breath. "The loss of Nathan I think has shaken him. I believe the one person who can save him right now is his wife."

"She is a strong woman," Estévan said, admiration in his voice. "I have watched her with him now for a number of years since I have worked the ranch. She loves him and she is always honest with him, even when he does not want to hear what she has to say."

Tomás nodded. "We will need every bit of that strength and love for him, both hers and ours, if we are to change the course that he is on."

They rode on in silence for a little longer. The trail took a turn toward the west and they could see the Kilpatrick Ranch in the distance. They spurred their horses to a lope and headed for the gate.

Eleanor was sitting in her rocker on the portal, taking a small respite while her children napped, when she looked up to see the three men coming through the gate. She recognized them straightaway and stood up to greet them. They rode up to where she stood and Tomás raised his hand in salutation.

"*Hola,* Eleanor, how are you this afternoon?" Tomás and the others dismounted and loose-tied their horses to the rail. "Do you have time to visit with us?"

"I can always make time for three of my favorite cowboys, Tomás," she said. "In fact, if you'd care to stick around, I'll be happy to feed you as well." The three men shot nervous glances at each other, as Eleanor had known they would. She understood that her culinary skills were infamous in the northern part of the territory, and she was not above using that reputation to give them a hard time.

"You know how much I appreciate your cooking," Estévan said with a straight face. "I am afraid, though, that we must get back to Cimarrón this evening."

"I do, in fact, know just how much you appreciate my cooking, Estévan," she said with a glint of mischief in her eyes. "I understand your need to get back to town. Why don't you come up on the porch and make yourselves comfortable?" Her voice took on a serious tone. "I know you didn't come all this way to give me a hard time about my cooking. What's on your minds?"

Tomás led the trio up on the portal and took a seat. When the others were seated, he spoke. "I do not want to waste time or mince words, Eleanor. We have known each other far too long for that. We are here because, like you, we are concerned about the path that Jared is going down. We want to help him before he goes too far."

Eleanor looked her old friend in the eye. She had known Tomás Marés since he was a boy. She loved him like a brother but now her eyes sparked with indignation. "So you thought you could ride out here and convince me to conspire with you against him, is that right?"

Tomás did not flinch. "I did not think of this conversation in that way, Eleanor. I am surprised that you see it in that way. We are yours and Jared's friends. Friends help one another when there is trouble." He paused. "And you know there is trouble brewing with what Jared is doing."

"Of course I know that, Tomás." Eleanor sighed. "It's just that Jared already feels like I'm against him. When he finds out that the four of us have been talking about how to stop him from doing this thing that is so important to him, he's going to feel betrayed." She looked at Estévan. "You know that's true. You were here when he said you and I were stabbing him in the back."

Estévan nodded. "You are right, that is the risk. But I would be willing to lose my friendship with Jared if it meant that I could stop him from making a mistake that will ruin his life."

Eleanor stood up and walked to the railing. "I know it would be hard for you to lose Jared's friendship. But I risk losing my husband and the father of my children. That's a much bigger loss to contemplate."

"Your risk is greater, there is no doubt," Estévan replied. "And yet it seems to me that you run that risk whether we try to help or not. You must know that what he is doing cannot end well."

No one spoke for a few moments. Then Tom Figgs cleared his throat. "Mrs. Delaney, I haven't known you or your husband as long as these fellers. Maybe I ain't got a right to speak but I'm here so I reckon I will, with your permission."

Eleanor turned and nodded at Tom. "Of course, Tom, tell me what's on your mind." She returned to her rocker and sat down again with an air of resignation. "We've already started this conversation. We might as well finish it."

Tom took off his hat. He turned it in his hands, an indication of how uneasy he was. "Like I said, I ain't known Jared Delaney as long as these boys but the man I know is a good man. He's brave and he's honorable." With a wave of his hand to include Tomás and Estévan, he said, "I told 'em I didn't understand him acting this way. They gave me a bit of the background. It sounds like things have changed a lot in the past eight or ten years." He paused, searching for the right words.

"That they have," Eleanor said, a wistful tone creeping into her voice. "We had come so far together, Tom. We have the life we've both always wanted. Now this horrible thing happened and everything has been turned upside down."

"It sure nuff looks that way, don't it," he said. "Here's the thing, though. I didn't know Jared before. What I do know, or at least what I believe to be true, is that the man I've ridden with and fought beside is a good man. Maybe he's hurtin' so bad right now that he's plumb confused but I reckon he'll come to his senses. I ain't about to step away and not try to help him just because it makes him mad at me." It was quite a lengthy speech for the taciturn farrier. He looked uncomfortable at having said so much and he twirled his hat even faster in his hands.

Eleanor smiled at Tom and reached out in a most gentle manner to take his hat. She set it on the porch, crown down. "I'm afraid you're going to wear the brim all the way down if you keep twirling that hat, Tom." Figgs blushed and Tomás and Estévan laughed at his discomfort. The humor took some of the tension out of the discussion. "And I think you're right that we all need to do the proper thing and speak up to Jared. It's just hard." She looked away for a brief moment. "Nathan was like a father to him . . . like the father he lost when he was a little boy. Now he has to live through that again and it's tearing him up inside. The only way he can think of to handle it is to seek vengeance against the men who killed Nathan."

Estévan leaned forward in his chair with a sense of urgency. "I think maybe I have the answer for what we need to do. Tomás was already thinking this way when he talked me into taking the job of acting sheriff." The other three waited, sitting forward in their chairs. "I just need to do my job. I need to catch those filthy *cabrónes* who murdered Sheriff Averill and bring them to justice. They deserve to die for what they

211

did. Jared is not wrong about that."

"They deserve to die after they have had a fair trial and been found guilty, brother," Tomás said. "That is what you meant to say, *qué no*?"

Estévan chuckled. "Of course, that is what I meant. I just need to find a way to bring them in before Jared has the chance to kill them." He paused, a frown on his face. "Or they kill him."

The words hung in the air like dust motes in the sunlight. Eleanor broke the silence. "So what do you propose we do? I can't keep him prisoner here and I don't think you can lock him up, Estévan. He's talked about doing something illegal but as far as I know, he hasn't, in point of fact, done anything. Yet."

"You can talk to him about what is right every time you have the opportunity," Estévan said. "I plan to have a long conversation with him as well. I will do my best to convince him to help me. I can deputize him if he is willing to follow my instructions." He cocked his head. "If not, maybe I will lock him up . . . for his own good."

"Good luck with that last part," Tom Figgs said with a chuckle. "Just let me know when you're plannin' on doin' it so I can be twenty miles away."

They sat in silence again but it was more comfortable now. Eleanor broke the silence.

"I don't know if we came up with any new ideas about how to help Jared but I feel a little bit better. At least I know I'm not in this all alone. Maybe if we all work together, we can get him to listen to reason." She stood up. "My offer of supper still stands."

All three cowboys bounded out of their chairs. "Gracias, Eleanor, but it is necessary that we be going," Tomás said. They hustled down from the portal and untied their horses. Once Tomás was mounted, he looked down at Eleanor. "You are right, we must work together to help our friend. I believe that if we do that, we can prevent this from coming to a bad end."

As they rode away, it occurred to Eleanor that they had worked together before and had been unable to stop bad things from happening. The thought was not comforting.

"So all you got to do is figure out who was behind all the rustlin', find enough evidence to convict 'em in a court of law, track 'em down, and arrest 'em." Tom Figgs chuckled. "Sounds like a piece a cake to me, Estévan."

"You are not funny, Tom," Estévan said.

He looked like he'd been chewing on a lemon.

"He *is* funny, *hermano,*" Tomás said. "What makes it funny is that he knows that it's impossible for one man to do." He shook his head. "I do not know what I was thinking when I urged you to take this job. You cannot do it by yourself."

Estévan cocked his head and looked at his brother. "Maybe you should have thought of that before you convinced me that I should become the second Sheriff Marés. I do not see anyone raising their hand to volunteer as my deputy."

An uncomfortable silence followed. Tom Figgs looked as if he wanted to speak and, in fact, opened his mouth twice but nothing came out. Estévan continued to look at his brother. Tomás stared back. After a long moment, he spoke.

"I did not think I would do this but I see no other way."

Estévan frowned. "What are you talking about, *hermano?* You are confusing me."

Tomás sighed deeply. "Maria will not be happy with me."

"You are doing that thing that you do, brother," Estévan said, his exasperation obvious. "Can you make your point before I die of old age, *por favor?*"

Tomás shrugged. "You need a deputy. I have experience. I will help you with this task." He shook his head and chuckled. "Not that it is that much less impossible with only the two of us."

Estévan was stunned. It took him a moment to find his voice. "Maria will kill both of us."

"If she does it fast, that might be the best way to go," Tomás said.

"I am serious, Tomás," Estévan said, his voice rising with emotion. "You know how she feels about this."

"Of course I do, Estévan. I feel the same way she does. I would rather take a beating than put on a badge again." Tomás looked up and stared at the sky. "But you are family and so is Jared Delaney. There is nothing else to do. She will see that."

Tom Figgs had been silent throughout the discussion. Now he spoke up.

"You boys just had to have this talk in front of me, didn't you?" He spit in the dirt. "Now I got to join up with you fellers or I'll feel like a weasel." He spit once more. "Thanks a lot."

The Marés brothers just shook their heads. They rode on in silence for quite a while. Tomás broke the silence. "I will tell Maria about my decision, brother. I expect you to talk to Jared and let him know that we are taking over his pursuit of justice."

"He will not be pleased." Estévan pondered the notion of talking with his friend. He laughed. "Still, I think I would rather talk with him than with Maria."

Tomás rolled his eyes. "Now *you* are the one who is not funny, *hermano.*"

This was even more difficult than Tomás had imagined. He had expected his fiancée to fly into a rage and perhaps even strike him. She had never struck him and he didn't think she would but he certainly had imagined she might fling some dishes at the very least. Instead, she had turned away from him in silence. He could see that she was crying from the way her shoulders were trembling.

"Please talk to me, *mi corazón,*" he said. "I know this is not what either of us wanted but Estévan is family. So is Jared when it comes down to it."

Maria shook her head and kept her back turned. Tomás had never felt more helpless in his life. He loved this woman with all of his heart and would chop off one of his own limbs rather than cause her pain. He walked over to where she stood and put his hand on her shoulder. She flinched and then relaxed. She turned toward him. There were tears streaming down her face. She tried to speak but no words came out at first. Tomás started to say something but she waved her hand at him and he remained silent. It took a minute but she found her voice.

"I knew this was coming." She shook her head. "I just did not know how to stop it."

"I do not know what else to do," Tomás said, shrugging his shoulders. "Like you, I felt helpless to change it." He shrugged again. "They are family." He looked as if he wanted to say more but he realized there was nothing more to say.

Maria looked up and held his gaze. She said, "Come back to me when this is done, my sweet Tomás. I cannot bear it if you do not return."

Tomás knew full well how dangerous this venture was. In the rational part of his mind, he knew he could not promise his love that he would survive and return to her. But in his heart, he knew what he had to say.

"I will come back to you, *mi corazón.*"

The next morning, Eleanor spent time straightening up the house a bit to take her mind off her troubles. The children were playing in the yard and she wanted some time to herself to think. She went over the conversation with Estévan and the others in her mind and it brought her a small measure of comfort. They were good men and she knew they loved Jared like a brother.

They were no easy answers; she knew that. There was a part of her that found it tempting to agree with Jared and cheer him on. The man or men who were responsible for Nathan's death were vicious killers and they deserved to die. If Jared hunted them down and killed them, she would not shed a tear or feel an ounce of remorse or compassion for them. Her chief concern was what committing this illegal and very dangerous act would do to her husband. She prayed that Estévan and the others could find a way to rein Jared in. Perhaps Estévan could deputize him so at the very least, he wouldn't become a criminal.

She was so preoccupied that it took a moment for her mind to register that the shouting coming from the stables was not the sound of children playing; it was her daughter screaming. Horrified, she raced out of the house and ran to the stables. When she got there, she saw Lizbeth lying on the ground, crying. Her brother was standing over her, yelling and waving his arms.

"Ned, what on God's green earth are you

doing to your sister?" Eleanor ran over to where Lizbeth lay and was relieved to see that she was not bleeding. She turned to her son. "Young man, I asked you a question. What did you do to your sister?"

"I hit her," he said. "She was telling me what to do so I hit her."

Eleanor grabbed the boy by both arms and shook him. "You don't hit your sister, no matter how mad she makes you, do you understand me?"

Ned tried to wriggle out of her grasp. "You can't tell me what to do either," he screamed at her. "That's all you do. You try to tell me and Papa what to do. You hate him and I hate you!"

Eleanor let go of the struggling boy's arms and took a step back. The tears came to her eyes. "Oh sweetheart, I don't hate your father and he doesn't hate me. We're just angry at each other. I know it feels bad but we'll get through it."

She could see her son's face begin to crumple. "Mama, I miss Papa." Then the dam burst and the tears came. Eleanor wrapped her arms around him and he crumpled against her. Lizbeth stopped her crying and came over to where they stood. She put her hand on her brother's arm and gently patted him.

In a soft voice, she said, "It'll be okay, bubba. Papa will come home."

Lord, I hope so, Eleanor thought. *In the meantime, I need help.*

She hugged and comforted Ned until his cries were replaced by snuffles. As she stroked his hair, she came to a decision. They needed a change of scenery. If she asked her neighbors, the Millers, to take care of the animals for a few days, they could get away from the ranch. She stepped back and said, "I'm going to town. Who wants to go?"

Both children began to smile, unsure as to what the adventure would entail. Ned said, "We do, Mama. Why are we going to town, though?"

"Because Miss Christy needs our help," she said. *And heaven knows, we need hers.*

CHAPTER 19

Sheriff Todd Little had put off his trip down to Romeroville as long as he could. The ranchers who had settled around the Romero mansion after Trinidad Romero abandoned it and moved on to Wagon Mound were getting more skittish as word of the cattle rustling had spread. The fact that all the rustling and killing had occurred north of Cimarrón and Springer didn't seem to make much difference to them. They were just plain scared. As a result, he figured he would have to make the sixteen-mile round trip down and back just to reassure the folks that they didn't appear to be in any danger.

He'd lollygagged around until midmorning because, in fact, he didn't really want to go. Now he realized that he might have wasted too much daylight. If he had any difficulty convincing everyone they were safe, he wouldn't be able to make the return trip in the same day. He would have to camp out on the trail coming back. His wife wouldn't be happy about this but he understood that if he didn't tell her, she would worry and he would catch the dickens once he did get home.

Little drug out his bedroll and tied it on behind his saddle. He mounted up and rode by his house on the way south out of town. As he'd expected, his wife, Alice, wasn't pleased that he wouldn't be home. On the positive side, the reason she wasn't pleased was because she enjoyed his company and hated being away from him. He figured it was worth catching a little grief if it reaffirmed the fact that she loved him. He told her he would head back as fast as he could and make it as far as possible before camping for the night. That way, he could get up early tomorrow and be home by late morning.

The sky was overcast and the temperature appeared to be dropping as he made his way down the trail. He skirted the foothills to the west as long as he could but within a few more miles, he'd have to head up into the trees where it would be even cooler. Although it was only October, it wouldn't be unusual to get a snowfall, which would slow him down if it came down hard and steady. He had his slicker and his mackinaw jacket so he was as prepared as he could be. At any rate, he had no control over the weather.

Little made good time up to the point where he needed to veer a little south and west to follow the trail up through the low hills. Although it was still plenty cool, the weather looked to be clearing up as he directed his horse through the tall pines. He rode along thinking about what he might say to the ranchers that would set their minds at rest. The fact was that there had been no rustling and murders south of Las Vegas in several years. All the incidents had taken place up farther north. In Little's mind, based on the facts it made sense to assume that the outlaws would not operate in their vicinity. Simply put, they had not shown any inclination to do so thus far.

Of course, a logical explanation such as this wasn't always enough to make people feel safe. He might need to impress upon them that most of the men who had been part of the gang responsible for the murder and mayhem had already been brought to justice. In truth, they'd been cut down in a fierce gun battle with Sheriff Tommy Stallings and his posse up northwest of Cimarrón only a few weeks before. The part of the story that he would leave out was that the leaders of the gang had not been caught.

That last thought sent a chill down Todd Little's spine. When Felipe Alvarado had paid him a visit in his office two days before, he had done his best to stand up to the man and give the appearance of being in control. The truth of the matter was that he had been terrified. As sheriff, he had faced down belligerent drunks and had separated men who were intent on beating each other to a bloody pulp. He hadn't enjoyed the experiences but he was confident in his ability to defend himself; and for the most part, he found that once the combatants calmed down, they were suitably remorseful.

As Little recalled the look in Alvarado's eyes when he gave him a final warning, a shiver went up his spine. He recognized that the man was incapable of remorse or compassion. Sheriff Todd Little knew that Felipe Alvarado wouldn't hesitate to kill him and would never look back once he did. Still, he questioned whether Alvarado was so brazen that he would murder an officer of the law, which would bring unwanted attention to Alvarado's activities from officials in Santa Fe. It wouldn't hurt to be on his guard for now. He felt an uncomfortable tingle between his shoulder blades and looked back at the trail he had just covered. Nothing. He laughed at himself for imagining things.

CHAPTER 20

Davey Good sat cross-legged in the middle of the trail with his hands resting on his knees. He looked about twelve years old. He stared up at Jared Delaney, who held his gun on him steady while studying him from about ten feet away. Davey felt a bit like a field mouse being scrutinized by a redtail hawk. He didn't relish that feeling. He figured he needed to do something to change the nature of their budding relationship, the sooner, the better.

"Why is Mr. Abreu so worried about you, Mr. Delaney? He told me to follow you all over and let him know everything you did." He grinned at Jared. "You dang sure got him spooked."

Jared lowered his gun but kept it in his hand. He frowned at the boy. "He's afraid I'm goin' to kill him."

"Are you?"

Jared cocked his head. "I'm contemplatin'

it. Depends on how things play out." He took a couple of steps closer to Davey and squatted down. "You said we had a lot to talk about. Start talkin'."

"Well, first thing I want you to know is that I got no love for Señor Jesus Abreu," Davey said. "He's got me over a bit of a barrel and he's forcing me to do his dirty work. Truth is, it wouldn't break my heart one little bit if you was to kill him."

"What kind of barrel does he have you over?"

Davey sighed. "I'm kind of on the run, sir. You remember I mentioned my daddy used to beat the hell of me?"

Jared nodded. "I heard you say that but I ain't clear on how that's got you over a barrel with Abreu."

"It's a bit of a long story and it's complicated. You sure you want to hear it?" The boy fidgeted. The ground was hard and his backside was beginning to ache.

"You sound to me like you want to parley. If that's the case, you got to lay some cards on the table, let me know what you got to deal with." Jared put his gun back in the holster. "We got plenty of time."

Davey shrugged. "Reckon we do. My daddy was an outlaw. A horse thief, bank robber, you name it. His belief was that if he wanted something, he'd just take it and the law be damned. He got me and my older brothers in the family business pert near as soon as we were old enough to ride."

"You sayin' you're a desperado?" Jared grinned. " 'Scuse me for sayin' so but you don't look all that terrifyin'. I doubt you shave more than once a week."

Davey laughed at that. "Mr. Delaney, I shave twice a week whether I need to or not. Fact is, though, I had no stomach for it. I did everything I could to stay out of that life and when I had to go along, I'd shoot in just about every direction except at the folks we were robbing. Daddy thought I was the worst shot who ever walked this earth." His expression turned serious. "I hated my daddy. Only reason I stayed around as long as I did was cause of my mama. When she passed, I was just biding my time and looking for a chance to get away."

Jared watched the boy's face as he talked, trying to get a feel for how straight he was being. In his current situation, it wouldn't be unusual for a fella to spin some tall tales to try to talk himself out of trouble, and yet there was something sort of innocent and almost childlike in his face as he told his story. *Why he's just a kid,* Jared thought.

"And here you are," Jared said. "Which I

reckon means you found a chance to get away. How did you happen to fall in with Abreu?"

Davey blew out air between his lips and shrugged. "Just call me lucky, I guess. My opening came in the middle of a bank job that fell apart. In the middle of the scuffle, I saw my chance to break free. I rode as far and as fast as I could away from that little town in southern Arizona. My daddy headed south to get away from the posse so I headed north. Wound up in Springer."

"Why Springer? It ain't exactly a garden spot," Jared said.

"I'd been living off the land for a month by the time I got there," Davey said. "Fact of the matter is, I was hungry and sore. I wanted a bath and a square meal. I had a little money with me, courtesy of the bank in Benson, Arizona. Springer was where I'd wound up. I figured it was good enough for the time being."

"So how'd you get hooked up with Abreu? Seems a bit odd, a runaway kid throwin' in with the president of the local bank."

"I can see why you'd think that but it made sense to me at the time. I needed a job and I saw a sign in the window of the bank that they were looking for tellers. I can read and write and count." Davey laughed.

"The head teller who interviewed me for the job asked me if I had any experience working in banks. I told him I sure did. Next thing you know, I was hired on."

Jared laughed out loud. "I don't suppose it occurred to the man to ask the nature of the bankin' experience you had, did it."

"It didn't seem to occur to him," Davey said with a grin. Then his face fell. "I wasn't counting on Mr. Abreu seeing my face on a wanted poster, though."

"How'd he happen to do that?"

Davey sighed. "He told me he liked to keep tabs on new people in town. He said he thought I looked like a suspicious character, being so young and all, so he went over to the sheriff's office and checked those wanted posters."

"Reckon he was right about that part," Jared said. "You were pretty shady."

"At first, I thought he was going to turn me in. Instead, he said he had some jobs he wanted me to do. When he told me the kind of things he wanted, I told him I didn't want nothing to do with it."

"What did he want you to do?"

"Different things," Davey said. "When we'd get a big deposit come in, he'd have me skim off a bit and change the books. He had me run errands for him, too. I took a few messages to a fella down in Las Vegas. I think he was somebody like me, just a chump who got in the way. I'm pretty sure he passed on whatever information I brought him to the big wheel down there."

Jared sat up straight. "Did you ever read the messages you delivered?"

"No, I was afraid to," Davey said. "He told me I'd better do everything he asked me to do or he'd turn me in. I believed him. I wasn't curious enough to take a chance on reading his notes."

"Too bad," Jared said. "It would be convenient to have some solid evidence against the man that I could use as leverage."

"Hmm," Davey said. "Just because I never read his messages before doesn't mean I couldn't now." He stretched his back. "Mr. Delaney, do you mind if I stand up? I don't plan to run from you and my rear end is getting sore."

Jared pondered the question. "I reckon that'd be all right. If you do make a run for it, I'll just shoot you in the leg. You might even consider that a favor as it would make you forget about your sore backside." As Davey stood up, Jared arose from his squat.

"I appreciate your concern for my sore behind." Davey chuckled. "And don't worry, I'm not taking off. I think you and I might have the makings of a beneficial partnership."

Jared studied Davey Good. There was something he found appealing about the kid. He was smart and it was clear he'd had some education. Having risen above a difficult and painful childhood himself, he appreciated it when he saw a young man trying to do the same.

"You talk like you been to school," Jared observed. "Most young outlaws don't use words like 'beneficial' all that much."

Davey nodded. "I didn't have much formal schooling but my mama taught me how to read and write. She used to make a game out of teaching me a new word every day. She had to be real careful and do it when my daddy wasn't around. He didn't think much of education. He figured as long as he could count the money and horses that he stole, he was doing all right."

"Sounds to me like your mama and daddy were a mismatched pair if there ever was one," Jared said.

"That's the honest to God truth," Davey said, shaking his head. "I only know bits and pieces of how they happened to get together. Seems like, as a girl, my mama was in a desperate situation and my daddy looked like a way out. I think she came to regret making that choice over time."

As Davey recounted his parents' unhappy marriage, Jared had a fleeting and painful thought. Was Eleanor coming to regret making the choice she had of marrying him? Until Nathan's murder and his decision to seek vengeance, it would never have occurred to him to ask that question. Eleanor's concern and disapproval of his course of action made him wonder if she would continue to stand by his side. The thought that she might not was too painful for him to contemplate. He brushed it aside.

"Davey," Jared said, "I've got a proposition for you."

"Yes, sir, Mr. Delaney," the boy said, "I'm listening."

"First thing, you can call me Jared." He grinned. "If we're gonna be partners, we don't need to be that formal."

"All right, Jared," Davey said. "What kind of deal are you offering?"

"We're gonna solve your problem of old Jesus Abreu havin' you over a barrel. Fact of the matter is, we're gonna get him over a barrel." Jared grinned even bigger. "Then he's gonna lead me to the real prize."

"How are we going to do all that?"

"I tell you what, Mr. Davey Good," Jared said. "Let's mount up and ride while I explain that to you."

From his vantage point up in the trees, Felipe Alvarado saw Sheriff Little glance back over his shoulder, as if to check to see if he was being followed. Alvarado sat still on his horse until the man returned his gaze forward. He laughed to himself as he thought about how often men see what they want to see rather than what is really there. Little didn't want to be followed; therefore, his eyes told him that he wasn't.

I think he knows what Delaney is up to, Alvarado thought. *I bet I can make him tell me before I kill him.* He laughed again, a soft sound, although had anyone been present to hear him, they would not have shared in the laughter. Instead, they would have been terrified.

Alvarado waited a little longer before he resumed tracking the sheriff, allowing the man to relax a bit with the mistaken impression that he was not being followed. He knew this country; there was only one way Little could go. There was a bend in the trail where he would have to turn north and go uphill a short distance, which would allow Felipe to catch up with him. He didn't believe there was much chance they would encounter anyone else on that lonesome stretch. With his plan clear in his mind, he began to anticipate the enjoyment of extracting the truth from the man.

Up ahead, Todd Little was unaware of the danger lurking right on his heels. In his mind, he was composing a speech so compelling that once he presented it to the ranchers, they would relax and he could head home without delay. Although he wouldn't arrive home until long after dark, he knew his wife would be surprised and pleased to see him, which opened up the possibility of a pleasant romantic interlude. He turned his attention away from the speech he was preparing and focused on the pleasurable prospects that might await him at home.

With his mind thus occupied, he was slow to react to the sound of hoofbeats on stone. Too late, he turned to see the specter of Felipe Alvarado a few feet away from him, his gun pointed at him and a cruel smile on his face.

"Good afternoon, Sheriff," Alvarado said. "What a happy coincidence it is that I have run into you up here. I have been wanting to ask you some questions."

Little's heart was in his throat. The drawn pistol made it clear that Alvarado was willing to cross the line of the law. He made an effort to sound casual as he replied.

"Somehow, I doubt that it's a coincidence that you ran into me." He stared at the gun for a moment, then looked up at Alvarado's face. "You know it's against the law to draw a gun on a peace officer, don't you?"

Alvarado laughed out loud. "Is that right? I'm so sorry, you know how concerned I am about following the law." His laughter faded as did his smile. "Step down off your horse. Be very careful, Sheriff. If you make any move toward me, I will shoot you. You can depend on it."

Little complied, moving with caution. As he did, he said, "You're making a big mistake, Alvarado. A number of people know where I went and they expect me back this evening. If I don't make it back on time, they'll come looking for me.'

Alvarado ignored the sheriff's comment. He said, "Lie facedown on the ground with your hands stretched out on either side."

Although reluctant, Little complied. When he was prostrate, Alvarado climbed down from his horse and grabbed his catch twine. He walked over to Little and placed the barrel of his pistol right at the nape of his neck.

He said, "Now put your hands behind your back. Cross them at your wrists. If you make a sudden move, I will shoot off your right ear."

Todd Little knew he was in a great deal of trouble. Once his hands were tied, he would be at Alvarado's mercy. Although it was a long shot, he figured he wouldn't have any better chance than he did right at this moment. He gathered himself and started to try to flip over. Alvarado had been anticipating this and was ready. True to his word, he shifted his pistol to the right and shot him in the ear lobe.

Little heard a deafening roar and experienced a pain that he had not previously imagined was possible. As he screamed and writhed on the ground in agony, Alvarado stepped away and savored his suffering. When his screams subsided to a low moaning, the outlaw stepped back over to where he lay on his back in the dirt. This time, he placed his gun right between Little's eyes.

"Let's try this again, Sheriff. Roll over and put your hands behind your back."

Unable to control his whimpering, Little did as he was instructed. Alvarado waited for a moment, then bent down and tied his hands. As he gave the knot a final jerk, Little cried out as the leather cut into his wrists.

Felipe Alvarado laughed. "You think it hurts now, *amigo,* just wait until we're done." He flipped the man over and told him to sit up, watching in amusement as he struggled to do so.

It took Todd Little a couple of attempts before he succeeded in sitting upright. He tried to disregard the pain and struggled to regain control of his emotions. As the agony ebbed a bit, his mind raced to consider options for escape. He glanced around, frantic for opportunity or inspiration. He found nothing. He began to come to grips with the desperate nature of his situation. His heart sank.

Alvarado read his expressions as they cycled through hope, comprehension, and despair. Once again, he laughed. "I think maybe you now appreciate what kind of trouble you are in, *amigo.*" He rubbed his hands together in anticipation. "We have work to do. I have questions that require answers."

"I'm not telling you anything, Alvarado. You're the one who's in trouble. If you let me go now, you may avoid spending the rest of your life in prison." Little tried to keep the panic-stricken tone out of his voice. He was unsuccessful.

The outlaw threw his head back and guffawed. "I like your spirit, Sheriff. Even this close to death, you act brave. We will see how brave you are once I am done with you."

Little stared at the man, his breath coming in short gasps. He did his best to push back the wave of terror that threatened to engulf him. "I don't know what you think I can tell you, Alvarado. If this is about Jared Delaney, you probably know as much about it as I do."

"Perhaps," Alvarado said. He smiled. "We shall find out. If you tell me everything I need to know, I will give you a quick death."

It dawned on Little that his life was almost over. He would not see his pretty wife that evening or any other evening. He did his best to die with honor but in the end, he begged for mercy and received none. When it was done and Felipe Alvarado wiped the blood off of his knife, he had to agree with the late sheriff. He hadn't known much more about Jared Delaney's plans than Felipe did. Still, it was worth it to hear him scream.

Chapter 21

"Let me get this straight," Davey Good said. "You want me to tell Mr. Abreu I heard you're planning to head down to Las Vegas to kill that Alvarado fella? How am I supposed to have come by this information?" They were riding north on the trail towards Springer.

Jared shot a cold stare on the young man. "You're supposed to be my partner in this enterprise. You figure somethin' out."

Davey frowned. "I suppose I could tell him I followed you to Cimarrón and overheard you telling someone about this. That's a little shaky 'cause I'd have to be pretty close to you to hear what you were saying. You're not supposed to know me, though, so maybe it'll wash."

"It's your job to make it wash," Jared said, his tone brusque. "If you can't sell it, you ain't much good to me."

The boy took a deep breath. "All right,

let's say I convince Mr. Abreu that you're riding down with your hair on fire to shoot Felipe Alvarado. Then what?"

"Then you offer to ride down to Las Vegas to warn Alvarado. You already convinced him I'm headin' that way, convince him you can beat me down there if you leave right away."

"Let's say he goes for it. What do I do then?

"You head out to Las Vegas. I'll be waiting here and you'll join me. Then we wait and watch."

Davey nodded. "I got it so far." He chewed on his thumbnail for a minute. "What are we waiting and watching for?"

Jared chuckled. "There ain't no way Abreu is gonna trust you to take care of this. Oh, maybe he will right at first but it won't take long before he'll start worryin'. He'll figure he needs to talk to Alvarado himself. Pretty soon, he'll decide to ride down and talk to Alvarado face to face."

"What happens when he does that?"

Jared had been smiling as he spoke to Davey Good. His smile vanished. "Then we take him."

Davey did a double take. "What do you mean by 'take him' . . . and what do you mean 'we'? How come I have to help you with that part?"

"I mean that when he rides for Las Vegas, I'll ambush him. I'll point my pistol at that son of a bitch and make him get down off his horse. Then I'll tie him up and get some answers from him. I want you there to help me hog-tie him so he can't get away. When I learn everything there is to know about his dirty dealin', I'll put a bullet in his brain."

"You're going to murder him?" Davey's face drained of blood, leaving him pale. "Why would you do that? You'll have a confession from him. Why wouldn't you turn him in to the sheriff and let the law handle it?"

Jared stared straight ahead as they rode north. "I've seen the way the law deals with these filthy devils. They get fancy lawyers and everything gets turned around. Too often, they get away with murder. It ain't gonna happen that way this time. I'm gonna make sure it don't. I plan to see justice done."

"That's not justice, that's vengeance. More than that, it's murder." Davey Good took a deep breath. "If you do this, how are you any different than the men you're tracking?"

The young man's question was answered

with silence. Not quite silence. Davey could hear birds chirping in the distance off the trail and there was a gentle breeze rustling the aspen leaves.

"Mr. Delaney, I know we just met and all but you don't strike me as the outlaw type . . . and believe me, I know the outlaw type. If my daddy could read and write, he would've wrote the book on it. I don't have much say over what you do in this matter," Davey said, a quaver now audible in his voice. "I reckon I'll have to help you with this scheme 'cause I'm afraid you'll do me harm if I don't." He turned his head and stared hard at Jared. "But I got to tell you, this is not right. You can call it justice but it's not. It's murder. And if you do it, you're not one bit different from those men you call devils."

Jared Delaney continued to stare straight ahead for a long moment. Then he said, "Maybe I'm not different, son; you might be right. Maybe that's what it takes to conquer evil . . . maybe I have to be even more evil."

The boy shook his head. "I don't think so, sir. Like I said, I don't know you but you just don't seem evil to me." He hesitated. "And I don't know how you'll live with it if you do this thing."

Jared had no response to this. As they rode on in silence, he fought an internal war. He knew what the boy said was true; he was not an outlaw. When he thought of what they had done to Nathan and before him, his parents, however, a rage came over him. When that happened, it was almost as if his loving wife and dear children didn't exist. All that mattered to him was to lash out at the vicious men who had taken away the ones he loved. He knew this wasn't right but he felt helpless to do anything different, even though it might cost him his family if he continued down this path. *Well, you got yourself in a hell of a mess, Delaney,* he thought. *You got no good choices. What do you do now?*

Eleanor and the children pulled up at the schoolhouse in the buckboard a short time after school had let out. It was Miss Christy's habit to spend some time grading papers and preparing for the next day's lessons before returning to her cold and empty home. Eleanor didn't know if Christy still followed this routine but she had to start somewhere and the schoolhouse made the most sense.

As they arrived, Eleanor was relieved to see Christine Johnson out front smacking the chalk erasers together. From a distance, she looked much the same as she always looked. It was only when the buckboard drew closer that Eleanor could see the new lines around her eyes and the downcast expression on her face.

As Christy looked up, Eleanor hailed her. "Take heart, the posse has arrived to save you."

Christy's smile was a bit uncertain. "Lord knows I could use saving." She cocked her head. "So what brings the three of you to town?"

"Why don't we put these two rascals to work cleaning those erasers for you? I'll come inside and tell you."

"I don't know," Christy said with just the hint of a grin. "Do you think they're old enough to clean erasers?"

"We can, we can, Miss Christy," Lizbeth hollered.

Ned scoffed. "Cleaning erasers ain't nothin', Miss Christy. We can do that with our eyes closed."

"I don't want you to do it with your eyes closed, Ned Delaney, I want you to watch what you're doing." In her teacher voice, she said, "And by the way, the proper way to say it is that 'cleaning erasers isn't anything.' You might as well learn proper language."

Ned got a defiant look on his face. "It's the way my daddy would say it. That's good enough for me."

Christy shot a quick glance at Eleanor and then looked back at the boy. "That's a good point, young man. Your daddy is plenty smart; he just talks like folks from Texas talk. There's nothing wrong with that."

Mollified, Ned said, "Can we really clean the erasers, Miss Christy? It looks kinda fun."

"It is kind of fun, Ned. You get to whack them together and make the dust fly." She smiled. "Try not to get yourself and your sister covered with chalk dust, though."

After some brief instruction in the fine art of cleaning erasers, Christy and Eleanor went inside the small residence that was attached to the schoolhouse. Christy walked over to the stove and pointed to the coffee pot sitting on the front burner.

"I just made this coffee right after the students left. Would you like a cup?"

"I would love one, Christy," Eleanor said. "Thank you."

Christy poured two cups and Eleanor followed her as she walked over to the parlor area where there were two overstuffed chairs. She waited for Eleanor to sit in one before handing her a cup. Then she set her cup on the table between the two chairs and took a seat. She studied the table, which was decorated with ornate carvings and appeared to be made of mahogany.

"Nathan was fond of that little table," she said, her voice subdued. "Most people didn't know how much he appreciated fine furniture. That was a side of him that most folks didn't get to see."

Eleanor could see that tears filled Christy's eyes, threatening to brim over. "There was a great deal more to Nathan Averill than his role as sheriff. Those of us who knew him best are the ones who know the depth of the man and suffer the terrible loss of him."

Christy nodded but remained quiet. They sat that way for a few minutes, then she looked over at Eleanor and spoke. "You and I knew him best, along with Jared. For me, there'll be no getting over that loss."

Eleanor sighed. "I know that's true, Christy, and yet we both know that Nathan would want you to carry on."

"And carry on I will," she replied. "I'll bear this burden of sadness to my grave but I won't let it conquer me. I do that to honor Nathan's memory because you're right; he would want me to persevere." Christy took a sip of her coffee then and looked over at her friend. "What brings you to town today? I know you didn't come just to bring me help to clean the erasers."

Eleanor laughed. "You're right about that, although I'm very happy to have some chores for my two savages to take on so they don't do damage to each other."

Christy looked startled. "What do you mean, are they really fighting? That's not like them. Seems like Ned is quite protective of his little sister even when she gets on his nerves."

"They're having a hard time right now, Christy," Eleanor said. "Jared has been gone a lot more than he's been home in the past days and when he is home, things have been very tense between us. They've seen a side of him that they'd never observed before . . . although you and I have seen it."

Christy nodded. "I had heard from Maria that Tomás and Estévan are very concerned about Jared. This thing about seeking vengeance for Nathan's death has got them both troubled. It's as if he's gone back to his ways from his first year in Cimarrón."

"That's exactly what it's like, Christy." Eleanor slammed her hand down on the arm of the chair. "I'm so upset with him, I don't care that he's been gone. He's so angry all the time and it's like a poison, especially for the children. I don't understand how he can do this to the children . . . or me, for that matter."

"You sound like you're at the end of your rope. Things must have gotten bad."

Eleanor hadn't realized how angry she was until this moment. "They have gotten very bad, Christy. I can understand how upset Jared is about losing Nathan but it's as if he can't see that there are others in just as much pain as he is. And besides that, he's treating the ones who love him the most almost as if it's our fault." Eleanor clenched both of her fists. "I didn't think I would ever feel this way but right now, I don't know that I want to go on being Jared's wife. There's no excuse for his behavior."

Christy drew in a deep breath. "That doesn't sound good, Eleanor. I would never have imagined things would turn out this way." She paused. "Do you want me to agree with you or do you want me to be honest with you?"

Eleanor stared at her friend for a moment. "I'm not sure what you're getting at but you know me . . . I want your honesty first and foremost. If I'm off target, I need to know it."

"I'm not saying you're wrong to be upset. Lord knows, when you see your little ones suffering, it makes it hard to carry on. And you're right; you can't make excuses for Jared's behavior." She paused and took a sip of her coffee. "But you know as well as I do that while there aren't any excuses for how Jared is acting, there is an explanation and to be fair, you need to take it into account."

Eleanor snorted in disgust. "So, because Jared's parents were killed when he was a boy, I'm supposed to just look the other way while he destroys his family? I don't think so. He's not the only one that's had a hard time in life. That doesn't give him the right to mistreat others."

"Of course not, but is it too much to ask that you think about this from Jared's point of view? Don't you think he feels a lot like that little boy who witnessed his father being murdered and felt helpless to do anything about it? Can you blame him for trying to make this turn out different?"

Eleanor took a deep breath and closed her eyes. When she reopened them, she said, "No, I guess I can't blame him for that . . . but I can't seem to make him see that the way he's going about things is not only destructive to those of us who love him but also poisonous to his own soul."

"You're right," Christy said in a soft voice.

"But if you can't understand the pain he's feeling and put aside some of your own anger, you'll never get him to listen."

Eleanor sat there motionless, then nodded. "This is why I came to see you. I knew you could help me figure this out." A moment later, she smiled. "The other reason I came to see you is that I need help with the children and you need something to do that makes you feel some hope for the future."

"I'm not sure what you mean." Christy cocked her head and stared at Eleanor. "How can I help you with the children and how will that change the future?"

"Before I answer that, I have to ask you . . . can the children and I stay here in town with you for a while?"

"Of course you can," Christy said. "I'm not sure how that will help but you are most welcome to stay."

"I think the children need a change of scene. They have too many memories, thoughts, and feelings about their father, all wrapped up in the ranch. If they're here, they can go to the school with other children. I think that will help get their minds off the trouble and confusion they're feeling."

"What about you?" Christy studied her friend. "How will that help you?"

"It will give me the freedom to go to Jared and try to help him find another way to do this thing." Eleanor's eyes grew moist. "You're right, I was so angry that I forgot for a moment that my husband is human. He's been so steadfast and decent for so long that I somehow missed how devastating this has been for him. I need to find him and let him know I love him." Eleanor grinned through her tears. "And then I need to keep myself from strangling him while I try to change his mind."

Chapter 22

"What do you think about Eleanor bringing the children to town, brother?" The brothers were installed in the reestablished sheriff's office in Cimarrón. Estévan Marés was leaning back in the chair with his feet up on the desk. Tomás cast a disapproving glance at his brother's casual disrespect to the furniture. Estévan looked at his brother and laughed. "You talked me into taking this job, *hermano;* you do not get to tell me where I can put my boots when I am in my own office."

"Fair enough." Tomás shrugged. "To answer your question, I think it is a good thing for everyone concerned. It is not good for Eleanor and the children to be isolated out at the ranch right now. I think having Miss Christy and the other children at the school around them will be a good thing for the three of them." He pursed his lips as he thought about the situation. "I also think this will be a good thing for Miss Christy as well. It will give her something that is important to focus on rather than wallowing in her sorrow."

Estévan scratched his head. "Those are excellent thoughts, brother, but they were not what I was thinking about when I asked you the question."

"What were you think about?"

"Jared is stalking this Alvarado fellow down in San Miguel County. I am worried that when he finds this out, which may have already happened, Alvarado will return the favor." Estévan shuddered. "Everything I hear about this *pendejo* tells me that he is an *hombre malo*. He has no soul. What is to stop him from going after an isolated woman and her children?"

Before Tomás could respond, there was an urgent banging on the door. Tomás got up and walked over to see who was making the commotion. When he opened the door, he found Ben Martinez, the telegraph operator and local busybody.

Ben rushed in. He was clutching a telegram in his left hand and he reached out with his right hand to grab Tomás by the shoulder. "Sheriff Marés, you got to see this. It's from Cisco Abeyta, the mayor down in Las Vegas."

With care, Tomás disengaged Ben's hand from its grasp on his shirt. "Ben, I am the deputy. Estévan is the sheriff now."

For a second, Martinez responded with a blank stare. Then he said, "*Madre de Dios,* I can't keep up with you boys. Tomás, you were sheriff, then you weren't. Tommy Stallings was sheriff, now he ain't. Estévan is the sheriff now . . . I guess until he ain't anymore." He threw up his hands in disgust. "It was sure a lot easier when Sheriff Averill was the sheriff. Things stayed the same back then. Now it's like a twister, things changing all the time."

"I know it is confusing, Ben. Things have been changing fast these days, there is no doubt." Tomás reached out and patted the telegraph operator on the shoulder. "Perhaps you should give Estévan the mayor's telegram and tell us what has you so distressed."

"You mean what's got me upset besides the fact that you fellas can't seem to make up your minds who wants to be sheriff from one day to the next?"

Ben looked as if he wanted to continue his rant about the revolving sheriff state of affairs. Estévan stepped forward and said in a quiet but firm voice, "Give me the telegram, Ben, and then be quiet while I read it, *por favor.*"

Ben started to sputter with indignation. Estévan raised his hand in a gesture suggesting that he stop talking. "*Por favor, Ben.*"

Martinez shut his mouth but his lips were compressed in a thin line reflecting his displeasure at being silenced. He tapped his foot as he waited for Estévan to digest the contents of the message.

Tomás watched with interest as his brother read and then reread the telegram. He saw his face cloud up like a monsoonal thunderstorm.

"What is it, *hermano*?"

For a moment, Estévan did not answer, then he swore in Spanish. "Someone has murdered Todd Little. I think we have a good idea who did the deed."

Tomás looked over at Ben Martinez. He knew that the telegraph operator would spread any information he gleaned from their conversation all over town in less time than it would take an average person to walk from one end of the village to the other. He made a motion to his brother similar to the one Estévan had just made to Ben.

"Ben, thank you for bringing this message to us. You realize what a terrible thing it is that happened down in San Miguel County.

I think the less said about it, the better, at least for the time being." Tomás did not look at his brother as he spoke, knowing he would be struggling not to comment on his ludicrous statement. "We do not wish to take up any more of your time." As he spoke, he gripped the telegraph operator and town snoop's arm and guided him to the door. Martinez looked as if he were about to protest but Tomás facilitated his exit with such alacrity that he barely had time to say *adiós.*

As he shut the door, Tomás turned to his brother and asked, "What did they say?"

"They said Sheriff Little had been found murdered," Estévan replied. "They took the time to add that his murder was 'horrible.' I am not sure what that means but I think we have an idea." As he spoke, Estévan clenched and unclenched his fists. "They want one of us to come down there and help them try to figure out what happened."

Tomás shook his head as he thought about the request. "That is not our territory or our job, *hermano.* I do not know if it is a good idea for either of us to be away from town the length of time it will take to ride down there and assist them with their investigation."

"Under ordinary circumstances, I would

agree with you," Estévan said. "It is clear, however, that this is the work of Felipe Alvarado. It is bound to tie in with everything that has happened up here. We might find out some information that could help us track down these animals." He paused for a moment as he contemplated the situation. "I wonder if Jared talked with Little in the recent past?"

"How is that pertinent?" Tomás watched his brother as he formulated his answer.

"If Jared talked with the sheriff in Las Vegas, I believe Felipe Alvarado would want to know how much and what kind of information the man shared with him. If, as I suspect, Alvarado found an opportunity to question Little away from town, he would then feel compelled to kill him in order to silence him." Estévan shrugged. "I suppose it is also possible that the sheriff was getting too close to some of Alvarado's other actions and he felt threatened by that. It might not be related at all. We will not know unless one of us goes down there and asks questions."

"And which of us do you think should make this journey? Tomás sighed. "And by the way, I know what you are going to say before you say it, *hermano.*"

Estévan grinned at his older brother. "I

can think of any number of good reasons why you should be the one to go . . . you have more experience at this sort of thing, you have a calmer disposition than I do, you have been lounging around town for too long. Should I go on?"

Tomás just shook his head. "And yet we both know that none of those are the real reason."

Estévan laughed out loud. "*Es verdad, hermano.* The real reason is that for the first time in my life, I am able to tell my older brother what to do."

Tomás shook his head. "Enjoy it while you can, brother. I took this job on a temporary basis and it is getting more temporary by the minute."

Continuing to grin at his brother's discomfort, Estévan said, "I am sure you will not deprive me of this moment of triumph."

"As long as you recognize the fact that it is, in truth, only a moment and without doubt, a very short moment," Tomás replied. He allowed himself a brief chuckle at his predicament before turning serious again. "If I am going, we need to have a clear plan in regard to how I handle the situation. A question that comes to mind right away is whether or not I should talk with Felipe Alvarado about his possible involvement."

"Would you not be concerned that this would alert him to our suspicions?"

Tomás shrugged. "He knows we suspect him. I think he needs to know that it is not just Jared Delaney who is coming after him." A scowl settled on his features. "This outlaw, this snake, seems to believe that he can do whatever he wishes and no one will lift a finger to stop him. I will do my best to convince him otherwise."

Estévan nodded, his playful mood gone. "You are right, *hermano.* This *cabrón* needs to know that the Marés brothers are breathing down his neck. I did not know Sheriff Little but I did know Nathan Averill. Unlike our compadre, Jared, I intend to follow the law as I try to apprehend this outlaw, but if he puts up resistance, as we both know he will, I will not hesitate to shoot him down like the rabid dog that he is."

"I think you are correct in assuming the man will not lay down his arms and surrender. I only wish there was some way we could convince Jared to work with us rather than at cross purposes." He sighed. "It would not only help us, it would without a doubt be in his best interests."

CHAPTER 23

"Aunt Christy, where is Uncle Nathan?" Ned Delaney had always called Christy and Nathan his aunt and uncle even though they were not related by blood. This was irrelevant to the boy . . . as far as he was concerned, they were family. He was helping his Aunt Christy rearrange the desk chairs in the classroom while his sister created her latest work of art on the tablet Mollie Stallings had given her for her very own.

The question hit Christy hard. The children and Eleanor had been with her for several days and up until this moment, neither of them had expressed any curiosity about the whereabouts of their Uncle Nathan. As she contemplated the question and tried to conquer her emotions, she realized that she should have prepared some sort of stock answer. How do you explain death to a young child?

"Uncle Nathan is no longer with us, Ned,"

she said. Hoping to avoid further discussion and questions, she said, "Here, help me move this desk over closer to the blackboard."

Ned stopped and put his hands on his hips. "I don't know what you mean, Aunt Christy. Did he go away?"

Christy sighed. It was clear the young man was not going to let her weasel out of answering his question. "I guess you could say he did, Ned. He passed away."

Ned looked confused. "I don't know what that means."

She shook her head. This was going to be even harder than she thought it would be. "Uncle Nathan was helping the sheriff track down some outlaws, honey. Outlaws are bad men who break the law."

"I know what outlaws are," Ned said impatiently. "Did Uncle Nathan go away with the outlaws?"

"No, Ned, he didn't." She could see that the boy was going to persist until he got his questions answered. *I hope I can get through this without bawling.* She walked over to one of the desks and sat down. "Come here, sweetheart, sit on my lap. I'll tell you what happened."

Ned loved to cuddle with his Aunt Christy. He ran over and plopped himself down on her lap, looking up into her eyes with expectation. As she looked into his innocent eyes, Christy thought her heart might break.

"Like I said, Ned, your Uncle Nathan was helping the sheriff chase some bad men." She tried to think of some way to soften the news but then she decided to just lay it out in as simple a manner as possible. "One of those bad men shot your Uncle Nathan. He was wounded and after a few days, he died." It took all of her self-control not to burst into tears.

Ned looked up at her, his eyes as round as dinner plates. "Uncle Nathan is dead?"

"Yes, honey," she said softly, "Uncle Nathan is dead."

The little boy put his hand on her cheek. "That makes me sad, Aunt Christy." He paused and looked at her face. "It makes you sad, too, don't it?"

She took a deep breath. "Yes, honey, it makes me very sad."

"I could give you a hug," Ned said. "That's what Mama does for me when I'm sad."

Christy's vision blurred with her tears but she smiled at the boy. "That would be wonderful, Ned. I would love a hug."

He reached up and put both arms around her neck, hauling himself up further in her lap. She wrapped her arms around him and soaked in the innocent and pure love he expressed to her without words. Christy was overcome with emotion as Ned squeezed her neck. *There are no words.*

As Tomás rode down to Las Vegas, a gloom came over him that left him feeling forlorn and distracted. Too many times he had confronted dangerous men who would just as soon cut him down without a moment's hesitation. He knew he was a capable lawman but he also knew he'd been lucky. Nathan Averill was as capable a lawman as had ever lived and he had been murdered. His own father had been killed only months ago and it was primarily due to bad luck. He was afraid down to the marrow of his bones that his luck had run out. To make matters worse, the unspoken dread in his future wife's eyes as she watched him ride away haunted him as he pushed his horse south.

He realized that he needed to stop dwelling on the hazards posed by his mission and instead come up with a plan. Tomás always felt better when he had a plan. Tommy Stallings used to hoorah him about this, saying a plan lasts until about the second gunshot in a fight, at which point everything tends to go to hell in a bucket. Still, he felt better with a plan if only because it gave him something concrete to deviate from when everything fell apart.

Cisco Abeyta, the mayor of Las Vegas, had sent the telegram informing them of Sheriff Little's murder. That would be the logical place to start. Tomás was acquainted with Cisco although he didn't know him well. In his few prior contacts with the mayor, he had found him to be pleasant and relaxed, if a bit passive when it came to supporting local law enforcement. Something seemed to have spooked him about this murder, though. When Estévan showed Tomás the telegram, a feeling of revulsion emanated from the words on the paper. Whatever had happened, it had made a profound impression on Cisco Abeyta.

Having left Cimarrón two days before, Tomás figured he would get into Las Vegas around midday. Although he was feeling hungry, he was inclined to go straight to the mayor's office and start asking questions. He was still not clear about what his role would be in the investigation since he, in fact, had no jurisdiction in San Miguel County. *A minor predicament.* Tomás calculated that if Abeyta wanted him to perform some official duty, he would find a way around the technicalities. *Is that not the way we do things here in the land of mañana?* We do as we please and then find some way to justify it after the fact.

Riding in from the north, Tomás wasn't sure where the mayor's office was but he had a vague recollection that it was on the main thoroughfare on the west side. He walked his horse down the right side of the street looking for a sign. Out of the corner of his eye, he noticed people watching him with suspicion. Word travels fast in small towns and he assumed everyone knew about the sheriff's demise. In all likelihood, there were folks who even had ideas about who had committed the deed. From what he knew about Felipe Alvarado, he had serious doubts whether anyone would come forward to bear witness against him.

He had traveled about six blocks when he saw a sign announcing the office of the mayor. He tied his horse out front and knocked on the door.

A voice from inside the office called out, "Come in, it is open." Tomás entered. A man stood up and walked around his desk toward him. "Sheriff Marés, we have met before. I am Cisco Abeyta, the mayor of our town. Thank you for coming."

"De nada," Tomás replied, "although I am

now Deputy Sheriff Marés. My brother, Estévan Marés, is the sheriff."

Abeyta shook his head as if trying to clear
it. "I had heard that things were changing
with such speed up in Colfax County it was
hard to keep up." He smiled. "No matter, I
am glad you are here."

"Now that I am here, what is it that you
would like me to do? We both know I have
no official jurisdiction down here in San Miguel County."

Abeyta waved his hand as if swatting a fly.
"And we both know you and the other lawmen in Colfax County have been taking a
close look at one of the citizens of Las Vegas
as a possible suspect in some robberies and
killings up your way." He walked around his
desk to his chair and motioned to Tomás to
take the seat across from him. "This has
gotten out of hand. I can look the other way
when someone is engaging in a little harm-
less cattle rustling but someone murdered
my sheriff." An angry look crossed his face.
"I think we both know who did it."

"Perhaps what you say is true, *amigo,*"
Tomás said carefully, "but my question
remains the same. What would you like for
me to do about it?"

"What I would really like for you to do
about it is to make the man who is respon-

sible for all this thievery and killing to go away . . . forever." Cisco Abeyta shrugged. "I suppose that is not realistic, *qué no*? For one thing, it is not legal. For another, the man we are talking about but whose name I do not wish to mention is one tough hombre. He is a hard one to make go away."

"So I hear," Tomás said. "Perhaps we could start by having you tell me what happened to Sheriff Little."

"His wife came to my house and told me he had not come home," Abeyta said. "He had ridden down to Romeroville to talk to some of the ranchers there about the robberies and murders and to let them know they were safe."

"Humph," Tomás grunted. "Sounds like he might have had the wrong information about that."

"Perhaps but I do not think he was wrong about the ranchers' safety. There has been no rustling down in that area. His error was in believing that he was safe because he was a lawman." The mayor shrugged. "Anyway, she told me that he had hoped to return the night before but he was not sure he would be able to take care of his business and get back. She was not worried until the next day when he did not return."

"Were there other times when the sheriff

was gone for periods of time without explanation?"

"No, Señor Marés, Todd Little was a devoted husband," Abeyta said. "He loved his wife and made it a point to never stay away any longer than necessary. That is the reason I took her concern seriously."

Tomás nodded. "So what happened?"

"Sheriff Little had no deputies. I sent my son and my nephew out on the trail to Romeroville to try to find him." Abeyta looked away. "Late that afternoon, my nephew rode in with his horse in a lather. He said my son needed me to come there right away because something awful had happened."

"So you rode out to where they discovered the body?"

"Sí," Abeyta said. "My nephew led me to where they had found him. He was lying in the middle of the trail. The murderer made no attempt to conceal his body."

"And what did you see?"

Abeyta shuddered. "It was horrible, *amigo*. He had been tortured."

"Tortured?" Tomás stared at the mayor. "In what way?"

"I hate to even think about it," Abeyta said. "*Madre de Dios,* his ear had been shot off. His arms were both broken and so were

269

all the fingers on both his hands; his face had been beaten to the point that he was unrecognizable."

"Are you sure it really was the sheriff?"

"*Sí,* he had his badge pinned on his vest and some papers in his saddlebags that confirmed it was him." The mayor took out his handkerchief and wiped his brow. "I have not even told you the worst part."

Tomás dreaded what he expected to hear next. "What would that be?"

"The man was gutted like a hog. I saw him myself when they brought the body in." Abeyta stopped talking for a moment. He looked a bit green around the gills. After a couple of deep breaths, he said, "The person who did this is a beast. He enjoyed it. We must find a way to stop him."

Tomás nodded. "There is no question you are right about that. The question is how do we do it?"

Abeyta shrugged. "I wish I knew, *amigo.*" He looked away. When he looked back, he had a defiant expression on his face. "People say I turn my head away from the shady things that are done in San Miguel County. They act as if I approve of this dishonesty and lawlessness. That is not true." He glared at Tomás for a moment as if he would challenge him. Then he leaned back in his chair, defeated. "I do what I can to make a difference. With this, I just do not know what to do."

Tomás felt bad for the man. From what he had heard, Cisco Abeyta was a well-intentioned if somewhat ineffectual mayor and he didn't seem to be involved in the types of graft and corruption that were commonplace in many villages throughout the territory. However, he had neither the skills nor the courage to challenge a dangerous man such as Felipe Alvarado.

"You are not alone in that, *amigo,*" he said. "We face many of the same difficulties in Cimarrón. Other people talk about what they think you should do about the problems but when it is time to step up and confront an outlaw, they are nowhere to be seen."

Abeyta cast a grateful glance in Tomás's direction. "I appreciate your understanding, *amigo.* I wish I had more answers for you. It is unfortunate, but I do not." He studied the nails on his left hand for a moment. "I was hoping that you might have some answers for me about what to do."

Tomás gave the mayor a rueful smile. "I have been searching for the same answers you are seeking for a number of years without finding them." He shrugged. "Still,

271

I am willing to keep searching." He stood up. "I think that I will now go pay a visit to our friend whose name you are reluctant to mention." He turned to head to the door, then looked back over his shoulder. "His name is Felipe Alvarado, by the way." His eyes flashed fire. "I will say it, even if you will not."

After Tomás left, Cisco Abeyta reflected on their conversation. *He seems like a brave man. It is a pity that this bravery will get him killed.*

CHAPTER 24

When Eleanor walked in to the schoolhouse, the first thing she saw was her daughter sitting at a desk in the back. Her head was down and she was engrossed in drawing a picture. This sight made her smile. Lizbeth loved to draw pictures and she showed a flair for it even at her young age. Eleanor was about to go ask if she could see what Lizbeth was working on when, out of the corner of her eye, she saw Ned sitting on Miss Christy's lap at the front of the room.

Approaching the pair, she said in a mischievous tone, "Looks like someone is getting some loving from his Aunt Christy." They both looked up and Eleanor stopped. Christy's eyes were red, and it was obvious she'd been crying. Ned had tearstains in the dirt that was a perpetual presence on his young face. Alarmed, Eleanor asked, "What's wrong?"

Christy kissed Ned on the top of his head

and looked at Eleanor. "I've just been telling Ned about what happened to his Uncle Nathan."

"Aunt Christy was sad, Mama," Ned said. "I was hugging her and trying to make her feel better." He wiped his face with his hand. "I guess I was crying a little bit, too. I'm sad about Uncle Nathan. I miss him."

Eleanor felt a stab of guilt. She hadn't known how to tell the children about their Uncle Nathan's murder. Rather than figuring out how to do so, she had just put it off. "I'm sorry Christy, I should have been the one to tell them. You have enough to deal with without having to bear sad tidings to my children."

"It's all right, Eleanor," Christy said. "I didn't mind telling him. We had a good cry together and he gave me some good hugs." She kissed the boy on the head again. "You're a good hugger, young man. I think you made me feel just a tiny bit better."

"You do?" The boy grinned and turned to his mother. "I guess you were right, Mama, hugs do help."

Eleanor smiled. "I guess they do, honey. They don't fix everything but they sure can make you feel a little better." She looked at Christy. "I guess we'll just have to keep hugging you and help you feel better a tiny bit at a time."

Christy returned her gaze. "I'll take all the hugs you folks want to hand out." One more tear trickled down her cheek. "I don't think there could be enough hugs in a lifetime to get me over this, though."

Eleanor smiled at her friend. "I guess we'll have to try it and find out."

As Tomás walked the four blocks down to the Imperial Saloon, he contemplated the wisdom of confronting Felipe Alvarado. There wasn't much danger of tipping their hand. The man was aware that Jared Delaney was stalking him so Tomás was certain that he would already be on his guard. It was a bit much to hope that Alvarado would be frightened, but if all it accomplished was to give him something more to be on the lookout for, it could be worth it. Besides, this was personal now. *I want him to know the Marés brothers are breathing down his neck.*

He walked into the Imperial Saloon and looked around, letting his eyes adjust to the lower light. There was a pretty sizable crowd for an early afternoon. He eased his way up to the bar. The bartender was at the other end of the bar wiping some glasses clean but when he saw Tomás, he smiled and walked his way in a brisk manner. He was a short man, stout in stature, with a handlebar moustache. His instincts told Tomás that the man was not Alvarado.

In a pleasant tone, he said, "Good afternoon, sir, what can I get you?" The bartender glanced down and noticed Tomás's badge. His smile dimmed a bit. "Oh, you're a lawman. You here on official business?"

Tomás found it interesting that right away the man thought he was there in an official capacity. It suggested that other lawmen had been around not all that long ago. "Why would you think that?"

The man grew uncomfortable, shifting from one foot to the other. He cleared his throat and said, "Uh, well, no particular reason, I just saw the badge and wondered." As he spoke, he had a hard time looking Tomás in the eyes. "What can I do for you?"

"I would like to speak with Felipe Alvarado, the proprietor. Is he here?"

Again, the man glanced away rather than meet Tomás's gaze. He hesitated, then said, "He's in the back. Do you want me to get him?"

Tomás smiled. "Since I am wanting to speak with him, yes, it would be good if you would get him." He noticed that a fine sheen of sweat had appeared on the man's forehead. *Interesting,* he thought.

"Oh, yeah, sure," the man said. "I guess that makes sense. Can I tell him what you want?"

Tomás's smile widened. "*Sí,* tell him I am here on 'official business.'"

The bartender's complexion turned a shade paler and he coughed. Then he nodded and said, "Sure thing, mister. I'll let him know."

As he waited for Alvarado, Tomás put his hand on his pistol. He touched the grip and then laughed at himself. He was no *pistolero.* Felipe Alvarado would be much quicker on the draw than he was. On the other hand, Tomás had been in enough gun battles that he knew how to take his time and fire with a steady hand. He didn't anticipate that this first encounter would result in gunplay, though. He figured it would in all likelihood involve verbal salvoes. He took a deep breath and let it out slowly to compose himself.

Felipe Alvarado sauntered out from a door behind the bar that appeared to lead to his office. He walked up to Tomás, a sneer on his face, and said, "My bartender tells me there is a lawman here to see me on official business. Have you seen him?"

Tomás smiled at Alvarado. "I am the man

he mentioned."

Alvarado looked him up and down. "I know Sheriff Little, the lawman in San Miguel County. You are not him."

"I am Tomás Marés, Deputy Sheriff of Colfax County. And in fact, Sheriff Little is no longer the sheriff of San Miguel County." Tomás's smile vanished. "I imagine you were aware of that fact, though."

As he continued to look Tomás up and down, he smirked at him. "That raises two questions then, *amigo.* One is why you would think I would be aware that Little is no longer sheriff, if indeed that is the case. The other is what is a deputy from Colfax County doing here? You have no authority in San Miguel County."

"You could hardly help but be aware that Sheriff Little was murdered several days ago," Tomás said. "And as an officer of the law in Colfax County, I do have authority to pursue those who are suspected of committing a crime there, even if they flee to another county."

"Are you accusing me of crimes, Deputy?" Alvarado managed to make the word *deputy* sound like an insult. "Do you have a warrant? If not, I must insist that you leave my establishment."

Tomás glared at Alvarado. "Let me be

278

perfectly clear, you filthy *cabrón*. I know you have killed and you have ordered others to kill. I just wanted to look you in the eye and tell you that the law is coming for you. You will pay for your crimes." Tomás turned and headed for the door.

As Tomás walked away, Alvarado yelled at him. "You two-bit *pendejo,* you have no evidence. You have no warrant. All you have is talk." As he walked out the door, he heard Alvarado shout, "You will pay for this."

Smiling to himself as he walked back to the mayor's office, Tomás thought, *that went well.*

"Come in," Cisco Abeyta called out when he heard the knock on his door. Tomás Marés walked in. Cisco could not tell from his expression how his encounter with Felipe Alvarado had gone. "What came of your conversation with Alvarado?"

Tomás smiled. "Cisco, have you ever taken a stick and beat on a hornet's nest?"

Abeyta looked at him with a puzzled expression. "No, that would be crazy. They come out angry and ready to sting you."

"That is true, *compadre,*" Tomás said. "But they *do* come out."

"What do you think he will do now, brother?" Estévan paced the floor in his of-

279

fice while Tomás sat motionless in a chair.

"A man like that will not tolerate disrespect. I believe he will go on the attack, perhaps even coming after us." Tomás spoke these words in a quiet voice and yet his unease was plain.

"So let me get this straight, *hermano.* You went out of your way to provoke a man who is a vicious killer so that he will come after us." Estévan shook his head. "Is that about right?"

Tomás chuckled. "I suppose that would be one way to describe it, *sí.*"

"And this is your idea of a plan?" Estévan had an incredulous look on his face. "Are you not the man who intends to get married in a few short months? Are you so eager to get out of that commitment that you have a death wish?"

Tomás laughed out loud. "I would appreciate it, brother, if you would not mention that thought to my fiancée. I do not want for her to think I am developing cold feet."

"I am glad you can joke about this," Estévan said. "Have you given any thought to what we should do now, since you have poked at this mountain lion with a stick? If you are right and he comes for us, what do you intend that we do?"

"It is not what *we* will do, brother; it is what *you* will do."

Estévan stopped in front of the chair where his brother sat and put his hands on his hips. "And what, pray tell, is that?"

Tomás smiled at his brother. His face was the picture of innocence. "You will find Jared Delaney, tell him that because of my impetuousness we are in danger and we need his help. No matter what else is going on with him, he will not turn his back on his friends. You will tell him that we need him to ride with us and the only way he can do that is to allow you to make him a deputy."

Estévan frowned as he thought about what his brother was saying. In a moment, the frown vanished. "You are much more devious than I remember you being when we were children." He smiled. "That might work."

CHAPTER 25

After Davey Good called him out on his plan to murder Jesus Abreu, they rode on in silence for some time. Jared chewed on what the boy had said. At one point, he found himself smiling as he contemplated the irony of the fact that a young man raised by an outlaw had a stronger moral code than he seemed to possess at the present time. He found himself torn about how to proceed. He still had a strong desire to avenge Nathan's death. He thought it was a bit odd that this young boy whom he had just met had managed to appeal to the honorable side of his nature when his wife, the person he loved more than anyone in the world, had been unable to do so.

Darkness was approaching and Jared decided they should make camp for the night. He saw a clearing off to the left of the trail and reined his horse over to it. Davey followed him without a word. Jared dismounted and began unsaddling his horse.

"What are we going to do?" Davey's eyes darted between Jared and the trail they'd just left.

Without looking up, Jared said, "We're gonna make camp, have a bite to eat, and get a decent night's sleep."

Davey rolled his eyes. "I can see that's what we're doing now. I mean, what are we going to do about Abreu?" He hesitated before he continued. "I don't want to be a party to a murder. I don't like the man and I want to get as far away from him as I can but I don't want to help you kill him."

"I know," Jared said. He turned to the boy who was still in the saddle. "Get on down, help me get a fire started." When the boy hesitated, he said, "Come on, get down. I ain't gonna hurt you and I ain't gonna kill Abreu."

Cautiously, Davey dismounted. "Well then, what are you going to do?"

"I don't know yet, we'll figure somethin' out. In the meantime, let's get a fire goin' and heat up some beans."

Davey gave him a skeptical look and then began unsaddling his horse. When he was done, he turned and said, "If you're not going to kill Abreu, what do you need me for?"

Jared had begun hobbling his horse. He stopped and addressed Davey Good. "I still intend to maneuver Abreu into helping us catch Alvarado. And like you said, I might be able to get evidence that would help put Abreu in jail." He turned and finished up with his horse. When he was done, he walked over to where Davey was starting a campfire. "That would help you out, wouldn't it?"

With a slow nod, Davey said, "I guess it would. If he's locked up, I won't matter much to him at all." He frowned. "So what do you intend to do when you catch up with this Alvarado fella?"

Jared was rolling out his bedroll. Without turning around, he said, "I intend to kill him."

Davey threw up his hands in exasperation. "Well how is that any different than what you had planned for Mr. Abreu?"

Turning towards the boy, Jared said, "There's a couple of things that are different about it. First off, Abreu helped plan all this trouble but Alvarado is the one who pulled the trigger. Second, from what I hear, Alvarado is a ferocious assassin. If I try to bring him in to the law, he ain't gonna go along without a fight. Either he'll kill me or I'll have to kill him."

The young man swallowed, his anxiety obvious. "Where am I going to be when you're having your showdown with this cold-blooded killer?"

"Relax," Jared said, "your part's done once you get me Abreu. After that, you're on your own. You can take off any time you like." He paused. "Don't get any ideas about takin' off before your part's done, though. If you want to get clear of this, you need my help."

Davey nodded and looked Jared in the eye. "I do . . . and you need my help just as bad."

Jared smiled. "You got that right. Looks like we're in this together, pard."

"Seems like I don't have a lot of choice in the matter." Davey shook his head. "Seems like you're kind of forcing me to do something that I don't have much stomach to do. I don't reckon that makes us pards."

Jared cocked his head and looked at the boy. After a moment, he said, "You may be right about that. Tell you what, if you got cold feet, you can slip off sometime in the night and try to make your getaway. I won't come after you. You just have to keep in mind that if I don't get the goods on Abreu and you double-cross him, I expect he'll try to make trouble for you." He fanned the flames of the small campfire so that the kindling flared up. "The other thing to keep in mind is that you will have passed up the chance to help bring two vicious murderers to justice. I thought you didn't like outlaws."

The boy stared at the fire, his face a mask of anger and confusion. He shook his head. "You're right, I don't like outlaws and I told you the reasons why. I'm no lawman, though, I just want to get away and start a new life."

"That's why you took off and left your daddy, wasn't it? You wanted to start a new life."

Davey hesitated, not sure where the question was leading. "I told you that, you know it's true."

Jared sighed. "But in your new life, you still ran smack-dab into someone else who was breakin' the law and was more than willin' to use you to further their wickedness. You think you're ever gonna find a place where that doesn't happen?"

"What are you saying?" Davey exploded. "Are you saying no matter where I go, someone is going to use me and try to lure me into their outlaw schemes?"

"What I'm sayin', Davey, is that if you don't learn to take a stand, it'll happen everywhere you go, for damn sure." Jared squatted down and put a skillet with tortillas and beans on the fire to heat up the evening's sparse grub. "So like I said, if you choose to leave, I won't come after you. You should only stay if you decide it's worth takin' the risk to bring Abreu to justice. If you're here in the mornin', that means it was your choice and nobody forced you into anything. If I see you when I wake up, then we'll be pards."

The young man stood there for a moment, then he sighed. "I don't know why life is so complicated, Mr. Delaney . . . I mean, Jared. I didn't ask for any of this trouble. I didn't ask to be born to a daddy who was an outlaw. I sure as heck didn't intend to fall in with a banker who turns out to be a cattle thief."

Jared chuckled. "You'd be surprised at how often luck . . . both good and bad . . . determines what you're faced with in life. You were born into trouble that wasn't of your own makin' and then you had the misfortune to run into our *amigo,* Jesus Abreu. You can spend a lot of time moanin' about your fate or you can figure out how to deal with it the best way you can and move on."

Now it was Davey Good's turn to chuckle. "I spent most of my life up to this point moaning about my fate. Seems like carping and complaining is what people do when they can't think of how to improve their circumstances."

Jared nodded. "That and lookin' for someone else to blame. Trust me, I know an awful lot about that."

Davey shot Jared a quizzical look. "You sound like you've had some experience with bad luck."

"That's a fact," Jared replied. "I've had a load of bad luck in my time. After a while, though, it was bad luck I made for myself. It took some patient and understandin' friends to help me figure out how to change that luck." Jared stared into the fire and Davey thought for a moment that he saw a tear fall. Maybe the smoke got in his eyes. "One of those folks was Nathan Averill, the man who was murdered by these outlaws, Abreu and Alvarado."

The boy squatted on his heels by the fire. "I'm guessing that's why you're so all-fired determined to bring justice to those men."

Jared didn't respond for a moment. When he did speak, his voice was thick with emotion. "What I've been so all-fired determined to bring down on their heads is vengeance. I ain't sure if that's the same thing as justice. I kinda think maybe it's not. You and some other people I know have been hammerin' a way at me to get me to look at this different. Maybe I need to start payin' attention."

Davey didn't know what to say so he said nothing. Jared got up and fetched two tin plates from his saddlebags. He handed one to the boy and spooned a helping of beans and tortillas onto it. He served himself as well and squatted by the fire to fill his belly. They sat in silence for quite a while, long enough for Davey to feel uncomfortable.

Jared stood up and turned to the boy. "As far as I'm concerned, you can feel free to go at any time. You don't need to sneak off in the night or nothin' like that, I don't have any desire to stop you. You're a good boy and you're right, none of this trouble is of your makin'."

Davey Good looked at Jared. He contemplated what the man had just said. "Nah, I think I'll stick around in the morning while we figure out what to do about this mess. I'd like to be free of the likes of Mister Jesus Abreu but I'd also like to see him get what's coming to him." He turned and went over to lay out his bedroll. He turned back and said, "I'll see you in the morning, pard."

Jared squatted there for a while longer as the boy turned in. Finally, he got up, dumped the rest of his beans, and went to get his bedroll. He spooled it out and lay down, staring up at the stars. As he looked up, he wondered if there was a halo moon tonight. He found the moon but this time; there was no cloudy mist around it. Of course, he realized, that doesn't mean that big changes aren't coming.

In the dream, Jared can see the halo moon but there are storm clouds gathering. Thunder rumbles and the temperature takes a precipitous drop. In the distance, he hears the harsh scream of the mountain lion as it hunts its prey. The sound makes his skin crawl. He has a sense of foreboding that his loved ones are in extreme danger but he can't find his way to their side. He doesn't recognize the landscape where his camp is set up and he has no notion of direction. He is consumed with an impotent and blinding rage. A part of him knows that this rage obscures his ability to think straight. He must be clearheaded in order to save his family. A memory surfaces from his childhood. He is huddled in the underbrush, hiding from the brutal men who have attacked his parents' home. He can see them slaughtering his mother and father, yet he is helpless to come to their aid. He is desperate to act but he's paralyzed with fear.

Jared awoke with a start. Davey Good

shifted in his bedroll and moaned but did not wake. Jared wondered if he had disturbed the boy by crying out in his sleep. From the old familiar emotions he was experiencing, he knew he'd had another one of his night terrors. As they always did, the dream left him feeling frightened and confused. He wished he could remember the details, thinking perhaps that would give him some clue as to what was disturbing him so. As usual, he had no clear memory, only murky images and disquieting emotions.

He shrugged his shoulders to release the tension and thought about his situation. He had a sense that he had been wandering around lost and wondered if that feeling was connected with his nightmare. As the words crossed his mind, he recalled that in his last conversation with his wife, she had indicated that she believed he had lost his way. He had refused to listen. Now, a young man whom he had just met was telling him the same thing. He wondered if it was that apparent. Even though he'd been unable to see it, if it was obvious to so many folks, maybe he needed to pay attention. He felt an overpowering urge to see Eleanor. If he was indeed lost, he reckoned the love of his life was the one who could lead him out of the wilderness.

Jared tossed and turned the rest of the night. Just before dawn, he awakened Davey Good. The boy opened his eyes and blinked several times. When he saw Jared, he recoiled in fear.

"It's all right, boy, I ain't gonna hurt you. I'll put on some coffee and then we'll talk a bit."

The boy seemed to relax. He didn't say anything but pulled his boots on and began to roll up his bedroll. Jared got the embers stirred, threw on some kindling, and soon had a fire going to provide heat for both the coffee and the two cowboys. Davey came over and sat on a log close to the fire. Jared handed him a tin cup full of coffee and they sat there mute for a time. A gentle breeze blew the smoke away from them.

After a while, Davey cleared his throat. "What is it you want to talk to me about?"

"There's been a change of plans," Jared said quietly. Davey shot him a look of alarm. "Nah, nothin' bad. We're just gonna change up the timing a bit."

"What do you mean?" Davey looked skeptical.

"I mean I've got to go check on my family before we take any further action to give these desperados what they got comin' to 'em."

"What are you going to do?"

"I've got to ride over to Cimarrón. That'll take me a couple of days."

"What in the heck am I supposed to do while you're doing that?" There was a haunted look in the boy's eyes. "Do I just stay here and wait for either you to come back or for Abreu and Alvarado to find me and kill me?"

"Nobody's gonna find you and kill you, boy," Jared said. "Abreu thinks you're out followin' me and I doubt Alvarado even knows you're alive. A couple of days isn't gonna change things for you." He paused. "There's a strong chance that it'll change things for me, though."

Davey looked confused. "I don't know what you're talking about. Seems like you're talking in riddles."

"Sorry, I sound like my friend, Tomás Marés." Jared smiled. "You remember I said as far as I was concerned, we're pards?"

"Yeah, I guess I do," Davey said, a look of suspicion on his face.

"Well pard, I'm asking you for a favor. I need you to give me this time and be ready to go when I get back. You can stay camped here; you got a stream close by and enough trees to shelter you from bad weather."

"I reckon I could do that." Davey frowned. "You're not planning on double-crossing me now, are you?"

"No, sir, I'm not," Jared said. He stood up and tossed his coffee on the fire. "In fact, when I get back, I think I'll owe you big time. I believe you've helped me clear up some confusin' notions I've had for a while. I'll be in your debt."

"I'm still not sure what you're talking about but I guess I can do what you ask." He cocked his head. "What if you don't show up when you say you will?"

"Give me three days," Jared said. "I should be back in two, but it might take a little longer than I think. If I'm not back in three days, you're free to take off. If I was you, I'd head north to Colorado and not look back."

The boy took a deep breath. "All right, I can do that. Whatever it is you're up to, I hope it works out for you."

"Me, too," Jared said in a soft voice. "Me, too."

Chapter 26

"*Tío* Felipe, I need to speak with you, *por favor.*"

"What is it, Ramon?" Alvarado was in the middle of checking his whiskey inventory at the Imperial Saloon and didn't have the time to speak with his nephew. The boy had been useful, however, so he indulged him.

"I heard some gossip around town; I thought I should check with you." He looked away, his nervousness evident. "People, they are talking. They say you murdered the sheriff."

Alvarado's eyes flashed. "Do you think that I give a damn about what people say? People talk all the time, it means nothing." He stared at his nephew with suspicion. "What is this to you? You have no *cojones*? Are you turning into some kind of *oveja*?" The outlaw snorted his disgust. "Will you start to say 'baa' like some little lamb now?"

Ramon blushed with shame. "I am sorry,

295

Tío, I was just concerned that someone might be suspicious enough to say these things to the law."

Felipe Alvarado laughed. "And who is 'the law' that they would say these things to? Sheriff Little was the law. Believe me, after what happened to him, I do not think anyone will be so eager to step up and fill his boots."

"That is true, *Tío.*" Ramon appeared relieved. "Maybe I put too much stock in this gossip. I just wanted you to know."

Felipe felt a small twinge of sympathy for his *sobrino.* Perhaps he'd been too hard on the boy. After all, he had proven himself to be quite useful. "I appreciate that, Ramon. I was just thinking that maybe you were developing a weak stomach."

"No, *Tío,* you do not have to worry about that." Ramon smiled. "I have learned well from you. A man must be hard if he wishes to move up in the world."

"You are right about that," Alvarado said with conviction. "No one gives you anything in this world. You have to take it. If you do not learn this, others will always bend you to their will." He smiled but it was not a pleasing sight. "If you do learn this lesson, you come to enjoy the power you have over others. There is satisfaction in imposing your influence."

Ramon smiled and nodded in agreement. Inside, his stomach was churning. Although he coveted the power that his uncle possessed, the man terrified him. He was pretty sure that if he disappointed him in some way, his *tío* would have no compunction about killing him and leaving his carcass for the buzzards.

"I can see that, *Tío* Felipe. It is without a doubt one of the things I admire most about you." Ramon worried for a moment that he had laid on the flattery a bit thick. His uncle was a cunning and intelligent hombre. If he perceived that Ramon was lacking in sincerity, he would not be pleased about it. The last thing he wanted was to displease his uncle. Just to be safe, he added, "You do not need my admiration, though, as we both know."

Alvarado waved his hand to dismiss this topic and begin the next. "No matter. I have a task for you. I want you to go to Cimarrón and find out what you can about the family of this Jared Delaney *cabrón*. He annoys me more every day. I need to do something to get his attention."

Ramon hesitated before responding. In fact, as his uncle suspected, he did have a bit of a weak stomach for violence. It was one thing for the man to murder a lawman who was supposed to be able to take care of himself. It was another to involve the wife and perhaps the children of a foe. He knew he couldn't say this to his uncle, though. Whatever qualms he had about the morality of his uncle's actions, or for that matter, his own, he had greater concern for his personal safety.

"I will leave immediately, *Tío* Felipe."

Ramon arrived in Cimarrón in the late morning. He had ridden well into the night and then arose before dawn. In part, he wished to please his uncle but his primary motivation was to get this task over with as soon as possible. He knew nothing about where Delaney lived but he'd heard that he sold cattle in Colorado. He'd given considerable thought to the question of how to find out the information he was seeking. He went straight to the livery. As he rode up, a man walked out to greet him.

"*Buenos días,* Señor," the man said. "I am Antonio Chavez and this is my livery. Can I take care of your horse for you?"

Ramon dismounted and shook Chavez's hand. "*Gracias,* Señor, but no. What I am seeking is information."

The smile faded from the man's face,

replaced by a look of suspicion. "What sort of information do you seek?"

Ramon continued to smile. "I represent a man who wishes to purchase some cattle. I was told that Jared Delaney deals in cattle and is an honest man. I was hoping you could direct me to where he lives."

The smile did not return but some of the suspicion faded a bit. "It is true that Señor Delaney is an honest man. I could direct you to where he lives but that would do you no good."

Puzzled, Ramon asked, "Why is that, Señor Chavez?"

"Because he is not there."

Ramon was feeling frustrated with the man but did his best to hide it. "Could you perhaps tell where I might find him then, if he is not at his residence?"

"I could not," Chavez said. "He is away at this time."

Unsure of where to go with this conversation, Ramon took a deep breath. "That is indeed bad news. I need to purchase a rather large herd of cattle for my employer. From what I have heard, this Delaney is a good man. I would hate for him to miss out on the sale."

Chavez studied the young man. After a moment's deliberation, he determined that he could be taken at his word. "Although I cannot tell you where Señor Delaney is, I can direct you to where his wife is staying. She might be able to help you."

Ramon felt a glimmer of optimism. "That would be very helpful, Señor."

"She is at the schoolhouse at the other end of town on this same street. She and the children are staying there with our schoolteacher, Miss Christy." He pointed north. "It is on the opposite side of the street. You cannot miss it."

So this Delaney did have children. A twinge of guilt passed through Ramon's mind but he did not dwell on it. If it were up to him, Delaney's family would not be dragged into this conflict but he understood with great clarity that it was not up to him.

"Gracias, Señor Chavez, you have been most helpful." Ramon tipped his hat to the man.

Chavez nodded back. "I hope you will be able to conduct your business with Señor Delaney. He is a good man with a nice family. Like all of us, he can always use the money."

Ramon smiled. "I think Señor Delaney will get what is coming to him." He turned to walk away, then he paused. Turning back, he asked, "Is the sheriff available at this time? I need to ask him about some reports I have heard about cattle rustlers and horse thieves."

Chavez shook his head. "Sorry, Señor, the last I heard, Sheriff Marés is out of town."

"Ah, well, it seems as if I have missed everyone then." Ramon smiled again, mounted up, and rode off to report to his *tío*.

Hours later, Ramon stood in front of his uncle and described the situation in Cimarrón. As he recounted the information that neither Delaney nor the sheriff were in town, but that he knew where Delaney's wife and children were, he saw a malevolent light appear in his *tío's* eyes.

"Gracias, Ramon, I will take it from here."

Davey Good sat by the campfire at dusk and wondered if Jared Delaney was going to come back. He was confused by everything the man had said to him and yet there was something about it that rang true. Having grown up with a bad man, he felt like he had a good sense about the difference between good and evil. Somehow, in spite of Delaney's desire for vengeance, Davey had the feeling that he was, at heart, a good man. He hoped that seeing his family would help him back onto an honorable path. He also hoped that path would lead Delaney back to where Davey waited. He wanted to extract himself from this trap he was ensnared in and he wouldn't mind seeing Jesus Abreu get taken down in the process.

CHAPTER 27

"Would you mind looking after my two renegade children for the day?" Eleanor sat across the table from Christy sipping her morning coffee. It was Saturday and Christy had the day off from her duties as schoolteacher. "The Miller boy has been taking care of the stock for me but I want to check to make sure everything is all right. I should be back around suppertime."

Christy smiled at her and said, "I would be delighted to entertain your well-behaved offspring for the day. We always have quite the time together."

Eleanor reflected on what Christy had just said. For whatever reason, she had noticed that her son and daughter, who were both so strong-minded that they often gave her fits, were always well behaved when they had the opportunity to be around other adults. In particular, they appreciated the company of their Aunt Christy and the affection was mutual. Eleanor was gratified that her hope that the children's presence would lift Christy's spirits was playing out in the manner she had visualized.

"I've noticed that," Eleanor said with a chuckle. "I've wondered if you might teach me whatever magic tricks it is that you're using on them to behave so well."

"No magic at all," Christy responded. "I'm their friend and for the most part, we just have fun together. You're their mother. You make them do chores, wash their hands, and go to bed whether they feel like it or not. My job is easy. Yours is a great deal more difficult."

"I'm not sure if that's true or not," Eleanor said with a laugh, "but it makes me feel better so I'm going to choose to believe it. I'll tell them that I'm leaving for the day and then be on my way." She laughed. "I suspect they'll be relieved not to have me around nagging them."

Eleanor made her way out into the yard where the children were playing and called them over. "Come here, my two wild savages. I need to tell you something."

They ran over to her. Ned giggled and said, "We're not savages, Mama, we're children." He turned and looked at his sister for a moment, then turned back to her.

"Lizbeth is kind of a savage, though, now that I think about it." The boy had his father's dry sense of humor; that was for sure.

"Am not!" Lizbeth caught up with her brother and ran to her mother for a hug. "What's a sage, Mama?"

Eleanor laughed. "It's 'savage,' sweetheart. Your brother and I were both making a joke. And you're not a savage; you are a darling child and the light of my life."

The little girl hugged her mother and then turned to her brother. "See, I am not a sage, mister smarty-pants."

Ned laughed at his sister. "It's not sage, you ninny, it's savage."

"Don't call your sister a ninny, young man. It's not nice."

"Yes, ma'am," Ned responded, looking not the least bit contrite.

"I have to go out to the ranch to check on the livestock," she said. "Will you stay here and take care of your Aunt Christy while I'm gone?"

"You're silly, Mama," Ned scoffed. "Aunt Christy is a grown-up. She can take care of herself."

Eleanor knelt down and took Ned's hand. "Sometimes grown-ups need to be taken care of, Ned. I want you and sister to be real good for your Aunt Christy. Do what she says and try to have fun."

"We always have a good time with Aunt Christy, Mama," Lizbeth said. "She makes up the funnest games."

"Funnest is not a word, sweetheart," Eleanor said. Having once been the schoolteacher herself, she never passed up a teachable moment. "You would say that she makes up games that are the most fun."

"Yes," said Lizbeth, "she does that, too."

Eleanor could only smile. "I'm sure she does. I should be back around suppertime so we can sit down and eat together. You can tell me about all the fun times the three of you have had."

She gave each of her children a hug and then Ned and Lizbeth ran inside. Eleanor went to hitch up her buckboard. When she had it ready, she went in to let Christy know that she was leaving. The children were engaged in a fierce game of checkers with their Aunt Christy and Eleanor thought that they probably wouldn't have noticed if she had just taken off without saying goodbye.

As Eleanor came to the final curve in the road that led to the ranch, she saw someone riding her way. It only took her a second to recognize the man riding proud and tall as her husband. She felt her pulse quicken and she wasn't sure if it was because of excitement or trepidation. She had no idea what he had been up to since she last saw him and she was afraid that he might have already committed some awful deed that could not be undone or taken back.

The distance closed between them and Jared waved to his wife. He drew up in front of the buckboard and dismounted, approaching her with a tentative smile on his face.

"I sure am pleased to see you, Eleanor my love," he said. He shrugged. "Don't know how you feel about seein' me, though."

Eleanor sighed. For an instant, she wished she could just close her eyes and when she reopened them, everything would be the way it was before Nathan Averill was murdered and her husband embarked on his mission of vengeance. Jared stood waiting, an expectant look on his face.

"Jared, I love you. I've missed you a great deal and so have the children. I just don't know what you may have done since I saw you last or how it will affect our lives." She shook her head. "I feel so many different ways, I don't know that I can say just how I feel about seeing you now."

Jared nodded. "That's fair, my love. If it'll

make you feel any better, I haven't done anything illegal up to now."

Eleanor felt a bit of tension release in her shoulders. She hadn't realized how tight they were until that moment.

"I suppose that's good news," she said. "I don't know if that means you've changed your plans in regard to this vigilante mission you've been on or if you just haven't had the opportunity yet to put your plan into action."

"I reckon it might be a little bit of both, to be honest." Jared took off his hat and ran his fingers through his hair. He was close enough that Eleanor could see the sunlight glint off the gray hairs at his temples. It seemed to her that there might be a few more of them than she remembered. "I've been doin' some serious thinkin' about the things you've said to me. I've also had the chance to talk with someone I recently met who has an interestin' point of view." A hint of a smile crossed his lips. "Sometimes a stranger can have a fresh take on a situation that changes your outlook."

A puzzled look crept across Eleanor's face. "I'm not sure what you're talking about. How did a stranger happen to have the opportunity to weigh in with you on . . ." Eleanor frowned and waved her hand. "I don't even know what to call what you've been doing. Threatening to take the law into your hands, seeking revenge, vigilante justice."

"Reckon all of those things fit. None of 'em sound all that noble when you line 'em up like that." He shrugged. "I been so blinded by my anger and desire for vengeance that I haven't been thinkin' with a clear mind." He shook his head and laughed. "I suppose that ain't news to you, though, is it?"

Her heart was pounding. Eleanor thought she saw a glimpse of the man she knew and loved instead of the different version she had watched ride off on a quest to break the law. She was afraid to get her hopes up and yet he sounded much like the Jared of the time before Nathan was killed.

"I love you. I know I said that already but I'll say it again. I'm not the only one either. Tomás, Estévan, those men love you like a brother. We've all been worried sick about you."

"I know you have, Eleanor my love, with pretty good reason." Jared moved a step closer to the buckboard. Eleanor could see the muscles in his jaw tense. "I gotta tell you, I'm still torn between wantin' to make those devils pay for what they did no matter what it costs me, as opposed to takin' a step back and leavin' it to the law." He spat in the dirt. "You know I ain't got much faith in the law to make sure justice is done and you know the reasons why that is. I can't seem to let this go and yet I know in my heart that what you've been tryin' to tell me is right." He shook his head. "I just don't know what to do."

Eleanor could see the pain and ambivalence etched in her husband's countenance. She felt that pain down to the depths of her soul.

"Jared, I know that of all the difficult things you've ever had to do, leaving this to someone else may be the hardest. There may be another way, though."

Now Jared looked perplexed. "What are you talkin' about?"

"I know you were upset when you found out Estévan had agreed to take on the job of acting sheriff."

"Yeah, I was, at the time," Jared said. "That's one of the things I've given some thought to since then. I know he was only tryin' to do the right thing, though at the time, I just felt like he was attemptin' to thwart my efforts." Jared looked down at the ground. Eleanor thought the expression on his face might be one of regret. "I reckon I feel bad about the harsh manner I spoke to him in."

"I know you thought that," she said. "I suppose in a way that was true." When Jared started to speak, she held up her hand. "Just like you, Estévan wants to hold these outlaws accountable for their heinous acts. He also didn't want to see your life destroyed in the process."

Jared sighed. "I know. I don't know why I couldn't see that at the time but I couldn't." He frowned. "What did you mean when you said there might be another way?"

Eleanor laughed. "I'm sorry to make light of a terrible situation but you, Estévan, and Tomás are all the same and I don't think you'll ever change."

"Now I really don't know what you're talkin' about," Jared said, "although I expect you're right about none of us ever changin'."

"Estévan realized that he couldn't handle this situation by himself. He needed help and he needed a few good men whom he could count on."

"Don't reckon I know where he's gonna find 'em," Jared said. "Tomás made it clear where he stood on that topic and I can't see Tom Figgs joinin' up without Tomás bein' a part of the deal. I can't think of anybody else left around Cimarrón who'd be much good in a fight like them boys."

"This will surprise you but Tomás agreed to be Estévan's deputy."

"What?" Jared was stunned by the news. "How did that happen? He was dead set against doin' that very thing and for good reason."

"I know. It seems like losing your father and not wanting to lose your future bride would be good enough reasons not to go off and do something crazy like this." The edge of frustration in her voice was unmistakable. "That's what he's going to do, though."

"Why on earth is he doin' that?" Jared was still dumbfounded. "Maria can't be happy about all this."

"She's not but she understands why he made the decision." Eleanor looked Jared in the eyes. "He loves his brother and he loves you like a brother. He couldn't let his brother ride out alone against vicious outlaws like these men and he couldn't stand by and let you make a terrible mistake that would ruin your life."

Jared didn't know what to say. He shifted from one foot to the other as he contemplated this set of circumstances. "I reckon that makes some kind of sense. Dang his hide, what's he thinkin', though. He's made more sacrifices than just about anyone in

Cimarrón. Don't know why he has to be the one to do this."

"He's not the only one," Eleanor said. "Tom Figgs has signed up to help Estévan, too."

"Oh, my Lord," Jared exclaimed. "What next?" He held up his hand and said, "No, don't tell me what's next; I don't know if I can stand it."

"Here's what's next," Eleanor replied in a quiet voice. "I can't believe I'm going to say this to you but I know what Nathan meant to you. Estévan would like to deputize you and have you join them in going after these men. What you would be doing would be legal."

"He told you that?"

"Yes, he did," Eleanor said. "I hate it because it'll be every bit as dangerous as all those other times you've gone out to track down evil men. Wearing a badge doesn't make you bulletproof. I know that there are times when you have to take the risks, though." She wiped a tear from her cheek. "This is one of those times."

"So Estévan wants me to come in so he can deputize me?"

"Yes," Eleanor replied, "just as soon as you can."

Jared looked off to the mountains in the

west. "I'll have to study on it a bit." He shifted, his discomfort obvious. "There's somethin' I need to take care of first, too."

"What are you talking about, Jared Delaney?" Eleanor was close to losing her temper. "You have an opportunity to accomplish what you were so desperate to do without breaking the law and ruining not only your life but mine and the children's' lives. What do you have to take care of that could possibly be more important than that?"

Jared hesitated. He considered telling Eleanor about his plan to entrap Jesus Abreu with the help of Davey Good, and with luck, get evidence that could be used against him. He hoped that Davey could convince him to write a note to Alvarado that would incriminate them both. If Abreu balked at doing that, though, he was afraid he might have to take Abreu captive in order to get his cooperation. He suspected if that became necessary, he would have to take some actions that his wife would not approve of in order to secure his assistance.

"I can't tell you right now, Eleanor my love, it's too complicated. If it works out the way I hope, though, you'll be satisfied." He shrugged. He knew there was nothing he could say that would make her feel all right about his riding away now. "I'm gonna need a few days to tie up some loose ends. I think you're right that joinin' up with Esté-van and the boys is the right thing to do but it's a little more involved than that."

Eleanor exploded. "I swear, Jared, I don't know how much more of this I can take. Just when I think maybe you've come to your senses, you give me some vague expla-nation that tells me nothing. Do you think I will tolerate this forever?"

"I'm not askin' for forever, I'm askin' you for a few days, that's all. I believe that things will line up so that I can do what you're askin' me to do. I just need to take care of something first."

Jared could see that Eleanor was furious. It broke his heart to leave her hanging this way after she had presented him with a chance to get back in her good graces. He had a fleeting memory of seeing that halo moon. He wondered if the change it por-tended was the dissolution of his marriage. He hoped with all his being that wasn't the case. He felt his heart sink as he searched for something reassuring to offer his wife. He couldn't find any words.

"I don't know if I can give you that time or not, Jared." Eleanor's jaw was clenched in anger. "I just don't know. If you can ride off now with that uncertainty, so be it."

Jared's spirits sank. "I hate it, Eleanor my love, but I don't reckon I've got a choice."

"Don't you dare say that to me," she flung back at him. "You always have a choice. I don't know what it is you're choosing over me and your children but that's what you're doing. You're putting us second. That tells me a lot."

Before Jared could respond, Eleanor slapped the horse with the lines and headed on toward the ranch. When he called out to her, she did not look back. As he turned and rode away, he felt like his heart had turned to stone in his chest.

Manuel Salazar was not a patient man. It had been too long since he'd heard anything from Jared Delaney. The need for revenge burned in his gut. The men who had murdered his mentor and friend, Nathan Averill, needed to pay for their crime. He had no idea what progress Delaney had made and it was driving him mad. He paced in his office as he obsessed about what he might do to speed things up.

He would have been happy to take matters into his own hands with Jesus Abreu. However, the man had not been seen at the bank for several days. It would appear that Jesus had a keen sense for smelling out trouble. He must have realized that Salazar was looking for him, and decided to make himself scarce.

Salazar had been checking in with Abreu's assistant at the bank several times a day but the man claimed to have heard nothing from his boss. The mayor was hedging his bets, though. He had spoken with Arturo Garcia, who ran the livery, as well as Jim White, the telegraph operator. The livery was on the north end of town and the telegraph office was on the south end. Between the two, Garcia and White knew almost everything that happened in town. If anyone could tell him of Abreu's whereabouts, it was one of those men.

As he paced, Salazar snorted. He could think of nothing more to do so he would have to do nothing. Manuel Salazar was not a man who was satisfied with doing nothing. He continued to pace and think. He would come up with something. These villains would pay for their foul deeds.

317

CHAPTER 28

Christine Johnson was feeling melancholy as she watched Ned and Lizbeth Delaney sitting at desks drawing pictures. Ned was drawing horses and he seemed to have the knack for capturing an authentic look of a horse in motion. Whatever Lizbeth was drawing was not immediately recognizable to the casual observer but she was pleased with it, and that seemed to be all that mattered. They'd just come inside after a rousing game of hide and seek that had lasted for over an hour and spanned the entire schoolyard. She figured the children needed some rest and she knew for a fact that she did.

Motherhood had not been in the cards for Christine Johnson. Cruel circumstances had resulted in her falling into a life of prostitution during her mid-teens and early twenties. She was not proud of that chapter of her life but she had no patience for the sanctimonious folks who condemned women who, out of desperation, eked out a living engaged in work lacking in meaning and dignity. The line composed of those willing to exploit these desperate women was long, and there weren't many who were keen to offer them a chance to rise above the squalor and degradation to find work that provided a living wage and a sense of self-worth.

As bad as her life had been at times, Christy had never lost her conviction that she was a decent human being with something more to offer the world than her sexual favors. She still had a vivid memory of the night she had turned against the vile men that exploited her and informed Sheriff Nathan Averill that they were planning to lure him into an ambush. Nathan had treated her with respect and, in the aftermath, had provided her with the opportunity to leave the profession of soiled doves and become the teacher that she was today.

She would never have imagined on that night that the sheriff's offer of assistance would blossom into a friendship and, in the end, a romance. Although there was a significant difference in their ages, Christy had never known a stronger or more honorable man. From the beginning of their relationship, she found herself more and more attracted to him. In the beginning, he had been uncomfortable with their age discrepancy but as time went on, he came to view it with good humor and equanimity.

She had loved everything about him. Her only regret was that they had never been able to conceive a child of their own. As she looked over at the Delaney children, she felt tears well up. She thought it was for the best that they'd never had a child since that child would now be fatherless. It was all she could do to bear that pain herself and she would have hated for a child to have to go through it. She knew how painful losing a parent was from her own childhood experience and wouldn't have wished it on anyone.

A knock at the door of the classroom roused her from her reverie. She frowned. It was unusual for anyone to knock when they came to visit her in her classroom. Most often, the caller was either a student or a parent and they knew that they were welcome to come on in. As she reflected on the question, she realized that since the death of her husband, people had been more respectful or at least more cautious about approaching her. Perhaps this was yet another citizen coming to express their sympathy and offer condolences. She cringed at the prospect.

She walked over to the door and opened it. A tall man stood there with his hat in his hands. He was smiling in an affable manner and yet a feeling of dread washed over her. There was something off about the man . . . something lethal and dangerous in his eyes.

"Señora Delaney?" The man's smile widened and yet the aura of menace he exuded did not subside.

Confused, she replied, "No, I'm sorry, I'm not Eleanor Delaney. I'm Christine Johnson, the teacher at this school. How can I help you?"

The man nodded as if recalibrating his thoughts. "Do you expect Señora Delaney back soon?"

Christy felt apprehension at this point although the man had not behaved in a threatening manner so far. "I'm afraid she's gone out to her ranch for the day, sir. I assume she'll be back later this evening." She cocked her head in curiosity. "May I ask what business you have with her?"

The man nodded and smiled at her. He then walked forward to enter the schoolhouse. Christy stepped in his way but the man pushed past her. Christy reacted with indignation.

"I beg your pardon, sir, you can't just

come barging in here like that."

The man turned and faced her. He replaced his hat on his head and she saw that he'd been hiding his pistol behind it. "Oh, Señora, you are wrong about that. I can barge in if I wish."

Christy felt the blood drain from her face. Against her will, she cut her eyes in the direction of the children. The man noticed and smiled.

"Ah, I see you are in charge of the Delaney brats today. That is good." He chuckled. "This may work out even better than what I had planned."

"Look here, mister," she said, bluffing in as convincing manner as she could muster. "The sheriff looks out for us. I expect he'll be around any minute to make sure everything is all right."

The man laughed out loud. "You should never play cards, you are not very convincing. I know that your sheriff is out of town, Señora."

Christy's heart sank. "What is it you want, mister? I don't have any money."

"I am not interested in your money, Señora. I require the pleasure of yours and the children's company for a time." He smiled as if he were asking her to go on a social outing. "I have some negotiations to engage in with Jared Delaney. You and those brats will make excellent bargaining chips."

In her mind, the pieces of the puzzle fell into place. This was the monster that had killed her husband. He had found out that Jared was tracking him and was attempting to gain a power advantage over his foe by kidnapping his family. Her thoughts raced as she tried to devise a strategy to extract herself and the children from this peril. Nothing came to mind.

Christy carried a derringer in her handbag but the bag was in a drawer in her desk. She was terrified at the prospect of getting into a gun battle with an outlaw when she was armed only with a two-shot weapon, but as Nathan had pointed out when he gave it to her, the Remington Model 95 with its .41 caliber rimfire cartridges could be lethal at close range. If she could figure out how to get her handbag, she might have to take the risk.

Christy looked the man up and down. As frightened as she felt, she had a hunch that the man would feed off of this emotion. There was a sadistic spark in his eyes and she imagined that it would turn to a fire if she fueled it with fear. She decided that whatever else happened, she would not give him the satisfaction of seeing her intimidated by him. In fact, having lost her beloved husband, she didn't much care what happened to her. If this man killed her, it would put an end to her constant emotional pain. She couldn't let anything happen to the children, though, so she knew she must proceed with caution.

In as matter of fact a manner as she could muster, she asked, "Where is it that you intend to take us, sir? Even though the sheriff is not here now, he'll be returning soon."

The man laughed. "I am tempted to wait for him so I can send him to his grave. However, that will not serve my purposes so I will have to wait." He looked over at the desk at the front of the classroom. "I assume you have writing implements in your desk. I would like for you to take down the words I tell you."

Christy felt her pulse quicken. If she could find a way to slip the derringer in the pocket of her dress while she was doing his bidding with the note, the odds might not be so heavily stacked against her. She walked over to her desk and sat down in the chair. She started to open the drawer where her bag was.

"Go slow, Señora," the man said in a firm voice.

With an edge to her own voice, she said, "If you want me to write a note for you, I'll need to get pen and paper out of the drawer. That means I have to open it."

The man's eyes flashed and he raised his pistol in her direction. For a moment, she was afraid she'd gone too far. "Do not be disrespectful to me, *puta*. Although I would prefer to keep you as a hostage, I could make do without you if I had to."

Taking a more neutral tone, she said, "I'm just trying to make sure I do what you want me to do." She couldn't help herself, though. She was becoming angrier at the brazen manner of this man. "You realize that if you shoot me, folks will come running. You can't believe that you're going to get away with this."

The man transferred his pistol to his left hand and drew a huge knife from a sheath on his belt. "I do not need to shoot you, Señora." His smile was terrifying. "I can kill you with very little noise with this."

Christy's heart was pounding in her chest and she was afraid she might faint. However, with great effort, she kept her wits about her. When the man looked down to return his knife to its sheath, she grabbed her derringer and, with one swift motion, dropped it in the pocket of her dress.

She took a deep breath. "All right, you win. What do you want me to write?"

He came a step closer so that he could see what she was doing. "You told me that the Delaney woman would be returning later today. And she will be coming back here, is this correct?"

"She told me she would be back in time to get the children fed and ready for bed, yes."

The man nodded. "Excellent. We will leave her a message right there on your desk."

"What do you want me to say to her?"

The man pursed his lips as he thought. "Tell her that if she would like to see her children alive, she needs to tell her husband to come get them from me."

Christy wrote this information down and then looked up. "Am I supposed to tell her where he should go to get them?"

He nodded. "He will need to ride towards Las Vegas. He knows the trail. About half of the way there, he will see a tall pine tree that has been struck by lightning. If he follows the path to the north from that tree, he will come to a cabin. That is where I will be."

It occurred to Christy that he had not said it was where *they* would be. She realized that once he took them away, he would no longer need them. The man's intention was to murder Jared and it was clear to her that he had no regard for her life or the lives of the children. The only reason she could imagine his not killing them right away once they were out of town was that he would want Jared to witness him murdering them in his presence. It was clear to her that the man was a sadistic beast.

If she was right in her theory that he intended to indulge his sadism by killing the children in front of their father, she hoped it would give her time to find the right moment to shoot this man down. She also realized that he might consider her disposable once he made it away from town with the children. She needed to convince him to keep her alive.

"How is it that you plan to get us to this cabin, sir? The children are too young to ride."

He smiled. "I saw your buckboard out back of the building. I will tie my horse to the back. I'm sure it will accommodate us."

Christy took a deep breath and felt her pulse quicken. She knew she had to be convincing. "You do realize that you need me, I hope. The children don't know you and have been taught to be careful around strangers. If you harm me and attempt to take them, they will cause a ruckus, I promise you. People will hear and some will come. I don't believe that will serve your purposes."

His eyes narrowed. "Do you believe that I do not recognize what you are trying to do, Señora? I know you are bargaining for your life."

"Of course I am," she said. "That doesn't make what I said any less true. If you want the children to remain calm, you need me."

Again, he smiled at her. Again, it was chilling. "I like your spirit, Señora. I think I am going to enjoy your last moments on earth. In fact, I will make sure I do."

Christy felt a wave of nausea wash over her. It took all of her willpower but she endured it until it passed. "I know who you are. You killed my husband. When you did that, I died, too. I know you intend to kill me but you're too late. You already did."

"Then you need to prepare to die a second time," he said in a soft, almost loving tone. "And in the end, when your death comes, you will welcome it, I promise." He waved his hand casually. "But enough about you and me. You are right; you can make yourself useful. Find a way to get those children into the wagon without a fuss. If you are successful, who knows? Maybe I will be merciful when your moment of reckoning comes."

Christy fought down her terror. She could not panic now; it would result not only in her own murder but in the murder of the children. She cared little about her own life but she would fight to her death to protect them.

"All right, I'll do the best I can to reassure them. They're children, though; you need to not do anything to scare them."

He bowed. "I am not a monster, Señora. I can be quite charming when I put my mind to it."

Biting her tongue to suppress an acerbic response, Christy walked over to where Ned and Lizbeth were sitting, her mind racing over the possible explanation she could offer the children that would be most reassuring to them. If they panicked, there might be nothing she could do to save them.

"Ned, Lizbeth, listen to me."

They looked up with quizzical expressions. Ned asked, "What is it, Aunt Christy?"

"This is Señor Alvarado," she said. She felt him stiffen beside her when she mentioned him by name. She hoped she hadn't overstepped her bounds but it was too late. "Your mama had to go somewhere and she

329

can't come here to get you. She asked him to take us to meet her. We're going for a ride in the buckboard."

Ned hopped up and said, "Oh boy, can I hold the lines, Aunt Christy?"

She felt a sense of relief, if only for a moment. It seemed as if they were accepting her story. "Well of course you can, Ned," she replied. She turned and spoke in a soft voice to Alvarado. "It's going to take me a few moments to hitch up the horse to the wagon. Please don't do anything to upset the children."

Just as softly, he replied, "As I said, Señora, I am not a monster."

Had the lives of the children not been hanging in the balance, Christy might have quarreled with the man about that statement. As it was, she knew it would be pointless, and, in all likelihood, fatal. She took the children by their hands and led them outside. Alvarado helped them into the wagon while she went over to the stable to get the placid old bay gelding. She felt her stomach turn when she saw him touch the children but there was nothing she could do.

Leading the horse over, she called out. "This will just take a minute, then we'll be on our way." Years of practice made her fingers nimble. Soon they were ready and on their way. The children seemed excited about going on an unexpected outing. Their innocence was heartbreaking.

As they reached the edge of town, she saw the mayor, Bill Wallace, coming from the opposite direction in his little buggy. He gave her a curious glance but she just nodded in greeting to him. She thought about trying to send him some sort of signal that she was in danger but she realized that he would be no match for the killer who sat on the seat with her. No point in putting anyone else in jeopardy. Now she had to bide her time and wait for an opening. She would only get one chance.

Eleanor was livid as she pulled up to the ranch house. She sat there for several minutes trying to calm down and clear her head. As she thought about the conversation she'd just had with her husband, she realized that the primary reason she was so upset was that she had gotten her hopes up that Jared had had a change of heart. When he expressed his unwillingness to commit to seeking out Estévan until he took care of his mysterious business, she felt like her hopes had been lifted only to be dashed in an excruciating manner. The fact that he wouldn't tell her the details of what he was up to just increased her suspicion and gnawed away at her trust of him.

She stomped her foot, which caused her horse, Tater, to toss his head.

"Sorry, Tater, didn't mean to spook you," she said. She climbed down from the buckboard seat and walked around to pat his nose and give him one of the carrots she carried in her pocket. He accepted her peace offering in his typical placid fashion.

Eleanor took a deep breath and walked over to the stables to check on the horses. There was hay strewn around and the stalls had been mucked out. It appeared that the Miller boy had been doing his job, which was not a surprise to her . . . he was good boy . . . but it was a load off her mind. The thought crossed her mind that this was not the particular load she would like to get off her mind but every little bit helped.

Looking around at this place that was her home, she felt a strange combination of anxiety and serenity. She loved her life here on the Kilpatrick Ranch with her husband and children. It was everything she could ever want and when she thought about it, it made her feel good down to her very soul. The notion that something or someone might rip all of this away from her engendered a sense of panic, and the fact that she couldn't seem to reach her husband alarmed her a great deal.

She stared up at the mountains to the west and pondered her dilemma. After a brief time, she concluded that there was nothing more she could do about it right then. What she could do was return to town and spend time with her children and friend. She gave Tater another carrot and then climbed aboard the buckboard and headed back towards town.

When she arrived at the school, she was expecting to see Christy and the children playing in the schoolyard. When she didn't see them, she thought they must have taken a break to rest. She laughed to herself, thinking that Christy would likely sleep well tonight after spending the day trying to keep up with Ned and Lizbeth. She pulled around the back and saw straightaway that Christy's buckboard was gone. She wondered where they might have gone and as she walked to the door, she hoped that Christy had left her a note.

The sun was already going down behind the mountains and the interior of the school was in semidarkness. She took the time to light a lantern and then went over to Christy's desk, which was where she would have left a note. Perhaps they'd gone over to the Marés Café to get the children a snack of sopapillas and honey.

A piece of paper lay on the desk and Eleanor picked it up. As she read the note, she felt as if her heart was going to explode out of her chest. For a moment she was afraid she would faint and she had to sit down to catch her breath.

The note was in Christy's distinctive handwriting. They had worked together long enough when Eleanor was still the schoolteacher that she recognized it right away. She reread the note to make sure she hadn't missed something or misinterpreted what she'd read. To her horror, the message was the same.

She had to find Jared but she had no idea where he might be. Thanks to his evasiveness about the mysterious task he had to take care of, she didn't have a clue as to what he was doing or how to contact him. In the meantime, their children's lives were hanging in the balance and he was gone. At that moment, she hated him.

CHAPTER 29

It was near dusk when Jared arrived back at Davey's camp. The boy must have heard him coming because he didn't seem startled when he rode up. He had a fire going and Jared was impressed with the fact that the campsite seemed organized and unclut-tered. You could tell a lot about a man based on the degree to which he maintained order in his personal space. Life could be messy but that didn't mean a man had to sur-render to chaos.

"Reckon you might've been about ready to give up on me," Jared said.

"No, sir," Davey replied. "You said you'd be back within a few days. I took your word on that. Would you like some coffee?"

Jared dismounted and loosened his horse's cinch. "I wouldn't mind a cup if you got it. Is it fresh?"

"I just made it a few minutes before you rode up." The boy walked over to the fire, poured steaming coffee into a tin mug, and handed it to Jared. He stepped back and looked at him. "Did you get done what you needed to do?"

As he pondered the question, Jared took a sip of coffee. It was hot and tasted fresh. You just couldn't do any better than Arbuckles' Coffee. He nodded his approval. "To tell you the truth, I don't know whether I did or not." Davey gave him a puzzled look. "I know that ain't much of an answer, it's just that some things are complicated. I do know what needs to happen next, though, and I know what help I need from you."

Davey walked back over to the log he'd been sitting on and took a seat. "Well, let's hear it then."

Jared walked over by the fire and squatted down. "First off, I want you to know that my plan has changed from the one I told you about before. This plan doesn't involve violence directed toward Jesus Abreu. If it does come down to fightin', it'll be because he starts it and leaves me no other choice."

"All right." Davey nodded. "That doesn't tell me much but still, it's important."

"I thought it was, that's why I started with that. Now let me tell you what I need you to do and see how that sets with you."

"You got my full attention," the boy replied.

"I want you to ride to Springer first thing in the morning and tell Abreu that you heard that I was plannin' to ride to Las Vegas and gun down Felipe Alvarado. You can also tell him that once I do that, my plan is to head to Springer lookin' for him." Jared took another sip of coffee. "You know that'll get him stirred up for sure. I reckon he'll decide he needs to warn Alvarado. Before he has much time to think about it, I want you to volunteer to ride to Las Vegas to carry that warning."

"And why would I be so willing to do that? Don't you imagine Abreu might be suspicious of my motives?"

"He will be unless you tell him straight up what your motive is. Here's the thing . . . you're gonna tell him that you'll do it but that this whole situation has turned out to be a lot more dangerous than you thought it would be. Tell him you can be ready to leave right away but that you're gonna need a hundred dollars to do the job." Jared smiled. "Your motive is greed. That's something Abreu understands all too well."

"And you think he's going to just hand me a hundred dollars to take a message to Las Vegas?" Davey looked skeptical.

"Of course not," Jared said with a chuckle. "He's gonna tell you that he'll pay you when you come back."

"And we both know that if I did what I told him I would do and came back, he'd never pay me." Davey nodded as he thought about what he'd heard so far. "To make it believable, I might argue the point with him a bit before I give in."

Jared nodded and smiled. "That's exactly right. If you make it too easy, he'll get suspicious. Just don't overplay your hand. Put up a little fuss but then give in. Here's the most important part, though. Tell Abreu you're worried that Alvarado won't take your word that you're representing him. Ask him to write you a note that explains your mission to give to Alvarado."

A look of comprehension appeared on the boy's face. "When I get this note, I gather that I'm supposed to bring it straight to you."

"That's right. I need somethin' in writing from Abreu that show he's in cahoots with Alvarado, somethin' that could be used as evidence in a court of law. The more specific it is, the better, although I don't know how much say you'll have over that part."

Davey was silent as he pondered the scenario. Jared waited. When the young man spoke, Jared could hear the suspicion in his voice. "So when I do this, are we done? Will you let me go on my way or will you think up some new scheme to involve me in?"

"Oh, we'll be done," Jared replied in a firm voice. "In fact, as soon as you give me the note, I'd encourage you to get on out of this part of the country as fast as you can."

"I think that's good advice," Davey said, "but just out of curiosity, why do you say that?"

"Because after you get the note and leave town, Señor Abreu is gonna stew about it for a little while and then decide that he doesn't trust you. He'll get his horse and follow you. When he does, I'll have the note and I'll be waiting for him on the trail down to Las Vegas just like I told you before. I'll take him into custody and hand him over to Estévan Marés in Cimarrón. You probably don't want to stick around for that. Like I said, I don't plan for it to turn violent but there ain't no guarantee it won't go that way."

Again, Davey contemplated Jared's scheme. "Can I ask you something?"

"Sure," Jared nodded.

"What made you change your mind about putting a bullet in his brain? He's still one of the men involved in killing your friend.

Maybe you will be able to get something in writing that shows he was a part of it. There's still the same risk of his hiring a lawyer and somehow getting away with it."

Now it was Jared's turn to be silent as he pondered the question. When he spoke up, he said, "You had a lot to do with my decision."

Davey looked at him with skepticism. "How's that?"

"I gave a lot of thought to how you talked about your daddy. It was clear to me that there was no love lost between the two of you. You had a low opinion of him. My guess is that if you never see him again, that'll be fine with you. And that's all on him because of the way he acted."

Davey nodded. "That's about right. So what's that got to do with you?"

Jared looked away for a moment. Davey wasn't sure but he thought maybe there might be a tear in his eye. When he looked back, he said, "I got two children, a boy and a girl. I love 'em more than anything else in the world. How could they be proud of their daddy if he was a murderer? If they never wanted to see me again, I don't think I could stand it." He shrugged. "When I thought about it that way, it wasn't all that hard to change my mind."

340

Davey nodded. "I guess I can see that. One big difference in my situation and yours, though, is that you love your children. I don't think my daddy has the first notion about what love is." He got a wistful look on his face. "I think they're pretty lucky."

They sat there in silence staring into the fire as the day cycled into the night. After a while, Jared stood up and said, "I'm gonna turn in. I'll get you up at first light so you can get a good start."

Jared walked over to his horse to get his bedroll. Davey sat by the fire a little longer, then he went over to where his bedroll was already laid out and crawled in it. It took him a little time to fall asleep as he pondered what was coming the next day. If things went according to the plan, he would escape the clutches of Jesus Abreu. An idea was hatching in his mind that might provide him with a stake so that after he made his getaway, he wouldn't be living hand to mouth wherever he wound up. When sleep did come, Davey had a smile on his face.

Estévan leaned back in the chair with his boots up on the desk in his office in Cimarrón. He'd been looking at some wanted posters but now he was mulling over a question that had been puzzling him. In the big

341

scheme of things, it wasn't all that important and yet he hated having loose ends. He thought he might have figured out the answer.

Soon after Tommy Stallings had assumed the duties of acting sheriff, the politicians had decided that since Springer was the county seat of Colfax County, the sheriff's office should be located there. Mayor Salazar had been adamant that Tommy move over at once. From the time that Estévan had taken over the job, the mayor had not said a word about the fact that he had remained in Cimarrón. He thought this curious until he considered that since Salazar had conspired with Jared Delaney to act as his vigilante in tracking down the murderers of Nathan Averill, the last thing he wanted was to have the sheriff right there scrutinizing what was going on. He smiled. Maybe he was getting the hang of solving mysteries.

His reverie was interrupted when the door flew open and Eleanor Delaney rushed in. He started to make a joke about her not knocking but then he noticed that her face was pale as death. Something horrific had transpired.

"What is it, Señora? What has happened?"

Eleanor Delaney tried to catch her breath.

Her fists were clinched by her sides, the knuckles white from the force of her grip. "They've got the children."

"Who has the children, Señora? What are you talking about?"

"The horrible monster who killed Nathan." Her voice rose. She was on the brink of hysteria. She clutched her fists tighter and took another deep breath. With a tremendous effort, she managed to calm herself. "It was that Felipe Alvarado, the man Jared believes shot Nathan. He took the children and Christy."

"Took them where? How do you know this?" Estévan realized that he was babbling. "I'm sorry Señora Eleanor; I will be quiet and let you tell me what you know." He got up and went to fetch Eleanor a chair. "Would you like to sit?"

"I can't," Eleanor said, pacing back and forth in front of the desk. "I don't have time to relax. This happened earlier in the day while I was out at the ranch. I'd gone out there to check on things. I left the children with Christy at the school."

"What time did you leave?"

Eleanor thought for a moment. "It was midmorning. I expected to be back before suppertime."

Estévan checked his pocket watch. "It is

about four right now. I suppose we have no way of knowing when this happened."

Eleanor shook her head. "No, we don't. Christy wrote a note, though; I recognize her handwriting. He must have dictated it to her. The note gives directions to a cabin off the trail to Las Vegas. He wants Jared to come meet with him."

Estévan chewed on his lip as he thought about this. "I am afraid I have no idea where your husband is right now, Señora."

"I have," Eleanor said, her face turning darker. "I saw him right before I got to the ranch. He was coming to tell me that he was giving up this mad plan to take the law into his own hands and kill the men who are responsible for Nathan's death."

"That is good news," Estévan said. "Where is he now?"

Eleanor exhaled, her frustration was unmistakable. "I don't know." Taking in Estévan's puzzled expression, she continued. "He told me that he was giving up on the idea of vigilante justice and was willing to work with you as a deputy if you were still interested. He said he had one more thing to take care of before he could do that, though."

"Well, what is it? Where did he go?" Estévan's frustration was rising to match that of

Eleanor's.

"He wouldn't say," Eleanor replied. The muscles in her jaws clenched. "Just when the children and I need him the most, he is off on some cockamamie mission." She paused. When she continued, her voice was tight with anger. "Right now, I hate him."

"I believe you have a right to." Estévan nodded. "At this moment, though, we do not have time for that. We need to go get the children." As he walked over to the gun rack, he said over his shoulder, "If you will give me the note with the directions, I will leave right away."

"I'm going with you. Can you get me a horse and saddle?"

"Señora, this will be dangerous. It would be best if you would leave it to me." Estévan checked the Winchester.

"Those are my children, Estévan," she said. "I'm going with you. It's not up for debate."

Estévan started to speak, then he shook his head. "You are right; we do not need to waste time discussing it. I know that look." He shrugged. "I can get you a horse and saddle from the livery where we keep our string."

"I'll take my buckboard there now; they can take care of my horse."

Estévan strapped on his pistol and grabbed an extra cartridge belt from the gun rack. "I have an idea. It will take a few extra minutes but I think it will be worth it."

"What is it?" Eleanor's impatience was palpable.

"I will ask Tomás to search for Jared." Eleanor started to protest but Estévan waved her protests away before she could voice them. "I do not care that you hate your husband right now, Señora. He is a good man to have by your side in a fight." He looked down for a moment. "And they are his children too. I know how he feels about them; I have heard him speak about it often. He would die for them."

Eleanor nodded. "I know he would." She turned her head for a moment. When she turned back, she said, "He might have to."

Estévan nodded. "We all might."

For the first time in the history of their relationship, Tomás Marés raised his voice to his fiancée, Maria Suazo.

"You cannot do this, I will not let you!"

Maria's eyes flashed. "What you *will not* do is raise your voice at me."

Tomás looked crestfallen. "I am so sorry. I know I should not have done that but I cannot let you put yourself in danger like this."

"You are putting yourself in danger for the people you love, *mi corazón*. Why should I not be allowed to do so as well?" A wicked smile crossed her lips. "You know that I am a better rider than you are, do you not?"

Tomás rolled his eyes. "Of course you are, that is not what I am worried about."

"Someone needs to find Jared," she said in a patient tone. "I can do that as well as you can." Another wicked grin. "In fact, better. You can go with Estévan and Eleanor and, if necessary, fight to save the children and Miss Christy." This time, her smile was affectionate. "And you do that well, *cara mia*. You have done it before, many times."

Tomás knew that time was short but he also knew that there were no guarantees that he would survive this next chapter in their unwavering struggle to vanquish evil. He took two steps towards Maria and took her in his arms, kissing her passionately. She clung to him in a fierce embrace.

"You are right, go find Jared and bring him to this cabin. We will approach them with caution. We cannot take any chances that might lead to the children being harmed."

Maria broke away from his embrace. "I

347

would love nothing better than to stay here and hold you but we have no time. I will saddle my horse and leave right away."

"You are right, *mi querido,*" Tomás said. "I believe the best place for you to start is to head over towards Springer. If you do not come upon Jared on the trail, you can ask about him when you get to Springer." He took a deep breath. "*Vaya con Dios, mi corazón.* We must save the children."

CHAPTER 30

Jesus Abreu's mind raced as he paced his office. After several trips back and forth, he turned to Davey Good and said, "Tell me where you heard this news."

Davey figured he should appear nervous to make himself more believable. As it turned out, he didn't have to pretend . . . he was as nervous as a field mouse with a hawk circling above it. "Sir, I went to Cimarrón because I thought he'd go back there to see his wife. Turned out I was right about that. I told some folks I was looking for Jared Delaney, that I had a message to give him. They said he'd been down at the Colfax Tavern the last they heard. When I went to the place, he wasn't there but I listened to what folks were saying."

Abreu leaned over and placed his hands on his desk, glaring at the boy. "And what were people saying?"

"The place was all abuzz," Davey said.

"All people could talk about was how Delaney had been in there bragging that he was going to ride down to San Miguel County and shoot Felipe Alvarado down like a dog. He told them he was headed that way right after he paid a visit to his wife." Davey hesitated. "I heard them say that he also was talking about heading back up to Springer to shoot you next. I don't know if he's serious or not but I figured you'd want to know."

Abreu stood up and began to pace again as he wracked his brain to come up with a plan. Part of him wanted to pack his old leather valise with all the money it would hold and take off for Colorado as soon as he could get this young scamp out of his office. Another part, the part that was terrified of his cousin, thought it would be wise to ride down to Las Vegas and warn him. Although he had no doubt that Alvarado would prevail over Delaney in a gun battle, he knew that if he failed to alert him and Felipe found that out, his cousin would not hesitate to kill him.

"Sir," Davey spoke up in a voice tight with anxiety, "I believe I could be of some help to you in this matter."

Stopping in mid-stride, Abreu asked, "What do you have in mind?"

"My horse is already saddled and I know the way to Vegas. If you want me to, I'll ride on down that way fast as I can and warn this Alvarado fella."

"And why would you do this for me?" Abreu's voice carried a note of suspicion.

"Well, sir, you been good to me and all, and I've done this much for you, it seems like doing this last thing would be the right thing to do." Davey cleared his throat and continued. "Of course, it would sure help me out if you'd give me a little money for my trouble."

Abreu nodded and smiled. "I understand now." He walked over to his desk. Without warning, he slammed his fist down on it. "Do you think you can shake me down?"

"No, sir," Davey said quickly, holding his hands up. "No, sir, not at all. It's just that I have gone to a lot of trouble to help you out. I was hoping you might be grateful for my efforts."

Abreu pondered the situation. He considered threatening to turn this young man into the authorities right on the spot, just to make him sorry he had tried to extort him. On the other hand, he didn't have much time to take care of this business and make his getaway. He decided he would play along for now, promising to pay the boy when he

351

returned.

"How much did you imagine my gratitude would be worth?"

"Uh, I was thinking that one hundred dollars would be a nice number." Davey coughed. "I mean, it's a long ride down there. I know you'll want me to get there as quick as I can."

"That's a lot of money," he said, stroking his chin. Abreu pretended to consider the request. "All right, I will do that. Once you return, I will give you the money."

"Well now, wait a minute," Davey protested. "I was thinking I would get the money ahead of time."

"I'm sure you were," Abreu replied, chuckling. "That is not how this will work, though. If you do this job and return, then you will get your money."

Davey made a pretense of thinking about the offer, then he said, "Well, all right, I guess I can do it that way. How's this Alvarado fella going to know I'm who I say I am, though?"

Jesus had already thought of that. "I will write a note for you to give him. Once you have warned him, ask him to sign the note so that I know you gave him the message." He stared hard at the boy. "You will not get a penny from me without this signature."

Right, Davey thought, *and I wouldn't get a penny from you with it either, you lying scoundrel.* He kept his thoughts to himself, though. "All right, I guess I can do that. Is there anything else you need me to tell him? I want to get back on the trail as quick as I can. I want to get this done with."

Abreu walked over and sat down at his desk. "Give me a moment and I will write the note." Wasting no time, he put pen to paper and then folded the note. With an intense look at Davey, he asked, "Do I need to tell you that you are not to read this letter?"

Davey shook his head with vigor. "No, sir, that would have never crossed my mind."

"All right then," Abreu said. "Do not waste any more precious time. I will expect you back by late tomorrow."

"Yes, sir," Davey said. "I'll do my best." With that, he rushed out the door.

As soon as he left, Abreu was once again consumed with ambivalence. Was it a mistake to trust the boy? Should he have ridden down himself to warn his cousin? Or should he leave without delay and head up to Colorado or maybe over to Texas? He just wasn't sure and for a moment, he was paralyzed by his doubt. He feared that regardless of the choice he made, things would not turn out well for him.

It didn't take him long to conclude that whatever else he decided to do about alerting Felipe Alvarado, the one thing he knew he had to do straightaway was to clean out the vault and prepare to leave town as fast as he could. When he thought about gathering his funds together, he smiled. It was his good fortune that he had just collected a number of mortgage payments from various ranchers. Had this transpired a week earlier, the contents of the vault would have proven to have been far less lucrative.

Jesus Abreu went to the vault and walked in, closing the door behind him. He walked over to the safe, entered the combination, and opened the door. He smiled as he raked the large quantity of cash into his old leather satchel. He hadn't been sure that he would be able to get all the money in it, but by stuffing it down, he cleaned out the contents of the safe. He set the bag just outside the vault and gave further thought to the question of whether or not he should be the one to warn his cousin.

As he imagined Felipe's potential reactions to the news that Jared Delaney was coming to Las Vegas with the intention of murdering him, he concluded that he had to ride down and give him the news himself.

Otherwise, Alvarado would perceive that he was frightened and had abandoned him. Abreu knew that his cousin would want to kill him if that was his perception. He decided that he would go pack his other leather valise with clothes so that he would be ready to ride away right after he returned to Springer. He would just make the one stop at the bank to gather up his money. Consumed with these thoughts, he walked out the back entrance to his office into the alley. He was so preoccupied that he forgot to lock the door.

It was all Davey could do to keep a smile off his face as he walked out of Abreu's office. Once he got to his horse and mounted up, he grinned from ear to ear. Riding south out of town, he opened the letter and read its contents. Sure enough, Abreu had written in some detail that Delaney had found out the truth about their having murdered Nathan Averill and was gunning for both of them. He didn't know the law right down to the letter but he was pretty sure there was enough information in the note to incriminate both men. He had two more tasks to accomplish before he set out for Colorado. He needed to get this letter to his friend, Jared Delaney, and he needed to get back to Springer undetected and pull his last bank job. He couldn't stop grinning.

"Get those whining brats into the cabin and quiet them," Felipe Alvarado snarled at Christy. "If I have to listen to any more of their whining, I will slit their throats right now."

Terrified, Christy hastened to gather up the children and hurried through the door of the one-room cabin. Even in the midst of her fright, part of her mind was curious as to why the outlaw had not already murdered all three of them. Once he had baited the hook with the note for Eleanor, she was sure that Jared as well as Eleanor would come as fast as they could to try to save them. Since Alvarado intended to kill them, he had no need of her or the children any longer.

While Alvarado was unsaddling his horse, she gathered Lizbeth in her arms and hugged her tight. She knelt down in front of Ned who was trying not to cry and not succeeding.

"Ned, I need you to look at me and listen like you've never listened before."

He took a deep, shuddering breath and looked at her. "Yes, Auntie Christy."

She could see the tracks of his tears on his dusty face and her heart almost broke into a thousand pieces. He was far too young to have to endure this and yet here they were. Although she couldn't see a clear way forward right now, she was determined to save the children's lives even if it meant sacrificing her own.

"The man outside is a horrible person. He may try to hurt us. I will do everything I can to keep him from it but I need your help. Will you help me?" She could see his face harden with determination and, in it, she saw the face of his father. In that moment, she felt her heart break.

"Yes, ma'am, I'll try." He frowned. "I ain't very big, though, Auntie Christy, I doubt I can beat him in a fight."

Christy smiled in spite of herself. "You don't have to fight him, Ned; you just need to do what I ask you. Let me handle the rest." Then, ever the teacher, she said, "And it's not 'ain't,' it is 'I am not' very big."

"You're bigger than me," Ned replied, "but I don't think you can beat him in a fight either."

Christy laughed out loud. "You're right; neither of us can beat him in a fight. We'll have to outsmart him. So I'm going to tell you what I need you to do. Are you listening?"

"Yes, ma'am," he replied. The look of

intensity on his face touched her heart.

"First, I want you to do your very best not to cry, no matter how scared you feel. Can you do that?"

"I'll do my best," he said. "I know my daddy would want me to be brave."

"Yes, he would," Christy said. "Your daddy is very proud of you and he loves you very much." She ached to take him in her arms and hug him but she'd gotten Lizbeth calmed down and she didn't want to have her begin crying again. "Now here's the other thing I want you to do. Are you still listening?"

"Yes ma'am, I'm still listening."

"I want you to take your sister's hand and go over in the corner. I want you to think of all the games you play together and I want you to get her to play with you. I know it will be hard to have fun when you're scared but that's what I want you to try to do. Play games with Lizbeth and try to keep her from being afraid. Can you do that?"

"Yes, ma'am, I can try." He started to pucker up and cry again but with a visible effort, he suppressed the tears. "I love Lizbeth, Auntie Christy. I know I'm mean to her sometime but she's my baby sister. I don't want nobody to hurt her."

Resisting the urge to correct his grammar,

she said, "I know you don't, Neddie. I don't either. So you just do what I'm asking. I'll try to take care of the rest."

Before they could say any more, she heard loud boot steps approaching on the narrow wooden porch. The door was flung open. "Go on now," she whispered to Ned. "Take your sister and go over in the corner."

"Are those brats going to cause any more trouble?" Alvarado gave her a menacing look. "I warn you, I have no more patience."

Christy stood up and faced him. "They'll be quiet." She shook her head. "You must understand that they're frightened."

"I understand," he said with an evil smile. "I just do not care."

Christy knew she was on quicksand. She couldn't challenge him in a direct manner and yet she felt like it would not go well for her if she played the helpless victim. Something told her he would relish that. In her heart, she knew he intended to kill them regardless; she could only hope to buy some time and search for a weakness to exploit. She decided to gamble.

"I know you don't care, which makes me curious."

The evil smile remained in place. "And what are you curious about, *chiquita*?"

Calling on all the wiles she had depended

upon to survive her days as a soiled dove, she flashed an impudent smile at him. "I'm curious why you haven't already killed us. Once I wrote the note and you got us out of town, you really had no further need for us. You know as well as I do that Jared Delaney will come riding down here as fast as he can once he sees the note."

"That is true," Alvarado said, rubbing his chin whiskers in mock contemplation. "Go on. I like this little game."

"He wouldn't know that you had killed us already. In fact, he would hope that you hadn't. We might be in your way when he gets here. What can you possible gain by keeping us alive?"

He stared at her. His eyes were cold. "I gain the pleasure of watching his face as I slit the throats of his urchins right in front of his eyes . . . right before I kill him."

Christy's blood turned to ice. It took all of her self-control to not scream. "And after you kill him, what about me?"

"You?" She'd thought his smile looked evil before but now the intensity was overpowering. "Oh, I have plans for you, *chiquita.* I will enjoy your death."

Maybe not as much as you think. She smiled back at him. "Thanks for letting me know."

CHAPTER 31

"This'll work," Jared said after reading the note. He had a big smile on his face. "How did you convince him to go for it?"

"I didn't have to do much convincing," Davey chuckled. "He kind of convinced himself. He's the sort of man who always looks for someone else to do the hard jobs. When I volunteered to ride back to Las Vegas, that worked for him."

"Did he agree to pay you?"

"Sure," Davey said. He smiled. "I have to say that his agreeing didn't fill me with confidence, though. He's not as violent as my old man but he's darn sure every bit as crooked."

"Well, this note couldn't be better if I'd written it myself. I believe this is evidence that'll stand up in a court of law." Jared frowned. "Do you reckon he's gonna follow you down?"

Davey nodded. "That'd be my guess. I

swear I could almost hear him having second thoughts as I walked out the door. He sure seems scared of this Alvarado fella."

Jared's expression grew hard. "With good reason. The man has no qualms about killing anyone whenever the mood strikes him. Fact is, he seems to enjoy it. I suspect Abreu knows that better than just about anyone."

"Is that a fact? Well, I can't say I'm disappointed that I won't be handing him this note then. Odds are good he'd kill me on the spot just for sport." He shuddered. "And if he didn't, I know for sure that old Señor Abreu wasn't planning to let me run free. I know too much."

Jared nodded. "I suspect you're right, which is why this seems like a good time for you to make tracks for someplace as far away as you can get."

"I guess it's time." Davey took a long breath and looked around at the camp. He shuffled his feet and then looked straight at Jared. "I'm not sure what to say to you, Mr. Delaney . . . I mean, Jared. I'd like to say it's been good meeting you but I expect that remains to be seen." He smiled. "It's been interesting, though, and that's the truth."

"I don't know what all these goin's-on will mean for you, Davey, but I know what it means to me. I was sure nuff headed down a blind trail. You played a big part in helpin' me open my eyes to see things clearer. I'm much obliged for that."

Davey shrugged. "I don't know about that, Jared. I wasn't trying to change anybody else's life, I was just trying to get away from the bad hand I'd been dealt and turn my own life around."

"Yeah, but there's all kinds of different ways a man can go about doin' that," Jared said. "Seems to me that you've tried to find an honorable way to go about it." If he noticed the strange look that crossed the boy's face, he didn't comment on it.

"Maybe so, I haven't taken much to time to ponder all that." Davey cleared his throat. "Speaking of time, though, I do believe I ought to be taking off. I have a feeling things are going to be heating up pretty quick. I'd like to be as far away as I can when that happens."

Nodding, Jared stuck out his hand. "Smart move. I wish you the best of luck wherever you wind up."

"Thanks," Davey said, giving a firm shake to Jared's hand. "I reckon I might need some luck along the way."

Turning away, Davey got on his horse and, without a word, swung around and headed back north. Jared wondered if he might go to Colorado. That's where he would go if he was a young man looking to start over. With that thought, he had to laugh at himself. He didn't feel like a young man but he sure felt like he was starting over. He knew he had a lot to make up for and he feared he might have exhausted the patience of his loving wife.

His original plan had been to wait for Jesus Abreu since he was almost certain the man would decide to ride down to Las Vegas to warn his cousin himself. He had intended to take him into custody and escort him to Cimarrón where Estévan could lock him up. Now he was having second thoughts. He had the note in Abreu's handwriting with his signature. Although he had changed his mind about doing violence to the man, he wasn't positive he could control his temper if he came face to face with him. His emotions were still raw about the murder of Nathan Averill.

Jared walked around the campsite cleaning things up and packing up his belongings. At some point he realized that he'd made the decision. He would leave Abreu alone for now and return to Cimarrón to give the evidence he possessed to the new Sheriff Marés. Then he would find his wife and beg for her forgiveness.

■ ■ ■ ■

Davey pondered his alternatives as he rode back towards Springer. He didn't know for sure if Abreu would feel compelled to go down to Las Vegas and talk with Felipe Alvarado in person. If he did, Davey didn't want to meet him on the trail, which meant that he would need to hide in the trees and wait for him to pass. On the other hand, if Abreu chose not to make the trip down to Las Vegas, Davey could waste valuable time concealing himself when he needed to put as much distance as he could between himself and all these bad hombres. And the most important consideration was that if Abreu didn't leave Springer, there would be no way he could get his hands on all that money.

The trail rose up to the crest of a hill and took a turn north. Davey was so deep in thought that he almost missed the telltale noises coming from just over the ridge. The sound of horse's hooves on rock snapped him out of his reverie. Someone was heading his way. He glanced to his right and saw a thick stand of trees about twenty yards off the trail. As fast as he could without making noise, he urged his horse to the cover. When he was ensconced in the shadows, he dismounted and waited. His heart was pounding and he felt nauseated.

Davey didn't have to wait long. Jesus Abreu came over the crest of the ridge striking an awkward trot on a little bay mare. He was bouncing around in the saddle and looked as out of place as a man could. Davey almost laughed in spite of his tense circumstances. *He rides like a banker.* Getting a grip on himself, he watched and waited for the man to pass. Abreu gave no indication that he noticed anything out of the ordinary, but Davey waited for almost a half hour before mounting up again and resuming his trek to Springer. No need to take unnecessary chances. He figured he would get to town by midafternoon, which would give him ample time to take care of his business and get back on the trail north. His plan was intact. He smiled.

Jesus Abreu was wracked with ambivalence. The closer he got to Las Vegas, the more he questioned his decision to ride down to warn his cousin about Jared Delaney. Felipe was quick to anger and prone to irrational violence once he was enraged. It was possible that he would blame Jesus for not finding a way to bring to a halt Delaney's

366

vigilante mission. If so, it would not go well for Jesus. On the other hand, if he failed to alert him, Alvarado would know he had taken the coward's way out and left him to face Delaney without any prior warning.

Although the day was cool, the sweat was pouring off of Abreu. His stomach felt as if it were tied in knots. He tried to clear his head and assess his best chance for survival. He had known for a while that his time in Springer was coming to an end. If he wanted to live, he needed to put as much distance as he could between himself and his murderous cousin. He also needed to leave no clues as to where he was headed. He pondered his choices. Maybe he would start out to the north and then double back to head down to Mexico. Felipe had heard him talk about Denver often enough that it would be the first place he would look when he came hunting him. Going in the opposite direction to Mexico would give him more of a head start. Maybe he could lose himself down south of the border. He would have enough money to live like a king.

He reined his horse in and looked around, checking the position of the sun. If he turned around now, he could get back to Springer by late afternoon. The bank would be closed but of course he had a key. He would let himself in, fetch his old satchel full of money, and get back on the trail. He felt the knot in his stomach loosen. He had a plan.

When Davey got to the outskirts of Springer in the middle of the afternoon, he dismounted and led his horse toward the alley that ran behind all the buildings on the main street, including the bank. There was a back entrance to Jesus Abreu's office and he intended to go through it. He didn't know if Abreu kept it locked but he'd seen the door and he was confident that he could break in if he needed to do so.

He tied his horse to the hitching post behind the bank and wasted no time walking over to the back door. His palms were sweating as he reached for the knob. When he tried to turn it, it caught for a brief moment. With his heart in his throat, Davey rattled the knob just a bit and then turned it all the way to the left. The door opened and Jesus Abreu's office lay before him. Davey shook his head in amazement as he thought about the man leaving the door unlocked. *He must have really been spooked to forget to lock the door. Oh well. His misfortune, my good fortune.*

He strode to the entrance to the vault,

almost tripping over an old satchel in the middle of the floor. Stepping around it, he opened the heavy door and walked in. The safe was in a corner and he approached it with caution. Pulling the piece of paper with numbers on it out of his pocket, he knelt down. Taking a deep breath, he began turning the lock in accordance with what was written on the paper. When he'd progressed through the sequence, he held his breath and turned the handle. The door opened. He almost let out a whoop of excitement but managed to restrain himself.

The inside of the safe was dark and he couldn't see anything. He squinted as he looked around but he came up empty. He saw nothing that resembled a large stash of money. His heart sank. As he tried to make sense of this appalling turn of events, it occurred to him that it was quite possible Abreu had already cleaned out the safe. Did he take the money with him or had he left it somewhere to pick up when he returned from Las Vegas?

Davey stood up and tried to collect his thoughts. As disappointed as he was, he realized he could still continue on with his plan of heading for Colorado; he would just have to do so without the financial resources he had hoped for. He would have to continue to scramble as he'd been doing most of his life and place himself at the mercy of others in order to get by. Minutes before, he'd been giddy with anticipation. Now he felt as low as he had in a long time. He shut the door to the safe and walked out of the vault.

Lost in his disappointment, he forgot about the satchel in the middle of his path. Before, he'd had to step around it; this time, he tripped over it. He almost fell to the floor but with an effort, was able to brace himself on the wall to keep from going down. With a curse, he kicked the satchel. It was fortunate that there was nothing hard in it and he didn't break his foot in the process. In disgust, he walked on.

He was almost to the back door when he stopped. Something was nagging at his brain, like an itch that he couldn't quite reach. In his dejection over the empty safe, he'd forgotten the possibility that Abreu might have hidden the money somewhere convenient so that he could pick it up on his way back through town. Davey had no doubt that the man had the same notion he did . . . to get as far away from the New Mexico Territory as he could as soon as possible. He turned around and considered the alternatives. Where would Abreu have stashed the money?

He wasn't sure where to start looking and a feeling of panic washed over him. He was pretty sure that Abreu would lose his nerve about facing Alvarado and turn back to return to Springer. He didn't think he had much time to search. He took a deep breath and continued to ponder the options. He realized that in his disappointment at finding the safe empty, he hadn't looked on any of the shelves in the vault to see if Abreu had put the money there. He wouldn't leave it loose, he would place it in a container of some sort. What would he put it in?

As he walked back toward the vault, he saw the satchel in the middle of the floor and with care, stepped around it. He'd taken two steps when he stopped. A smile spread across his face and he began chuckling. The chuckles turned into a full belly-laugh and it took him almost a minute to get himself under control. When he did, he turned around, bent down, and opened the satchel. It was stuffed so full of money that a handful of cash fell out on the floor. With the big smile still on his face, he stuck it back in the satchel and zipped it up. Grabbing it by the handle, he stood up and headed for the back door.

Davey had his hand on the doorknob but

he stopped before he opened the door. As concerned as he was about Abreu making an ill-timed return, he felt compelled to leave him a message. He set the satchel down and strode over to Abreu's desk. Finding a pen and paper, he started to write a note. He paused as he considered what he was doing and then set the pen and paper aside. He pondered the situation for a moment and then he smiled. Grinning, he went over to the satchel and took out a hundred-dollar bill. Returning to the desk, he placed it under the paperweight. *That pretty much says it all.*

Straightening up, he walked toward the door, picked up the satchel, and walked out to his horse. He used his catch twine to secure the satchel behind his saddle, then he mounted up. He felt the impulse to ride north through the alley at a gallop, whooping the entire way. He resisted that whimsical notion and nudged his horse into a respectable trot. And thus Davey Good began his new life as a wealthy man.

Maria kept up a steady trot but she didn't push her horse too hard. With any luck, she might meet Jared on the trail coming from Springer but she couldn't count on that. If she had to ride on to Springer and perhaps out into the countryside searching for him, she didn't want to risk having her horse pull up lame.

As she rode, Maria thought back over the years of her association with Jared and Eleanor Delaney. When they'd first known each other, Eleanor was the schoolteacher whose last name was Coulter. Jared was a young cowboy who'd just ridden in from Texas. Maria was married to Juan Suazo, and her husband and Jared were both hands on the Kilpatrick Ranch. In the beginning, they had been friendly rivals. Over time, the rivalry receded while the friendship grew. In the end, they became partners in the Kilpatrick Ranch following the deaths of Ned and Lizbeth Kilpatrick.

Their business had prospered as they drove herds up the trail to sell to the miners in southern Colorado. For a time, there seemed to be no limits to their good fortunes; then Juan was murdered by cattle rustlers who were backed by one of the scoundrels from the corrupt Santa Fe Ring. They sought justice through the legal system but as was often the case, money and power prevailed. It appeared that the evildoers would get away with murder, but in the end, Nathan Averill had made sure that didn't happen. For that alone, she was forever indebted to the man.

For what seemed like an eternity to her, she had staggered under the overwhelming burden of her grief. Most days, it was all she could do to get out of bed, and many was the time that she questioned whether she wanted to live without her Juan. Throughout her ordeal, Miguel and Anita Marés had been there to support her, taking her in and giving her work at their café in town.

Over time, she began to notice their elder son, Tomás. He was at all times polite and attentive to her. At first, his presence irritated her. Over time, she came to appreciate that his gentle and shy ways were genuine. A more decent man would be hard to find. Her feelings transitioned from irritation to affection and, at last, to a strong and comforting love. While she would never again know the passion and excitement she experienced with Juan, she knew in her heart that Tomás would walk through fire for her.

Although she was deep in her thoughts and memories, Maria kept one part of her mind focused on her task and on the trail ahead of her. As she came to the top of a rise, she saw a rider approaching in the distance. It was too far to identify the man but she could see that he was a cowboy. She hoped it was Jared but was prepared in case the rider presented a danger. She patted the pistol tucked in her belt.

As the distance closed between them, it became obvious to Maria that the rider was indeed Jared Delaney. She spurred her horse and galloped up to him.

"Jared, I am so glad I found you."

"Maria, is that you?" Jared's confusion was reflected in his voice. "What are you doing here?"

"I came to find you," she said. "A terrible thing has happened. Come with me, I will tell you about it as we ride."

CHAPTER 32

Jesus Abreu had hoped that once he made the decision to turn around and return to Springer, his acute ambivalence would vanish and be replaced by a sense of relief. Such was not the case. Now he was wracked with second thoughts about how Felipe Alvarado would react when he discovered Jesus had not come to warn him about Delaney. He hoped that Delaney would kill Felipe but he was not confident about the likelihood of that happening. He feared that Alvarado was too mean to die. Contemplating all of these thoughts motivated him to spur his horse into a brisk trot. He wanted to get back to Springer, collect his money, and leave town as soon as possible.

Bouncing with great discomfort as his horse trotted along, the thought flashed through Abreu's mind that perhaps he needed to get a horse with a smoother gait. His hands were slick with sweat, a reaction both to his fear of Alvarado and his anticipation of starting a new life in Mexico with the money he had stolen. Up ahead, the buildings that made up the business district of Springer came into view. On the west side of town, he veered off to the right and turned into the alleyway that ran up behind the bank.

Tying his horse to the hitching rail behind his office entrance, Abreu pulled out his key and inserted it into the lock on the door, turning the knob as he did. To his surprise, the door opened before he could turn the key. *I could have sworn I locked this,* he thought. *I must have been in a bigger hurry than I realized.* He walked in and glanced over to where he had left the satchel. His blood froze in his veins. The satchel wasn't there.

Abreu ran over to the spot where he knew he had left the satchel, hoping somehow that it would appear out of nowhere. It didn't, of course. He stood there shaking in despair, trying to envision where the satchel might have gone. His knees felt weak and he walked over to his desk to sit down. As he did, he saw what appeared to be a hundred-dollar bill underneath his paperweight. Bewildered, he reached for the paperweight, removing it from the bill.

Struggling to catch his breath, Jesus also struggled to get his mind around the notion that Davey Good, that little *pendejo,* whom he had thought of as a pawn, had somehow managed to outsmart him and steal his money. He just could not accept it. He looked at the bill again and glanced over to the spot where the satchel full of money no longer sat. He blinked, looked away, and then looked back, but the satchel still wasn't there. He felt like he might be sick to his stomach.

He started as he heard a knock on the door. Before he could respond, the door opened and his assistant stuck his head in.

"Señor Abreu, I thought I heard you in here. You have a visitor."

Abreu opened his mouth to tell his upstart assistant that he wasn't accepting any appointments at the moment. Before he could utter a word, Manuel Salazar walked in, strutting as usual.

"*Hola, Buenos días,* Jesus," he said in a hearty voice. "I heard that you might be in town. We have business to discuss."

Jesus sputtered a couple of unintelligible responses before he was able to produce a coherent reply. He shook his head and said, "This is not a good time, Manuel. Perhaps you could come back tomorrow."

"No," Salazar said in a firm voice, "we will discuss this business right now. As you know, I am the chairman of the board of stockholders of your bank." There was a wicked glint in his eyes as he continued. "In fact, as I recall, you insisted that I assume that position."

Abreu waved his hand as if swatting at a fly. "Manuel, I must tell you again, this is not a good time." *How did this cabrón know that he had come back to town? It was as if he was waiting for him. He must have spies.*

Forging ahead over Abreu's objections, Salazar continued. "I have spoken with the other stockholders. They have expressed concerns about what they perceive as irregularities in how you operate. They have authorized me to conduct an audit." He smiled. "The audit will begin right now."

Jesus Abreu sat back in his chair. He sighed and put his head in his hands. *So this is how it ends,* he thought.

"You must calm down," Maria said in a firm voice. "Your children's lives depend on having a clear head."

"I'll kill that son of a bitch." Jared gripped the handle of his pistol so tight that his knuckles were white. He spurred his horse and began pulling away from Maria.

"Jared, slow down," she called as she galloped to catch up with him. "We need to have a plan. We cannot ride in like a mountain thunderstorm. I will tell you again, your children's lives depend on how we do this thing."

Jared slowed to a trot. Maria rode along side of him. "I'll slow down long enough to come up with a plan, then I'll be ridin' hard. You can join me or go on back to town, it don't matter to me."

"All right," Maria said. "Let us be swift then. The note said you knew the trail to Las Vegas. There is a tall pine tree that has been struck by lightning. This *bandido,* Alvarado, he says you would know it."

Jared thought for a moment. "Yeah, I know where it is. What happens when we get there?"

"He says there is a path to the north, it leads to a cabin. That is where the children and Miss Christy are being held."

"All right," Jared said. "We'll go as fast as we can between here and that tree. Once we get there, we'll take it slow and sneaky." An agonized expression crossed his face. "How do I know that monster hasn't already killed 'em all?"

Maria was silent for a moment, then she spoke. "You don't."

Jared spurred his horse. Maria followed close behind.

Sunlight shone through a window of the cabin and woke Christy. The image of a full moon with a halo around it flashed through her mind. She must have seen it out that same window during the night. *Change is coming and it's not good.* She shifted, aware that she was very uncomfortable.

As her mind cleared, she recognized the source of her discomfort . . . her hands and ankles were bound. It came back to her that Alvarado had tied her up the night before as a precaution to prevent her from attempting to escape. *I wouldn't have tried to escape,* she thought, *I would have tried to blow your brains out.* Turns out he did her a favor. With her hands bound in front of her, she was able to reach and pat the derringer that was still tucked away in the pocket of her dress. Two shots should be lethal at close range. She only hoped she got the opportunity to find out.

"*Buenos días, chiquita,*" Alvarado said. "Shall I untie you? I will if you promise not to misbehave."

Christy realized that the man had been watching her while she slept. This made her skin crawl. She knew she couldn't show any signs of vulnerability, though, so she smiled.

"Why would you think I wouldn't behave myself? We've been getting along pretty well so far, haven't we?"

Alvarado chuckled. "I like you, *chiquita.* It pains me that I must kill you."

Christy continued to smile at the murderer. *If I have anything to say about it, it will pain you very much,* she thought. She kept the thought to herself.

"Who knows, maybe you'll change your mind," she said. "To answer your question, though, of course I'll behave myself. If you untie me, I'll look after the children."

Alvarado pondered the prospect and then took out his knife. Christy drew an involuntary breath. He saw it and smiled.

"Not yet, *chiquita.*" He continued smiling but his eyes were cruel.

He cut the bonds from her wrists and ankles. It was apparent that he expected this business to be concluded before the end of the day and didn't think he would have any further need for them. Christy's heart raced as she contemplated the reality that her life would in all likelihood end this day. She took a silent vow that if it did, she would not go alone. She would do everything within her power to take Felipe Alvarado to

the grave with her. If she gave her life
protecting the children, so be it.

CHAPTER 33

Eleanor and the Marés brothers watched the cabin as the sun rose over the mountain. So far, they had seen no signs of activity. At dusk the night before, they had made it to the pine tree that had been struck by lightning and had made a camp there. Eleanor had wanted to push on but Tomás had insisted that they stop, warning her that stumbling upon the cabin could prove fatal to the children. She had relented but only after he promised her that they would be up at the first hint of light so they could make their way up the trail to the north and find the cabin. Now they were in position, hidden in a grove of trees about thirty yards away from the front of the cabin.

Estévan reached over and touched her arm. "I think I saw some movement in the cabin. I believe they are awake now," he whispered. He shrugged his shoulders to work some of the stiffness out of them. "We must watch with great care now and look for an opening."

Before they fell into a fitful sleep the previous night, they had discussed strategies. Estévan had favored storming the cabin in hopes that they would catch Alvarado unaware. Tomás, always the more cautious of the two, had advocated waiting for Alvarado to come outside and attempting to take him down with his rifle. They both looked to Eleanor to make the final decision.

"Be ready, Tomás," Eleanor said, her voice tight with tension. "If he shows his face, you need to blow him straight to hell."

"I am ready," Tomás said. He was stretched out on the ground, his rifle resting on a log to steady it. "I need to see more than his face, though. I must have a clear shot. We cannot wound him and risk his going back in the cabin with the children and Miss Christy."

"That is why as soon as you take your shot, I will charge the cabin," Estévan said. "I will finish him with my pistols if you do not kill him right away." He looked at Eleanor. "I will not let him get back into the cabin, Señora, I promise you."

Eleanor nodded. They waited.

Jared and Maria arrived at the lightning-ravaged pine about a half an hour after the sun had ascended over the mountains. They found the path heading north with no difficulty and headed up it, slowing their pace in order to minimize the noise they made. As they rode, they talked about how to approach the cabin.

"I think we should try to sneak up on this *cabrón,*" Maria said. "We wait for a chance to get a clear look at him and we shoot him down like the dog that he is."

"Maybe," Jared said, pondering the idea. "He knows I'm coming, though. I'm afraid he'll be on the lookout and we won't be able to get the drop on him. If he sees us sneaking up on him, we'll never get a good look at him. He'll use the children as a shield."

Maria shrugged. "There is no clear answer. The children and Miss Christy are in mortal danger; we know this is true."

"The man seems to have a pretty high opinion of himself." Jared pursed his lips as he pondered the situation. "If I play this right, call him out *mano a mano,* I may be able to get him to come out without the children. Maybe his pride will prevent him from using them as a shield."

"I do not know the answer," Maria said. "Whatever you decide, I will do it. We are wasting time; we need to head up the trail to the cabin."

Jared pulled his horse up. Maria looked at him. "What?"

"You don't have to go any farther, Maria," he said. "I owe you my gratitude forever for finding me and coming with me this far. I don't want to take the chance of you getting killed. If you go with me to the cabin, that's a very real possibility." He looked at the sun as it continued to climb higher over the mountains. "You and Tomás deserve the chance to have a life together. You've both lost so much; I don't want to risk you losing that chance."

Maria shot him an incredulous look and then burst out laughing. "I love you like a brother, Jared Delaney, but sometimes you are very stupid."

Jared sat back in his saddle and studied the woman whom he had known for a lot of years now. He shook his head and grinned. "I'm sure you're right, Maria. Would you mind explaining all this to me?"

It took Maria a moment to stop laughing. When she did, she said, "Tomás is either on his way here right now or maybe he is waiting up at the cabin with his brother while you and I are down the trail talking. He will be calm and he will be patient until he has the chance to kill this evil man, then he will pull the trigger. He will do this because he is a good and brave man, and he will do it because you are his brother as well."

Jared nodded. "He's my brother, too. You know I would do the same for him."

Her eyes brimmed over with tears; one lone tear trickled down her cheek. "If we are lucky, we will kill this monster. If we are not, he will kill us. I lost one husband and had to carry on. I will not do that again." She clenched her jaw, a look of defiance on her pretty face. "If anything happens to Tomás, I will kill the man who is responsible or die trying."

Jared took a deep breath and exhaled. "Well, I guess that's that. Let's go."

Eleanor was getting impatient but she told herself she needed to calm down and wait. Any premature movement or noise might alert Alvarado and result in the death of her precious children. If that happened, she didn't think she could carry on. She thought about Jared and wondered if Maria had been able to find him. A part of her hoped he was on his way but another part felt a resentment that bordered on hatred at the things he had done that led them to this point in time. If he hadn't chosen to strike out in seeking vigilante justice, Alvarado would not have taken their children. In her mind, it was as simple as that.

She was about to whisper a question to Tomás, asking him if he saw any signs of life in the cabin, when a voice rang out loud and clear. Horrified, she looked in the direction from which the voice came and saw her husband, mounted on his horse about ten yards from the door of the cabin. Maria was a little behind him and off to the side.

"Come on out, you gutless dog." Jared yelled at the top of his lungs. His voice echoed across the valley. "You wanted me, well, here I am."

Jared climbed down from his horse. There was silence for a moment, then the sound of laughter drifted out to where he stood.

"I told you to come alone, *cabrón*. You did not follow directions. You must think me a fool if you believe I will walk out alone into an ambush." More laughter. "That is not how we will do this."

Eleanor looked at Tomás and Estévan, both of whom had confused looks on their faces. Tomás shook his head and then put up his hand to signal that they should be quiet and remain where they were.

"You think this is funny, you yellow coward? I thought you were a bad hombre, not scared of anything or anyone. You think this lady is goin' to hurt you?" Now it was Jared's turn to laugh. "She just came to watch you die."

What is he doing? Eleanor was baffled by what her husband was saying to the outlaw inside. It was clear he was doing his best to provoke the man. All of a sudden, she realized that he was trying to goad him into charging out in a fit of rage to separate him from the children. It didn't seem to be playing out the way he intended.

"I think you brought a woman along to do your work for you, *pendejo,*" Alvarado said with a chuckle. "If that is what you want, I can play that game too."

The door to the cabin opened and Alvarado walked out holding Christy in front of him as a shield. His left arm was around her chest, his pistol was in his holster, and he held a large hunting knife to her throat with his right hand. They took a couple of steps forward and then stopped.

"See, *cabrón,* I have a woman, too." Alvarado laughed once more and this time there was a maniacal sound in the laughter. "I have something else you want even more than this woman. Inside, tied up and waiting to be butchered. Do you want to see what I have?"

Jared looked around, an agonized expression on his face. His plan had failed. Alvarado held all the cards. He tried once more.

"So you're such a dangerous man that you hide behind women and children? You afraid you can't take me in a fair fight, man to man?" Jared was trying to needle the outlaw into facing off with him one on one. It wasn't working.

Eleanor felt panic rise in her chest. She couldn't just sit there; she had to do something. She looked over at Estévan, who was watching her. She pointed to the right, indicating that she wanted him to flank the combatants and get a decent angle from which to shoot. He understood and began to work his way in that direction under the cover of the few scraggly bushes. Eleanor turned to convey this to Tomás and saw that he had recognized what they were doing and was already mirroring his brother's actions by sneaking his way to the left. Her mind raced as she tried to think of anything else they might do to help. Nothing came to her. It seemed like all they could do was get in a more strategic position and wait.

Jared's mind was racing too, as he tried to think of a way to inflame Alvarado into facing him. He didn't know if he could take him one on one but if it would free Christy from his clutches and keep the children out of harm's way, it would be worth it. If the outlaw gunned him down, he was confident that Maria would kill him. The problem was that Alvarado wasn't buying any of it. It was a standoff.

"Jared, shoot this son of bitch." Christy yelled at the top of her lungs, her face twisted with rage. "Don't worry about me, kill him now before he hurts the children."

Felipe Alvarado increased the pressure with his knife, breaking the skin on Christy's neck. She cried out in pain and fear in spite of herself.

"I do not think he wants to see you with your throat cut, *chiquita.*" Alvarado tightened his grip across Christy's chest. "Hombre, you do not wish to see this lady die, I think."

Jared didn't respond; his mind raced as he tried come up with a plan. He noticed Christy's hand moving down to the pocket of her dress and he wondered what she was up to. His eyes widened in astonishment as he saw her draw a derringer out of the pocket. It seemed like she was moving in slow motion as she pulled it out. She couldn't raise her arm because of Alvarado's grip so she reached behind her and fired two shots in rapid succession into his right thigh. He screamed in pain and reached toward the wounds with his right hand, the one with the knife in it. Christy struggled to get loose from his grasp but he held tight with his left arm. With a scream of rage, he raised his right hand and plunged the knife into her chest. She slumped in his arms and he let her fall.

No one moved. For a brief moment, it seemed like they were all frozen. Then pandemonium ensued. Jared drew his pistol and emptied it into Felipe Alvarado. Maria did the same. When Jared's gun was empty, he realized that there was more gunfire blazing toward the outlaw with a thunderous roar. He looked to his left and saw Estévan Marés wreaking a fusillade of bullets on the man with both of his pistols. Looking back to his right, he saw Tomás emptying his Winchester into Alvarado. And halfway between the two, he saw his wife taking deliberate aim with her pistol, firing in a focused and resolute manner.

Alvarado's body jerked with the impact of each bullet in what appeared to be a macabre dance. When the shooting stopped, he stood there for a moment longer, a perplexed expression on his face. Then he fell sideways and crumpled to the ground. Smoke hung in the air; the acrid smell of black powder filled the nostrils of all the combatants still standing.

The moment Alvarado fell, Eleanor sprinted for the door of the cabin with Jared right behind her. Tomás and Maria ran over to check on Christy. Estévan just stood there, stunned by what he had witnessed.

"She has a pulse but it's very weak," Tomás told Maria as he bent over the woman and put his fingers to her throat. "We need to try to stop the bleeding."

Without hesitation, Maria tore a large swath of cloth from her dress and applied pressure to the wound in Christy's chest. She cried out in pain and opened her eyes. For a moment, she was disoriented but then she recognized Maria.

"Maria, I'm glad you came," Christy said in a weak voice. "Are the children all right?"

"I think they are, Eleanor and Jared are checking on them now," Maria responded. "You need to be quiet and save your strength. We will take care of you."

Christy smiled but her eyes were sad. "I'm afraid it's too late for you to take care of me. I think I'll be going to see my Nathan soon."

Tomás knelt beside Maria and took Christy's hand. He tried to speak but his voice faltered. Finally, he found the words. "You are the bravest person I have ever known. The children owe their lives to you. Sheriff Averill would be so proud."

"I think I'll be finding out pretty soon," Christy said, the sad smile still on her lips. "I can't wait to see him and talk about everything that's happened."

"Please do not give up, *amiga*," Maria said with a ferocious urgency. "We can stop the bleeding, maybe we can save you."

"No," Christy said in a voice that was just audible. "It's too late for that. I love every one of you. You've been my family. Thank you." She closed her eyes.

Tears streamed down Maria's cheeks. She looked at Tomás, grief etched in her features. "No," she said. "I do not want to lose anyone else. We cannot let her go."

Tomás let go of Christy's hand and took the hand of his fiancée. "I am afraid we have no choice in the matter, *mi corazón*. Some things we cannot change." With his other hand, he put his fingers to Christy's throat, searching for a pulse. There was none. He reached up and with a gentle touch, closed her eyes.

Eleanor exploded through the door of the cabin, glancing around in a panic. It took a moment for her eyes to adjust but then she spotted the children in a corner. There was a rope around both their waists, pulling them close together. The other end of the rope was tied to an iron woodstove. Their feet were bound as well. Ned has his arm around his sister, who was crying. He looked up with terror in his eyes but it transformed to hope and joy when he recognized who had burst into the cabin.

"Mama?" Tears began to flow as the reality unfolded before him. "Papa? Is that you?"

Eleanor rushed to his side and enfolded him in her arms. "Yes, my love, it's me. You're safe now."

Jared loosened the rope around their waist, lifted it over Lizbeth's head, and snatched her up, hugging her to his chest. Eleanor struggled to free Ned from the rope without letting go of the embrace she held him in. Everyone was crying and laughing at the same time.

"Mama, you came," Ned cried. "I knew you would." He looked over at Jared. "I thought you would, too, Papa, but it's been a long time since I saw you." He shuddered as a sob escaped. "I was afraid you had forgotten about us."

Jared staggered back as if he had been struck. He glanced at Eleanor, who maintained a neutral expression. He reached out his arms to his son and Ned came to him. "Neddie, I would never forget about you. I think about you all the time." He squeezed him tight, then pulled back and looked him in the eyes. "I love you and I love Lizbeth. I've just been gone working."

Ned hugged his father as if he would never let go, his arms around his neck. Jared looked over the top of his head at Eleanor, a question in his eyes. What had she told the children? Eleanor met his gaze for a moment and then looked away. Neither of them seemed to know what to say. At that moment, Estévan came into the cabin.

"Are the children safe?" He was breathing hard. It was difficult to tell if it was from the exertion of the gun battle or the emotional aftershock.

"Yes, they are," Eleanor answered. "Thank you, Estévan, for everything you did. I . . . we," she stumbled with her words for a moment, "appreciate what you've done more than you'll ever know. We'll always be indebted to you, Tomás, and Maria."

Estévan took off his hat and ran his hand through his hair. He shrugged. "I do not know what to say to you. You are *familia*. There was nothing else to do but what we did." He took a deep breath. "I have bad news." He frowned. "No, I have terrible news. Miss Christy is dead."

Jared and Eleanor were stunned. Although they had seen Alvarado stab her, they had been in such a frantic rush to find the children that neither of them had thought about the outcome. Now the cruel reality set in.

"Mama," Ned asked in a small voice, "is Auntie Christy all right?" He looked back and forth between his parents, neither of whom had responded. "She was so brave; she told us she would save us from that bad man. I told her he was too big for any of us to fight but she said not to worry. She said she would take care of us."

The cabin was quiet. The adults looked at each other, none of them knowing quite how to proceed. Finally, Jared cleared his throat.

"Ned, I've got really sad news to tell you." He stopped and looked at Eleanor. She nodded her head. He continued. "Auntie Christy did fight with the bad man. She hurt him and thanks to her, we were able to stop him." He realized that his description was incomplete and inadequate. "We had to kill the bad man, son. If we hadn't, he would have killed you and all of us." He looked up at the ceiling searching for words. "It's a terrible thing to have to take someone's life but sometimes that's what you have to do to keep your family safe."

Ned nodded. Once again, he asked, "Is Auntie Christy all right?"

Jared fought back tears as his mind was flooded with all the memories of his long and sometimes tangled relationship with Christine Johnson. He struggled to remain in control of his emotions.

"No, son, she's not all right." He stopped again to collect himself. "Like I said, she hurt the man so we could stop him from hurting you. When she did that, he stabbed her with a knife. I'm afraid . . ." Again, he stopped, choked up with an unbearable sadness.

"Papa?' Ned reached out and took his father's hand. "Where is Auntie Christy?"

"Son," Jared said, choking the words out, "your Auntie Christy is dead."

"No, Papa," Ned cried out. "I don't want Auntie Christy to be dead." He burst into tears.

Jared took his son in his arms and rocked him.

"Neither do I, son." Tears streamed down his face. "Neither do I."

CHAPTER 34

Tomás and Estévan loaded Christy's body in the buckboard and covered her with a blanket they found in the cabin. Estévan agreed to stay behind with Alvarado's corpse and wait for Tomás to return to help transport him to Las Vegas. There was some confusion about who to report the circumstances of his death to since Sheriff Todd Little had been murdered, in all likelihood by Alvarado himself. Estévan didn't know if someone else had been appointed as acting sheriff but he figured he would take the body to Las Vegas and dump it at the office of the mayor.

Jared tied Eleanor's horse to the back of the buckboard and Eleanor took the lines with the children in the seat beside here. Jared rode alongside. Tomás and Maria made a point of riding ahead a little ways to give Jared and Eleanor some space to deal with their traumatized children, not to mention each other. They made their slow and deliberate way from the cabin back to the main trail to Cimarrón traveling in stunned silence. As they came to the pine tree that had been struck by lightning and made the turn north towards home, Jared eased his horse a little closer to the buckboard.

"How are you holding up?" He looked at his wife, searching her face in an attempt to read her emotions. She stared ahead at the trail. Jared waited.

"Now's not the time to talk about this, Jared," she said at last. She glanced at the children, both of whom had fallen asleep on the seat and were leaning against her. "We need to get them home and safe."

Jared started to say something, then he stopped. He nodded and eased his horse back away from the buckboard. They continued in silence. Up ahead, Tomás and Maria were talking in quiet but intense voices.

"My heart almost leaped out of my chest when I saw you behind Jared," Tomás said. "I do not know why he brought you along. You were only supposed to find him and give him the message. You were not supposed to take part in the fight. What was he thinking?" He was so agitated that he threw up his hands repeatedly. "For that matter, what were you thinking?"

"Jared told me not to come, Tomás," Maria said in a calm voice that was in contrast to Tomas's tone. "I told him that I would stand with you or die with you. He had no say in the matter. It was my choice."

Tomás started to protest but then he stopped. He looked at his fiancée and tears filled his eyes. "I love you, Maria. I would stand or die with you as well. I suppose that is just how it is." He wiped his eyes with a sleeve. "Thank you."

They rode for a while without words before Maria broke the silence. "What I would really like is for us to run the Marés Café and make some babies. I believe I would enjoy that much more than this 'standing and dying business.' " With a twinkle in her eye, she said, "It would be much safer."

"I like the idea." Tomás turned to her with a grin on his face. "Most especially the part about making babies." They rode on toward home.

The children were both asleep in their beds. Ned had fallen asleep as Jared carried him from the wagon into the house, but Eleanor had to stay with Lizbeth and hold her close for a time before exhaustion overcame her emotional turmoil. Eleanor lay beside her for several minutes before she got up, careful not to wake her daughter, and joined Jared on the portal. They sat there without speaking for a while.

"What do we do now?" Jared posed the question in a quiet voice but he was gripping the arms of the rocking chair so tight that his knuckles were white.

Eleanor exhaled a large breath and stared at the mountains to the west. "To be as honest as I know how to be, I'm not sure." She turned to look at Jared. "You hurt me and the children." Jared started to protest but she waved her hand at him to cut him off. "You need to listen to what I have to say. That's one of the ways you hurt us. You stopped listening."

Jared's anguish showed in his eyes. For a moment, it appeared that he would argue but then he sighed. "All right, I'll listen."

Eleanor nodded. "You became so consumed with vengeance that neither the children nor I mattered to you." Again, he started to protest. Again, she waved him off. "If you can't be quiet and listen now, after everything that's happened, then we need to stop and you need to leave."

Now panic showed in his eyes. "I'm sorry, I won't say another word until you're done."

Eleanor looked hard at him for a moment

before continuing. "You were so single-minded in your plan to go after Alvarado that you couldn't think of anything else. You never stopped to consider that he might come after me and the children, you just pursued him like a hound from hell."

Jared raised a finger and said in a subdued voice, "Can I ask you a question to make sure I understand what you're saying?"

Eleanor nodded. "Go ahead."

"You can't be saying it's my fault that Alvarado kidnapped the children." His voice caught in his throat. "You can't mean that you think I'm responsible for Christy's death."

"That's exactly what I'm saying," Eleanor said. Her voice came up and she slapped her hand on the arm of her rocker. "You didn't stop for a minute to consider what might happen if you went after this monster all on your own." Jared sat back in his chair. He looked as if he'd been punched in the face. "You could have worked with Estévan and Tomás, maybe Tom Figgs. At the very least, you could have made sure someone was watching over us while you traipsed all over northern New Mexico on your quest for revenge. You were so determined to do things your way that you left us unprotected. How could you do that?" Eleanor struggled to hold back her tears.

Jared sat there shaking his head. Finally, he said, "I don't know how to answer your question. I don't agree with everything you said but I reckon there's plenty of truth to it. I'm gonna have to spend some time thinkin' about all of this before I can give you an answer."

Eleanor brushed away a tear that had escaped from her eye and began trickling down her cheek. She steeled herself and looked him in the eye. "You'll have to take that time somewhere else. I can't have you in the house right now. You've done so much damage, I don't know if you're going to be able to fix it." She looked away toward the mountains and then returned her gaze to him. "I just don't know if we can go on together after this."

Now tears filled Jared's eyes and spilled over. For a moment, he trembled, then he regained control. "That's not what I want, Eleanor darlin'. I'll do whatever I need to do so that we can be together. I don't know yet what that is but I'll figure it out and I'll do it. You'll see."

"I just don't know if it's possible," she said.

"I understand," Jared said as he stood up. "You just need to know that I'll do whatever

I have to do to make this right." He walked down the steps of the portal, turned, and looked at her. "I'll leave now but I'll check back with you in a day or two. I'll let you know what I've been thinking and find out how you and the little ones are doing. I will make this right."

He walked away in the direction of the stables and found a fresh horse. Without looking in Eleanor's direction, he saddled up and rode away.

CHAPTER 35

Jared rode on the trail to Springer until it was almost too dark to see before he made camp. He needed to close this chapter of his life before he could move on and make amends with Eleanor. That meant he needed to settle up with Manuel Salazar. He owed him a report on what had taken place at the cabin north of Las Vegas. Beyond that, Salazar needed to know the consequences of his part in their blind pursuit for vengeance.

He rolled out his bedroll and stared up at the sky. Once again, he noticed that there was a halo moon. It seemed ominous. He shivered, perhaps from the chill of the night or perhaps from the prospect of the changes that were coming. He had no idea what those changes would be. Sleep was a long time in coming.

The forest was ablaze. Jared couldn't find his horse and had no idea which way to run. The flames were so bright he was blinded and his eyes felt like they were burning. The smoke was thick and he had trouble breathing. He began to shake as the panic set in. It was accompanied by an overwhelming sense of sorrow as he realized he would never see his wife and children again. He wished he had been able to tell them how sorry he was for the things he'd done.

Jared started awake and covered his eyes. The morning sun was glaring in his eyes with an intensity that let him know it was midmorning. How in the world had he slept so late? He'd used his coat as a pillow and somehow one of the sleeves had shifted in the night, covering his nose and mouth and making it hard to breathe. He felt like he'd been having a dream but he couldn't remember what it was about. *Probably just as well.*

He still had several hours to ride before he reached Springer. He knew he should get going but he felt groggy and sluggish. He built a small fire and heated up some coffee. While he waited for it to boil, he gnawed on some jerky and pondered his situation. None of it was good. When the coffee was ready, he poured some in his tin cup and took a sip. It was bitter. *Maybe it ain't the coffee that's bitter,* he thought.

Maybe that's just the way my life tastes.

He wasn't sure yet what he wanted to say to Manuel Salazar. A part of him wanted to rail at the man for sucking him into this ill-fated undertaking but he understood that he was a grown man. He'd gone along with the scheme of his own free will . . . in fact, with a passion that bordered on the obsessive. He was accountable for his actions and had to bear the consequences for them. Perhaps he wanted some company in shouldering that load. He wasn't sure how he would convince Salazar to do that, though. As he saddled up, he concluded that he would just report what had transpired and let the mayor draw his own conclusions.

Jared rode into Springer in the early afternoon and tied his horse to the rail in front of the mayor's office. He knocked once and heard a voice summon him in. As he entered, he saw Manual Salazar sitting behind his desk. The man's face brightened as he recognized him.

"Señor Delaney, it is good to see you. Do have any news?"

"I do, Mayor." Jared took off his hat and walked over to the chair opposite the man. He sat down and exhaled. "I suppose you'll think of it as good news. Quite a bit of it ain't so good, though."

Salazar leaned forward, his eagerness apparent. "Does this mean you have dealt with Felipe? I cannot wait to hear about it. I have news for you as well." He rubbed his hands together, barely able to contain his excitement. "Please tell me your news first, though."

Jared felt a surge of anger and had to resist the urge to smash the man in the face. A good woman was dead, his children might never be the same, and his wife couldn't stand the sight of him; yet all Salazar cared about was hearing of how he had killed Felipe Alvarado. He struggled to control his emotions, reminding himself that Salazar didn't know about the fate of the innocent victims.

"Alvarado is dead, but it got bloody."

Salazar sat back. "What do you mean that it got bloody?"

With great effort, Jared controlled the storm of feelings he was experiencing. He spoke in a monotone. "Alvarado kidnapped my children and the lady they were staying with at the time. Before we could take him down, he killed the woman."

"What?" Salazar sputtered as he tried to ask several questions at once. "Alvarado kidnapped your children? He killed a woman?" He shook his head as he tried to

410

comprehend what Jared was saying. "How did this happen? Are your children all right?"

"My children are alive," Jared said. "I don't reckon they're 'all right' though. I don't know if anything will ever be the same for 'em. They were scared out of their minds."

"Señor Delaney, I am so sorry, I cannot find the words to express it. I never thought something like this would happen."

Jared wanted to blame the man. He wanted to hate him and convince Eleanor to hate him. He wanted to be absolved of his own sins and have the full burden of what they had wrought together placed on the shoulders of Manuel Salazar. For a brief moment, he pictured himself telling this to Eleanor. The image passed. He knew it was a lie.

"I know you didn't, neither did I. The difference is that it wasn't your job to think of such a thing, it was mine. They ain't your kids. You might feel sorry about it but I'm the one who bears the blame."

Salazar sat speechless for a few moments, then he said, "I am sorry nonetheless and I do share the blame, no matter what you say." He shook his head. "What of Alvarado? You said 'we' took him down. Who else was involved?"

Jared described the bloody confrontation, explaining who the others were and how it transpired. He explained that Estévan and Tomás intended to take Alvarado's body to Las Vegas and deliver it to the mayor there. As far as they were concerned, he was the person most qualified to sort out the jurisdiction mess.

Salazar listened in rapt attention. When Jared stopped, he shrugged. "I do not know of a better resolution than that. Felipe Alvarado was a resident of San Miguel County so I suppose, in the end, it is their problem." He sat up straight. "I almost forgot; I have news of our other villain. We have Jesus Abreu in custody over at the bank." He shook his head. "I would have liked to have put him in a cell and locked it tight but our jail cell does not lock. His office at the bank had to do."

"What do you mean that you have him in custody? Did you accuse him of a crime?"

Salazar smiled. "The bank vault was empty. Someone took all the cash." His smile turned into a frown. "We could not find the money, though; it appears that Jesus must have hidden it. He claims a former bank employee stole it but that sounds like rubbish to me. It may not matter. The board of the bank conducted an audit and found many irregularities. I think we will be able to charge him with several crimes."

As he contemplated Abreu's story, Jared almost missed the last few words Salazar had said about a former bank employee taking the money. He sat up straight as he wondered . . . did Davey Good have it in him to pull something like this off? Jared smiled. *That young rascal; I reckon he just might.* He laughed out loud.

"What is so amusing, Señor Delaney?"

"Oh, I was just rememberin' somethin' important. You sounded a little uncertain about whether or not you had enough evidence to nail Abreu." Jared reached into his vest pocket and pulled out a piece of paper. "This will solve that problem for you." He handed the note to Salazar.

Salazar read the note and looked up, his eyes full of astonishment. "This is a confession of his involvement in conspiracy to commit murder. We have him." He pounded his fist on his desk. "We have that *cabrón.*" He jumped up and ran around his desk to where Jared sat. "Let us go tell him the news. I cannot wait to see the look on his face."

They walked the two blocks to the bank and entered the building. Salazar walked up

413

to the young man seated at the desk closest to the door. Jared saw a look of alarm pass over Salazar's face.

"Why are you not with the prisoner?" He spoke with a vehemence that drew the attention of everyone in the bank.

The young man stammered, "He's locked inside the vault. There's no way for him to escape. I needed to relieve myself so I left him in there." He looked around as if one of the tellers might help him with his explanation. "I had a few things I needed to take care of at my desk."

Salazar snorted in disgust and strode over to Abreu's office door. He flung it open and looked around the room. The vault door was open, the vault was empty, and the back door was ajar.

Salazar ran to the door and looked out. There was no sign of Jesus Abreu. He turned to the young man in a rage. "I suppose it did not occur to you that Señor Abreu might have a second set of keys in the vault in case he accidentally locked himself in."

The assistant glared at Salazar. "No, Mayor, *no one* thought of that possibility."

"You ignorant *pendejo,* he is gone." He whirled around to face Jared. "We cannot let him get away, Señor Delaney. You need to ride after him right away."

Jared shook his head. "No, sir, I don't need to do that."

"Did you not hear me?" Salazar was in a rage. "The man is getting away. We must follow him without delay. Do you not want to avenge the death of Nathan Averill?"

The people in the bank were staring at Manuel Salazar, their mouths hanging open in astonishment. Jared looked around at them and then back at Salazar.

"No, sir, I don't reckon I do. I've seen the price of vengeance. I can't afford any more of it."

He turned and walked out the door, leaving Salazar there trying to make sense of it all. He walked the two blocks back to the mayor's office, untied his horse, and mounted up. He knew what he had to do; he just had no idea how to do it or how long it might take. He would find a way to atone for his many transgressions. Nothing else mattered.

ABOUT THE AUTHOR

Jim Jones is the author of five novels set in northern New Mexico in the late 1800s: *The Lights of Cimarrón, The Big Empty,* and the Jared Delaney series, including *Rustler's Moon, Colorado Moon,* and *Waning Moon.* His novella, "Scarecrows," appeared in the Five Star Anthology, *Perilous Frontier.* His songs and books are about the West . . . cowboys, horses & cattle, cattle rustlers, the coming of the train . . . songs about people and land, rivers and mountains, the beauty of the Western sky. With the 2021 release of his new album, *Good Days Are Comin',* Jim has produced eleven Western/Folk albums and three award-winning children's character education videos. His book *Bolo the Brave* was a Western Writers of America Spur Finalist in the Storyteller/Illustrated Children's Book category. He was the Western Music Association's 2014 Male Performer of the Year and winner of the

International Western Music Association 2019 Song of the Year, the Academy of Western Artists 2016 Western Song of the Year, and the Western Writers of America 2013, 2017, and 2021 Spur Awards for Best Western Song. Jim lives in Rio Rancho, New Mexico.

The employees of Thorndike Press hope you have enjoyed this Large Print book. All our Thorndike, Wheeler, and Kennebec Large Print titles are designed for easy reading, and all our books are made to last. Other Thorndike Press Large Print books are available at your library, through selected bookstores, or directly from us.

For information about titles, please call:
  (800) 223-1244

or visit our website at:
  gale.com/thorndike

To share your comments, please write:
  Publisher
  Thorndike Press
  10 Water St., Suite 310
  Waterville, ME 04901

CPSIA information can be obtained
at www.ICGtesting.com
Printed in the USA
BVHW030625220623
666185BV00003B/3

9 781432 892692